Books by Phyllis A. Whitney

STAR FLIGHT
THE EBONY SWAN
WOMAN WITHOUT A PAST
THE SINGING STONES
RAINBOW IN THE MIST
FEATHER ON THE MOON
SILVERSWORD
FLAMING TREE
DREAM OF ORCHIDS
RAINSONG
EMERALD
VERMILION
POINCIANA
DOMINO
THE GLASS FLAME
THE STONE BULL
THE GOLDEN UNICORN
SPINDRIFT
THE TURQUOISE MASK
SNOWFIRE
LISTEN FOR THE WHISPERER
LOST ISLAND
THE WINTER PEOPLE
HUNTER'S GREEN
SILVERHILL
COLUMBELLA
SEA JADE
BLACK AMBER
SEVEN TEARS FOR APOLLO
WINDOW ON THE SQUARE
BLUE FIRE
THUNDER HEIGHTS
THE MOONFLOWER
SKYE CAMERON
THE TREMBLING HILLS
THE QUICKSILVER POOL
THE RED CARNELIAN

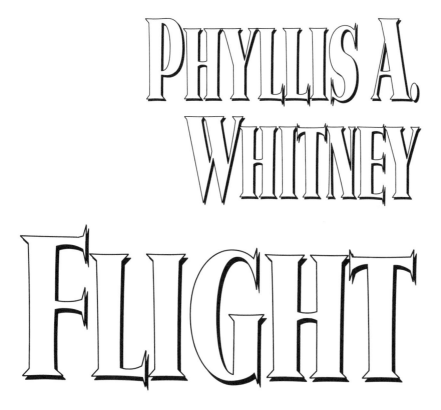

PHYLLIS A. WHITNEY

FLIGHT

CROWN PUBLISHERS, INC.

New York

Published by Crown Publishers, Inc., 201 East 50th Street, New York, New York 10022. Member of the Crown Publishing Group. Random House, Inc., New York, Toronto, London, Sydney, Auckland.

CROWN is a trademark of Crown Publishers, Inc.

Manufactured in the United States of America

Library of Congress Cataloging in Publication Data
Whitney, Phyllis A.
Star flight / Phyllis A. Whitney.
1. Motion picture actors and actresses—North Carolina—Fiction.
2. Women detectives—North Carolina—Fiction. 3.Family—North
Carolina—Fiction. I. Title.
PS3545.H8363S7 1993   93-8728
813'.54—dc20   CIP

ISBN 0-517-59499-4

10 9 8 7 6 5 4 3 2 1

First Edition

For Julie Fallowfield,
for so many years my
friend, agent, and
counselor. Thank you.

Foreword

THE MOST exciting part of discovering a new setting for a novel is the role played by the unexpected. When my daughter and her husband drove me to Asheville, North Carolina, I had never heard of Lake Lure. I'd read about Chimney Rock, but had dismissed it as being out of my reach, with too many steps to climb. (To my delight, there is an elevator!)

When we started out from Asheville, our direction was chosen arbitrarily. We drove along the Blue Ridge and down into Hickory Nut Gorge. The gorge itself was beautiful, but nothing spoke to me until we came out upon the shore of a narrow lake that stretched below the flank of a rock-scarred mountain. We drove into hills above the water, where we could better view the entire enchanting scene. I knew immediately that I'd found my setting, even though at that moment I had no idea of the treasures that waited to enrich my novel. Lake Lure and Rumbling Bald

Mountain provided the atmosphere and legends that would build my story.

A number of people helped me along the way. Edward J. Sheary, Director of Libraries for the Asheville-Buncomb system, made me welcome and helped with information and introductions. Laura Gaskin, of Central Adult Services in the Pack Memorial Library, furnished me with the names of those who might help in my search and provided me with numerous copies of articles about the area.

Martha Schatz, Director of the Rutherfordton County Library, became my main contact after I returned home, sending me packets of material on all aspects of Hickory Nut Gorge and Lake Lure. Her enthusiastic report on my manuscript was the first reading I received. Thank you, Martha.

Joanne Okpych, innkeeper of the Esmeralda Inn, sent me information about the historic inn, where early movie stars came to stay when they were making pictures in the area. Since I am a movie buff, my imagination took off and I created my own movie stars.

Dale Miller, then a manager at Lake Lure Inn, gave us a tour of the inn, where so many notables of the past had stayed. He also showed us the kudzu-covered barn behind the inn where square dances were once held. The barn was being used for storage, but I cleared it out with a flick of my typewriter and held a costume ball in that cavernous space.

Of special help to me were Laney Harrill and his wife, Lyvonne. I met Laney on top of Chimney Rock, and we were invited to his home on Lake Lure. There I could catch the feeling of what it would be like to live on the shore of that mountain-framed stretch of water. Laney also introduced me to some of the marvelous legends that abound in Hickory Nut Gorge.

For every book I write, I visit the local chamber of commerce. In the chamber's little building in the village of Chimney Rock, I struck a special lode of gold. Ann O'Leary took us up the mountain to see the set of the Indian village that was used in the movie *The Last of the Mohicans*. We took photos and videos of that remarkable and very complete Huron village, so that when I was working at home, I could visualize it again. For the movie, sadly, much of the village ended up on the cutting room floor. I'm glad that I could preserve more of its detail in my story scenes.

Thank you, David Easton, for loaning me your miniature pig. Sigmund von Hogg brings his own individual personality to several scenes. I met Siggy when he was a rather large baby. Now at one hundred pounds he is full grown, but still is considered miniature.

My special thanks to Edith Edwards of Kudzu Konnections in Rutherfordton. I once wrote about the destructive qualities of kudzu in a book called *The Glass Flame*, but now I have learned about its virtues. *The Book of Kudzu* provided me with a fascinating collection of recipes, not only for culinary purposes but for healing as well, all helpful in my fiction writing.

The handsome drum in the story was the work of Edward King, who makes each drum an individual work of art. I acquired one of his drums for myself so that I could hear its varied tones whenever I wished, and try to catch the sound in my own amateur thumping.

Two scenes in the story take place in Asheville itself. One is set in the famous Grove Park Inn high above the city. The other takes place in the Captain's Bookshelf, a delightful antiquarian bookshop. My thanks to Chandler Gordon, son of the original "captain," and to his wife, Megan Gordon, who created the wall decoration of a Japanese silk dragon that I've described in the bookshop scene.

Randy Williams drove us around the Fairfield Mountains vacation complex, where I was able to set some of the action in my narrative. He also took us to the unique Mountains Library— where my books were on the shelves. Dorothy Dunlap, the librarian, and a volunteer, Eileen Harrison, made us welcome and provided me with still another scene.

I have taken a few liberties with the geography of Lake Lure's shoreline, building houses as I pleased, and setting down paths where there may be no paths. For a writer, the imagined and the real are so mingled by the end of a book, that it's difficult to know which is which. For more than a year I have lived in these pages with this setting and these people. I hope they will come to life for my readers as they have for me.

Prologue: The Legend

FOR NEARLY sixty years, the mountain had kept its grisly secret. In North Carolina's early days, the mountain had been called Old Bald. No trees grew along a rocky space near the top, so the name was born naturally. But that was before the "disturbances" occurred in 1874 and again in 1880. On the first date, the mountain's time of notoriety arrived.

Farmers in the valley were alarmed when rumbling sounds emerged from deep inside Old Bald and smoke was seen rising above its massive spread. A religious revival began and preachers called sinners into church to save their souls before the coming of doomsday. Rumors of volcanic activity flew quickly, so that newspapers sent reporters from nearby Asheville and from as far away as New York City to investigate. Soon scientists swarmed in to begin arguments that would never entirely resolve the mystery of what was now being called Rumbling Bald Mountain.

The theory most accepted was that long-ago earthquakes had caused fissures to open inside the mountain. When great boulders crashed into these hollow caverns, the rumbling sound resulted. The smoke that caused alarm among the residents was simply dust rising through crevices when huge rocks fell precipitously from great heights within the mountain.

In those days, there was no lake, only a long, deep valley along the foot of the mountain. The valley was part of Hickory Nut Gorge, through which flowed the Rocky Broad River. In the 1920s, the vision of a newcomer, Dr. Lucius W. Morse, would become a reality and change the valley and the surrounding countryside forever. Dr. Morse had come to North Carolina from St. Louis for his health and stayed because the country suited him. The results of Dr. Morse's dream began to transform the area with the building of a hydroelectric dam that created Lake Lure. Soon this part of the state became famous for its beauty and its reputation as a resort flourished.

Film companies in a budding industry heard about the beauty of these Appalachian mountains and, in particular, the spectacular appeal of the gorge. Actors and crews came to stay at the Esmeralda Inn and the Lake Lure Inn came into being to entertain the wealthy and famous.

The mountain had been quiet for more than a hundred years and the volcanic theories that had proliferated during the brief period of geological activity had long since been ridiculed and dismissed, so no one who now lived in the area had any concern.

Interest moved to another source when the resort's first widely publicized scandal and tragedy occurred in the late thirties. Victoria Frazer, a beautiful and glamorous film star, had come from Hollywood to make a picture with Roger Brandt, already famous for his cowboy roles in Westerns. The very combination of these two opposites in the same picture excited the imaginations of moviegoers across the country and the movie magazines had a field day.

It was inevitable that two such beautiful and dynamic people, cast in intimate scenes, should fall in love. Victoria possessed a passionate quality that played well on the screen, while Roger was an educated and well-read man—something seldom revealed in his movies, most of which featured monosyllabic dialogue. The two were magnets for each other.

As inevitable as their falling in love might have been, Roger was already married to a young woman of Spanish descent from a fine old California family, and no divorce was likely. The studio stood on its ear trying to avoid a scandal that might destroy two valuable properties. In those less-than-tolerant days, repercussions had to be avoided at all costs.

The studio was not entirely successful. While in North Carolina, Victoria gave birth to a baby girl who was quickly spirited away to adoptive parents in California, a childless couple who were friends of Victoria. Perhaps all might have been saved, even then, had Victoria lived, but she chose instead to drown herself in the lake at the foot of Rumbling Bald Mountain. Her scarf was found wrapped around the pilings of a dock. She had left an unfinished letter to the daughter she had sent away, and the message had been interpreted as a suicide note. In any case, the divers who searched the deep waters of the lake never recovered her body. And whatever the mountain knew, it wasn't telling.

Juicy reports of the scandal appeared in magazines and newspapers across the country, and Roger's career plummeted. At the age of twenty-three, with one of the most recognizable faces in

America, no studio would touch him. Movies were made in a few months in those days, and when his last picture was released—one made shortly before Victoria's death—audiences booed and walked out. The public, which had accepted him as the pure and noble rescuer of maidens in distress, could not handle the reality presented by the press.

The behind-the-scenes story was as romantic and tragic as any screenplay, but the truth was not to be known until many decades later.

Oddly enough, Victoria's roots were in North Carolina and quite a few Frazers still lived there. She'd been born in Asheville, where a talent scout, home for a holiday visit, had discovered her while she was very young. So, in a sense, she had come home to die. Roger Brandt, on the other hand, was a native Californian. While *Blue Ridge Cowboy* was being filmed, he rented a house on the lake and brought out his wife of two years to stay with him until the end of the picture. Rumor had it that Camilla Brandt had come to Lake Lure to keep an eye on her husband. If so, her presence had no effect.

After the scandal broke and Roger Brandt became an untouchable in Hollywood, he defiantly bought the Lake Lure house he had rented and moved in permanently with his wife. No one could ever figure out why he wanted to live near the scene of a tragedy that had destroyed his career. Equally mysterious was how he had persuaded Camilla to uproot herself from her family and move to so isolated a spot in America's South. Since Roger answered no questions and never allowed reporters near his wife, no one knew their reasons. Soon the Brandts had a son and the family became as much a part of Lake Lure's legend and scene as the mountain itself.

Over the years, the romantic story of the two ill-fated lovers grew. To this day, when visitors are taken on pontoon boats to tour the lake, they are shown the very place where Victoria Frazer drowned. The house where Roger Brandt still lives is pointed out as well, though boats are asked not to approach its dock. One guide even began to add his own embellishments. He claimed that in the early-morning hours, when mists rose along the water, a lovely white spirit appeared, drifting at the foot of the mountain. A spirit that always whispered the same name over and over— that of Roger Brandt. Of course, when Brandt got wind of the story, he immediately put a stop to such nonsense. As a longtime resident whose privacy was accepted and respected, he had influence. Strangely, the uprooted Camilla made herself more a part of the community than her husband was willing to do.

Not until more than fifty years later did the daughter of the baby who was sent away—the granddaughter of Victoria Frazer and Roger Brandt—come at last to Lake Lure. Only then did the mountain give up its terrible secrets—though not without a good deal of travail for those who were involved with Roger and Victoria's past.

O ⋆ N ⋆ E

SOMETHING AWAKENED me so suddenly that I sat up in bed, my heart thumping as I stared at the unfamiliar reflection of water rippling across the ceiling of my room. Being disoriented by my surroundings wasn't my problem—I knew where I was well enough. Back home in Palm Desert, there was no nearby water to cast ceiling reflections, so I began to wonder whether there had been something out there on the lake—some strange ambience that had reached out to disturb my dreaming—or whether I simply found it hard to sleep in the watery surroundings.

As I came fully awake, I dismissed the former notion. I was here in North Carolina to find the answers to important questions, some of which had plagued me for years. I knew I needed to search for solutions with logic and good sense. A sound plan, certainly, but one that made me smile as I considered it. I wasn't sure that I was capable of such a sensible approach. Confusion and concern were too much a part of my emotional baggage at the moment.

I'd arrived at Rumbling Mountain Lodge in the early evening, after a long flight from California, with several changes before I finally reached Asheville and picked up the rented car that had brought me here. A glance at my watch told me that it was a little before 3:00 A.M. locally, though not yet midnight at home.

Finding myself sleepless, I put on a robe and slippers, opened the door to the long balcony that ran past several rooms, and stepped outside. The late-September day had been warm, but the night air of the mountains felt wonderfully refreshing. Driving here while there was still some daylight, I had realized how lushly green everything was, very different from the desert browns I was used to. Leaves were just beginning to turn, with the promise of even greater beauty to come.

I had never *meant* to come here. I knew the story behind my mother's birth and had absorbed some of her prejudice against the man who still lived at Lake Lure and was my grandfather. I knew about my grandmother, who had sent her child away to old friends in California before her own suicide. All this was a part of my family history and responsible, I was sure, for the uneasiness I was trying to dismiss.

Even though my real grandparents had never been a part of my life, I had grown up curious about them, my young imagination fired by the glamour of those two legendary figures. Once, when I was sixteen, I had said to my mother, "Don't you *want* to know the truth about your mother's death?"

But her sense of having been rejected was too strong and her guard was always up. To the day of her own death, she remained unforgiving toward a past she really knew very little about. She had wanted a life that was safe and secure, and her foster parents had given her that. I remembered them as loving but old, with whatever young leanings toward adventure they might have had long subdued.

As I stood on this balcony, high above the very waters where Victoria Frazer had drowned, some disturbing enchantment seemed to fill me—as though something in me already knew that how and why she had died would have a startling effect upon my own future. What did Roger Brandt really know about her death?

I was the one who wanted to *know.* Once, I sneaked into a movie theater where one of Roger Brandt's old pictures was playing. In spite of all that seemed sentimental and corny to me, I'd been able to catch a bit of the fascination he must have held for the audiences of his day. He'd been very much a man's man, strong and vital in his adventure pictures, yet women, too, were clearly susceptible to his special charm.

A veteran of more than thirty movies since his teens, he would have been in his early twenties in the film I saw. He appeared tall and lean—perhaps *lanky* was the word—yet possessed a natural grace of movement that was appealing. The camera loved him. His eyes said more than any lines they gave him, and a crease in one cheek brought an interesting twist to his smile. He had a special way of walking off with his back to the camera and then pausing to look over one shoulder, almost mischievously, as though some secret existed between him and the audience. Of course, his prowess on a horse was famous and the palomino in his films belonged to him. All these things I knew about from old fan magazines I'd picked up in secondhand stores, hiding them from my mother.

My father, I didn't remember at all; he'd died in an accident when I was only two, so he held less reality for me than my grandfather did.

Unfortunately, I had never seen the movie *Blue Ridge Cowboy*, which starred both of my grandparents. Those same old magazines had shown me her entrancing, tender young face with those great eyes that must have held me spellbound. I knew they were green, because the magazines said so, though all the photographs I saw were in black and white. My own eyes were green as well, and sometimes I'd felt a certain pride of distinction because they'd come from my famous grandmother. She must have been a glorious shooting star across the film screens of the world, only to have her light quenched in the dark waters of Lake Lure. At least she would never grow old. Roger Brandt was over seventy, and probably growing feeble, with all that young charisma long gone. Yet I was curious about him.

My room at the lodge was on the second floor, at the rear, above the lake. The building was set among tall evergreens, oaks, and maples that offered shade by day and a certain dusky seclusion by night. Beneath my balcony, the hillside dropped steeply to the water. With the lodge's lighted standards all around, I could make out wooden steps leading down to a slanting walkway that ended where a house stood near the water.

My coming here still seemed strange and unreal to me. It had less to do with Victoria and Roger and the distant past than with the death two years ago of my husband, documentary-film maker Jim Castle, in this remote place. Nevertheless, what was happening now seemed strangely fateful and destined—if one believed in such things.

Jim's interest in Roger Brandt had been sparked by the fact that he was my grandfather, but it had quickly grown to be more. He had watched his films and read hundreds of books written by Hollywood insiders, and those invariably made some mention of

Roger Brandt. When Jim decided to travel here to get footage of his film's subject, I had refused to accompany him.

As a film writer, I had worked on some of Jim's past efforts, but I'd wanted nothing to do with this one. I was still resisting destiny. When he died on that trip, I'd suffered a good deal of guilt, perhaps because our marriage was no longer close. I kept thinking if I'd come here with him, Jim would still be alive.

The startling letter that finally had brought me here was nearly anonymous. I knew the few lines by heart, and as I looked out over the water toward that great crouching mountain, they ran through my mind:

> Lauren Castle:
>   Your husband's death was not an accident, as I have only just learned. If you want to know what happened to him, you must come to Lake Lure as soon as possible. Stay at Rumbling Mountain Lodge, and I will find you.
>   N.

The note had forced my hand. I had comforted myself knowing I could come as Jim Castle's wife, so that my connection to Roger Brandt would remain a secret, except to one person. Gordon Heath, who had been working with Jim and who was an old friend of his, still lived here. But Gordon's presence in these parts and his knowledge of my family history was something I wasn't ready to deal with yet. I had written to Gordon to say I was coming—though not why or when. I didn't want him to know more than that for now, but I was aware I would need his help. So where was I to find cool logic to guide me now?

Gordon had sent me a letter at the time of Jim's death—a

letter that had been kind but impersonal. Clearly, what had happened between us eleven years ago in San Francisco was to be ignored. He wrote that Jim had been filming a scene for his documentary on an abandoned movie set—an Indian village on the mountain above Hickory Nut Gorge. A heavy beam had fallen, killing him instantly.

Gordon had returned Jim's possessions to me—everything, that is, except the work he'd been doing on the documentary. After I received his letter, I had written to him, but there had been no further communication between us. His silence had spelled disapproval of me. Yet here I was and the first person I would need to find was Gordon Heath.

As I stood at the rail, someone turned on a light in the house near the water's edge and my attention returned to the present. I wondered who lived there and why they were up so late. Someone else must also be sleepless.

However, I had no patience for idle speculation at this hour. Tomorrow—today!—I must find Gordon Heath and talk to him, whether I liked the idea or not. I hoped he could identify the N who had written to me. I also wanted him to show me the place where Jim had died and tell me more about the accident.

A door opened in the house below and someone came out to stand on a walkway that led down to a boathouse. The figure was tall and wore a long robe, but I couldn't tell whether it was a man or a woman. When the person looked up in my direction, I realized that I was visible against the lights of the lodge.

"So you're not sleeping, either?" a woman's husky voice called up to me. "If you want to come on down, I'll fix us tea and a snack. Don't bother to dress—I'm in my pajamas."

Her manner seemed so assured that I didn't feel I could refuse.

Intrigued by her informal invitation, I stopped only to put on shoes before starting down steep wooden steps to the walkway. When I reached the landing that passed her door, the woman held out her hand in a clasp that seemed as assured as her words.

"You're Lauren Castle, the guest who came last evening, aren't you? I knew your husband. Mrs. Adrian, at the desk, told me you'd arrived. Come on in and we'll get acquainted. I'm Gretchen Frazer."

I'd known, of course, from the lodge stationery that Victoria Frazer's sister owned and managed Rumbling Mountain Lodge, but I wasn't prepared for this sudden impromptu meeting with the woman who was my great-aunt. I didn't intend to reveal myself to her, or to anyone else. Not yet. I would play everything by ear for a time until I began to get a feeling for the place and the people. First I must know what had really happened to Jim—assuming, of course, that there was more to the story than I knew.

She led me into a big room that was clearly the main living space of the house—both kitchen and dining area. Following a wave of her hand, I sat down at a round oak table and watched her prepare tea. Blue pajama legs showed beneath a comfortable-looking plaid robe that she had tied around her waist with a frayed cord. She was tall and bony—a bit gaunt—but her body gave the impression of great strength. Her face—a somber, life-worn face—wore a map of deep lines. It seemed a little forbidding in its cast—or at least that was my first impression.

By now, Victoria Frazer would have been in her early seventies—a few years younger than Roger Brandt. This woman must have been a younger sister to Victoria, for she seemed active and ageless. When her sister died, she could have been no older than seventeen or eighteen. I counted myself lucky to meet her informally as Jim Castle's wife, since she might be a source of much that I wanted to know about my mother's family.

When Gretchen Frazer had set down a tray with two blue glazed mugs, into which she had poured a dark brew, accompanied by a plate of brown cookies, she joined me at the table.

"Tell me what you think," she said, and when I looked at her blankly, she smiled. All the lines of her face lifted, so she now seemed less formidable and austere. "I mean the tea. It's made from kudzu. And so are the cookies—from kudzu flour, that is. I don't imagine you've tasted kudzu before?"

Of course I hadn't, though I knew the reputation of the voracious vine from Japan that was devouring the South. "I don't think we have kudzu in California," I said. "I didn't know it could be eaten."

"It's time people found out instead of just sitting around cursing it," she said pleasantly.

The aroma of the tea was inviting, and I flavored it with a little honey and sipped. "It's quite good."

"And not full of caffeine. It will help you sleep."

I realized suddenly that she was staring at me. Her eyes were a deep, dark brown and for a moment they held me. Then she blinked and relaxed, releasing me.

"Your eyes are an unusual color, Mrs. Castle. I've seen eyes like that in only one other person in my life."

I knew she meant her sister, Victoria, so I leaned forward to take a cookie, avoiding a reply.

"Your husband told me that you are a film writer, Mrs. Castle. I hope you don't plan to continue his work on the Brandt story."

I wasn't sure why she would oppose this, but I tried to reassure her. "Those aren't my skills. I write mostly for television, and I like to get away now and then and find fresh settings to write about. Jim's description of Lake Lure in his letters made me think I might find something for my own work here."

"You waited long enough to come," she said, sounding tart.

I had planned my story, my excuses. "It would have been too painful to come sooner."

She seemed to accept this. "In the old days, when I was young, this area attracted a number of film companies. We were quite famous before World War II. Then everything fell apart."

"It seems remarkable that Roger Brandt still lives here." I hoped that I sounded casual.

She shook her head as if puzzling. "I expect you know the local stories about Roger and my sister, Victoria?"

"I've heard some of them," I said, and changed the subject slightly. "Since Jim got to know Roger Brandt through his work and admired him, I'd like to meet him sometime."

"I don't know if you'll succeed. He doesn't take much to visitors. He and I are not exactly friends, as you might expect. Though his wife, Camilla, is all right. Sometimes I feel sorry for her."

I let this talk about the Brandts pass and finished my tea. "Thank you," I said. "I'd better get back to bed now."

She rose and came with me to the door. "If you're looking for a good setting for a story, you've come to the right place. You must be sure to take one of the boat tours around the lake."

I followed her onto a long, open porch that ran across the front of the house. From there we descended steps to the big flat roof that covered the boathouse. Metal railings protected us from the water and outdoor chairs and benches had been set about invitingly. The night was less than quiet, with water sucking rhythmically against pilings beneath us, while the orchestra of insects on the shore seemed to herald the end of summer.

A cloud covered the moon, making me aware of a sudden enveloping darkness in which the even darker mountain shapes around the lake were visible.

Gretchen Frazer pointed. "You can't see the place from here, but way down there across the water is a building that was used in the movie *Dirty Dancing*. Several scenes were shot here—so Hollywood has discovered us again. And of course some of the mountain scenes around Chimney Rock were used for *The Last of the Mohicans*. They even built a village of longhouses up there. Huron Indians in North Carolina! But it's all good for business."

Reference to the village caught my attention. "Miss Frazer, can you tell me anything about my husband's death?"

Her shoulders seemed to droop a little. "I'm sorry, I shouldn't have reminded you of such sadness. I only know that he died in that very village. I've never wanted to go there myself. I liked this place better in the old days. In the twenties, everyone came to Lake Lure—Franklin Roosevelt, F. Scott Fitzgerald, Emily Post, Frances Hodgson Burnett. The list goes on and on. You must be sure to visit the Lake Lure Inn—you'll find a lot of history there. Of course we enjoyed a long, peaceful time without visitors, but we need the money outsiders bring in, and it's good to see everything opening up again."

A wave of tiredness swept through me and I turned toward the walk leading back to my room. Gretchen came with me as far as her house, where we were stopped by a large animal that came through the screen door it had apparently managed to open. It trotted over to snuffle around my ankles, startling me.

"Behave, Siggy," Gretchen told the creature. "Don't mind

him, Mrs. Castle. He'd like to sit on your lap, if you'd let him—he's very friendly. Spoiled."

Since the fat bronze-colored animal seemed to weigh a hundred pounds at least, I didn't mean to offer him a lap. Siggy looked up at me hopefully with bright little eyes and I could have sworn he was smiling.

"He's a miniature pig," Gretchen explained, "and full-grown. Meet Sigmund von Hogg, Mrs. Castle. He's housebroken, of course, but very mischievous, and smarter than most people."

Gretchen's manner had softened, grown affectionate, and I liked her a little better because of the pig. I ventured to pat his head and felt stiff bristles that were definitely piglike. Siggy wriggled with pleasure when I scratched, and showed signs of becoming even friendlier.

"That's enough now," Gretchen told him. She opened the door and pushed him inside with her foot. "Thanks for coming down, Mrs. Castle. I was glad to have company and meet you. I'd better get back to bed now myself, since I have a patient coming early this morning."

"Patient? You're a doctor?"

"Hardly. But people come to me and I try to help."

She explained no further, so I said good night and climbed back to my room. When I got into bed again, I was no longer as aware of the rippling water reflections on the ceiling. It was interesting to have met my grandmother's sister so quickly. There were doors to be opened there, but Jim was my first concern and upon waking I must find Gordon Heath.

I went to sleep almost at once, and I was still sleeping soundly when a maid knocked at my door with breakfast rolls, fruit, and coffee. I sat up in bed to thank the young black woman as she set her tray on a drop-leaf table.

When I'd showered, I sat down hungrily to enjoy my breakfast. Then I dressed in jeans, tucked in a white shirt, and put on sturdy walking shoes; ready or not, it was time to start looking for Gordon.

In the lobby, I found Mrs. Adrian again on duty at the front desk. I asked her whether she knew Gordon Heath and she smiled.

"Everyone knows Gordon. But I think he's on vacation now, so I'm not sure where you'll find him. His mother runs a gift shop down the road a piece, just opposite the landing. You might talk to her. She'll know where he is. Her name is Finella Heath, and she calls her shop Finella's."

I thanked her, but before I started on my way, I asked a question that had been puzzling me. "I had a cup of tea with Miss Frazer late last night and she mentioned seeing a patient this morning, though she told me she isn't a doctor. What did she mean?"

Mrs. Adrian's face lighted. "Isn't she wonderful! At her age, she can outdo most of us. She can put her hands on you and make you feel better instantly. It's a gift. And she knows all the right herbal remedies. She's taught herself. I suppose you'd call her a healer."

I had wondered what it might have been like to be the younger sister of a woman as famous and beautiful as Victoria Frazer, and I was glad Gretchen had her own remarkable talents.

I thanked Mrs. Adrian and went out to the parking area, where I'd left my rented Ford. When I'd backed into the drive, I followed a narrow road that wound down through thick woods that showed a few splashes of brilliant color where oak and maple had begun to turn. I felt an exhilaration about waking up in a new place and discovering wonders I hadn't been able to see on my arrival the night before. I didn't want to think that part of this feeling might be the anticipation of seeing Gordon again. What had been between us was over long ago, and our last meeting had hardly been amicable. But since he had been Jim's friend, I knew he would see me. I wondered whether he, too, had suffered guilt because of what had happened in San Francisco.

At the level of the water, the highway led past open spaces that formed a parklike area on the lake. Several large willow trees with drooping branches added to the beauty of the scene. Moored to the landing was a long pontoon boat that bore the name *Showboat,* and the flowing water knew nothing of old tragedy.

I drove along slowly until I saw a rustic building on my left. It had probably been a barn at one time and was still painted bright red, with a sign above the door that announced FINELLA's in large white letters. A smaller sign on the screen door told me the shop was open. I parked at the side of the building and sat for a moment considering. It was unlikely that Gordon had ever told his mother about knowing me eleven years ago in San Francisco. Yet, for me, that episode of my life had changed my destiny. Jim had promised a more certain life and we had the film industry in common. A life with Gordon had seemed riskier, a question mark, and I hadn't been brave enough to take a chance with him. It was a few years before I realized I'd made the wrong choice. Not that I was sure Gordon would have been right—but Jim was wrong for me and I for him.

I left the car and climbed several wooden steps to a small landing. As I opened the screen door, a bell chimed musically.

T ★ W ★ O

THE SHOP'S interior was spacious—indeed a barn, with plenty of room for well-spaced tables and counters filled with enticing treasures. At once I was enveloped in light and color. A golden radiance shone from pine floors and walls, and I looked up into shadowy reaches where oak beams crossed empty space. Color glowed all about me, in woven hangings on the walls, in scatter rugs of Indian design, and, of course, in all the rich contents of cabinets, counters, and display tables. Yet there was no sense of crowding—just an overall effect of cheerful, open light.

I was prepared to like Finella even before I stumbled over her. With my gaze fixed high and wide, I didn't notice the woman kneeling on the floor beside a pine counter until I almost stepped on the painting that lay before her.

She raised a hand to stop me and looked up, smiling—a warm, friendly smile for a stranger.

"Hello. Come in and browse, if you like. I'll be with you as soon as I've finished mounting this watercolor."

Finella's hair was vividly red and cut in what used to be called a page boy. When she moved her head, her hair swirled thickly and settled in its own shining pattern. Her mouth, touched with a soft red, was generous in size and the dimple her smile encouraged deepened as she looked up at me. I remembered just such an indentation near her son's mouth and for a moment I was distracted. Her look and manner were so vibrantly young that it would be difficult to guess her age without knowing that she had a son a little older than my thirty years.

I returned her smile, but instead of moving to look around the shop, as she suggested, my attention was caught by the watercolor she was about to frame. Clearly, the mountain the artist had depicted was Rumbling Bald, its long, uneven top and rock-scarred flank easily recognizable even in the storm that appeared to be crashing over its summit. The lighting was strange—almost too vivid, as though the artist had caught what must have been a momentary flash of lightning as it illuminated the scene. I could sense a wind that bent the trees at the mountain's foot, where lake waters were whipped into white-frothed waves. The painting possessed a wild power that made me shiver—as though it threatened me in some way.

"Does the mountain really look like that in a storm?" I asked.

Finella nodded. "Her work is strong, isn't it? Do you see what's happening on top?"

I looked more closely and saw that an elliptical lighted shape appeared to be tilted dangerously toward the mountain.

"It looks as though a plane is about to crash in the middle of a storm."

"Mm," said Finella, sounding enigmatic.

She was still on her hands and knees, and I knelt beside her to get a better look and to search for the artist's name in the right-hand corner. The painting had been signed with a first name only: Natalie. I was startled but decided it would be too coincidental if the first name I came across that began with *N* happened to be the person I was looking for. Still—there was the matter of serendipity that was forever fortuitous and unexplainable.

"Who is Natalie?" I asked.

"She's a very talented artist. I'm showing several of her paintings in my shop, but they're hard to sell, since she picks such wild, disturbing subjects. They're uncomfortable to live with. Of course, what's happening in this painting is straight out of Lake Lure legend, of which we have many. That's not a plane that's about to crash. Look again."

I studied the tilted shape and smiled. "Not a UFO?"

"Right out of history."

"You mean that people around here really saw such a thing?"

"Or thought they did. A few were absolutely positive, even though they were doubted and pooh-poohed. Natalie's father—a teenaged boy at the time—and her grandfather are positive about what they saw. Because of the storm, they couldn't get to the top that night. This was in the fifties, when such sightings were popping up frequently."

"Did they go back to investigate?"

"They tried to the next day, but army intelligence was already on the job, brought in by helicopter. So no one was allowed to go up. Because of army maneuvers, they were told. Days later, when a party of the curious climbed the mountain, the government men were gone and the whole episode—if anything *did* happen—

was swept under the rug. There was nothing to be seen except a circle of scorched earth. But Roger and Justyn are convinced that a spaceship came down that night."

"*Roger?*" I couldn't help echoing the name.

"Roger Brandt, Natalie's grandfather. Though she doesn't like to use the name Brandt, since she's determined to make it as an artist under her own steam. I think that shows a lot of good sense; she doesn't need any of that old baggage hanging around her neck. I suppose you know about Roger Brandt and Victoria Frazer?"

"I've already met Gretchen Frazer at the lodge," I said evasively.

"Gretchen's a remarkable lady. I like the title Natalie has given to this painting: *Star Flight.* Perfect, don't you think?"

I stood up and began to move about the shop. I still hadn't introduced myself and I didn't want her to see my face. *Natalie Brandt?* It might make a weird sort of sense if she had been the one to send me that note. She would have no idea that Roger Brandt was also *my* grandfather. Jim had promised me that he would tell no one. Only Gordon Heath had known back in San Francisco. In any case, I realized that I must meet Natalie Brandt as soon as possible. First, however, I still had to talk to Gordon.

I continued wandering about the shop, busy with my own thoughts. One corner of the large main area had been partitioned into a small separate room, and I walked over to the door to investigate. A sign read: COME IN AND MEET KUDZU, THE FRIENDLY VINE.

I looked back at Finella. "Friendly kudzu?"

She stood up, stretched widely, and came toward me. I had seen only the back of her jacket and pants as she knelt before the painting, but now I received the full effect of bright patches of green and rose set into the denim jacket that fell smartly from her shoulders. Big square pockets vibrated with yellow and green. Vivid color suited her, bringing a sparkle to lively blue eyes that matched the denim.

"Kudzu isn't appreciated," Finella told me. "Some of us are trying to change that. Nobody is using the vine as it should be used. Go inside and look around."

I was interested, but now wasn't the right time. I had postponed introducing myself to Gordon's mother long enough—perhaps because I couldn't turn back once she knew who I was.

"I'm Lauren Castle," I said, walking toward her. "Jim Castle's wife."

She came at once to shake my hand warmly. "Gordon said you might be coming, but we didn't know when."

"I was able to leave suddenly," I said.

"We were very fond of Jim. As you know, he and my son were old friends. The accident shocked us terribly. I'm so sorry, Mrs. Castle, but I'm glad you've come. I don't know why, but I always felt you should."

Nothing in her words suggested that her son had told her how well he had known *me* out in California. Jim had told me that Gordon had married and then divorced, but that was all I knew about what he had done over the past eleven years. Most of the time, Jim and I had an unspoken agreement not to discuss Gordon.

"Where can I find your son?" I asked.

Finella shook her head and her glossy red hair swirled again. "I can't tell you offhand. He works for Chimney Rock Park, but he's taken ten days off, and when he's not working, I never know where he's likely to be during the day. However, we share a house on the lake, so I'll see him tonight, if not before."

"Then perhaps you can tell him I'm here and staying at Rumbling Mountain Lodge."

"Of course. I know he'll want to see you as soon as he can."

"When Gordon wrote to me, he mentioned a movie village as the place where Jim died. I'd like to go there, if you can tell me how to find it."

"That's easy enough. It's only a short drive from here, though the road up is rough and bumpy. Just follow the gorge beside the river to the next little village of Chimney Rock. Watch for the small chamber of commerce building up an embankment on your right. If you drive around behind it, you'll find a dirt road leading up the mountain. Keep going until you come out at the Indian village. The movie trucks used to bump over that road with all their heavy equipment, and the ruts are still there."

She accompanied me to the door and touched my arm in a reassuring gesture. I thanked her and said I'd like to come back to explore her shop later.

"I'll tell Gordon you're here as soon as I can, and do come back whenever you like."

I went out to my car, feeling slightly dazed. Everything was happening faster than I expected. I felt excited about the discovery that N probably stood for Natalie Brandt, to whom I was related through our mutual grandfather. My first cousin! I cared very little about the man who had betrayed Victoria Frazer, aside from a natural curiosity. According to my mother, he was the villain of this piece. And her prejudice, naturally, had become mine.

Once I'd driven past the end of the lake, the gorge lived up to its name: Steep mountains crowded each side of the narrow road. The Rocky Broad River tumbled over huge boulders below the highway, making this a road that could never be widened. This must make a fine bottleneck in the tourist season. I watched for the chamber of commerce sign and turned off, making my way behind the small building to where the dirt road started.

It was as rough and jarring as Finella had warned. The car rattled as it climbed around twists and turns, until the road came out at a large, flat, cleared area that stretched ahead. A steep mountain rose on one side and a drop-off that looked out over a valley descended on the other. There were ten or more structures of various sizes rising from bare, dusty white earth edged by the remains of crops that had been planted here and there—to lend authenticity, I supposed. A wide path led straight ahead past very real log and bark structures that had weathered to gray.

I left my car, walked twenty feet, and passed into another time and culture. These were not the wigwams of the western plains, but the traditional Huron longhouses of the North. Several were truly long and covered with strips of bark over sapling frames bent to form rounded tops. Trapdoors used to let out smoke were propped open in the roofs. During inclement weather, they could be closed against rain, but now they stood open, oblivious of the elements. The movie company had come and gone, carelessly abandoning the historical details they had so carefully constructed.

One structure, still unfinished—perhaps for the purposes of the movie—showed the open basketwork of the walls which normally would have been covered by bark. Whole tree trunks had been split and laid side by side to form a floor that was set a foot or so up from the ground.

Several buildings were smaller than the longhouses—more like huts with rounded domes. One large structure caught my attention. It was disguised as a longhouse on the side that would face a camera, but behind that facade it was built with the anachronism of two-by-fours. Looking in, I could see that its big central room was large enough for tables that would serve the crew, with a proper roof to shelter them. It still housed an abandoned refrigerator.

Outside, in the realm of the cameras, the hide of a deer had been stretched against logs for drying. On an open porch, I glimpsed a weathered pile of skins left behind, having served their purpose as props. Here and there, all about the village, were round cribs built of intertwined branches and still holding dry cobs of corn that looked as though they had been stripped long ago by foraging mice. Meticulous attention seemed to have been given to details. Later, when I saw *The Last of the Mohicans*, I discovered, sadly, how little of all this had been used. As I stood looking about this deserted place, a curious sense of having entered another time possessed me. As though, just out of sight, Indian women were busy with their cooking fires, awaiting the return of their men from the hunt. Strangely, I felt as if I were part of some play that had yet to begin. I had no idea of my role, but soon the curtain would go up and I would find myself onstage. Would I know my lines when the time came?

I shook myself free of such fantasies and walked on. In the center of the village, I saw a circle of white stones on the ground. Tall poles had been set in the center of the circle and lashed together, reaching more than seven feet into the air. A stake, perhaps, for burning an enemy? This seemed a little too real for my taste. A weatherworn blanket had been tied around the poles— perhaps to spare an actor's back from discomfort during long filming? I had no idea how the illusion would be managed in the movie, but I recalled such a scene in my long-ago reading of *The*

Last of the Mohicans. Curiously, placed a little ways in front of the stake, there was a second, smaller circle of stones, with evidence of hardened ashes at its center. At a loss to explain any of this, I kept walking.

The thickly forested mountain towered above the village, creating a magnificent backdrop on one side. On the opposite side, where the village looked out toward other mountains, a cliff dropped off steeply to the valley below. Only an occasional bird broke the deep, peaceful silence—a silence empty of any human intruder except myself. Hickory Nut Gorge was out of sight here, though I could look out to see the high, jutting pillar of granite that was Chimney Rock. Directly across from the village, a water-fall streamed down a steep mountain.

Certainly all this must have made a marvelous setting for actors in a movie, but for me it was frighteningly real. This was the place where my husband had died—where some malevolence might have touched him, if the note from *N* had any truth to it.

I discovered a long, thin tree trunk, supported at either end by the crotch of a growing tree. I perched myself on the rough bark of the makeshift bench to rest and wait. Though for what, I wasn't sure. Perhaps for the play to begin, so I could discover the part intended for me. Or had this play begun eleven years ago in the city of San Francisco?

I found myself returning in memory to a time when I was nineteen and engaged to marry Jim Castle. He was nearly ten years older than I was and already successfully established as a creator of documentary films. I aspired to scriptwriting and he had become a mentor when I took some special courses that he was teaching at Berkeley.

Jim had seemed to be all the *safe* things my mother wanted

for me. His attention was flattering and he was fun to be with. We had common interests and I thought I was falling in love. When he asked me to marry him, I agreed. My mother met him and approved, assuring me that he was nothing like my father, who had taken off on his own when I was small, and had died in a car accident.

My life had seemed comfortably settled, and then Jim had introduced me to another instructor, a graduate student who had become a good friend of his. I still don't know exactly what happened. An immediate recognition seemed to strike fire between Gordon and me. The attraction was immediate, and it was more than physical. This was something I'd never experienced before. What I felt for Jim paled beside this shattering new emotion.

Jim was going to Los Angeles for two weeks to meet a producer about a new project he was planning. He relegated the task of looking out for me to Gordon, never dreaming of the spark that had lighted between us—something we were both trying to resist. That was the most devastating part—the way Jim had trusted us. Gordon was finishing up a harried year of graduate work and teaching that had left him little time to see the fascinating city across the bay. We agreed that I would show him San Francisco, since he'd be leaving the area in six weeks.

In so many ways, Gordon was Jim's opposite—more rugged, yet not nearly so good-looking or easy to be with. Gordon was unsettled and unsettling. He wasn't sure what he wanted to do with his life. In fact, life seemed to him something to taste, to savor, to experiment with. Nothing about him seemed "safe." But for me everything seemed exactly right and as it should be. His face, wide at the cheekbones, had a serious cast, with a lot of determination in the chin. His eyes could dance with a secret

amusement—not laughing *at* me, but delighting in me and what
we had every time we were together. My first feeling was one of
alarm and then denial. I wasn't brave enough, or wise enough at
nineteen, to deal with what was happening to me, so I convinced
myself that Gordon and I were destined to be good friends and
nothing more.

I could still remember the words Gordon said to me the first
time we were alone. "I've known you somewhere, Lauren—I'm
sure of it." I hadn't yet experienced the mystical side of him, but
even as I said I didn't think so, I felt the same way. I *knew* this man
very well indeed.

The sense of recognition continued between us. Sometimes
each knew what the other was going to say. We liked the same
books, movies, causes. We both loved animals and the outdoors.
Gordon read some of my writing and thought it was promising—
but told me that I still had a lot to learn.

For nearly two weeks, we went about together—innocently
at first. We explored not only San Francisco but the wonders we
found in each other. I don't think we forgot Jim Castle as we
wandered the streets and picnicked in the park. Except for clasping
hands as we walked, or Gordon's arm draped casually around my
shoulders, there was no physical contact in the beginning. Perhaps
we both knew, without conscious awareness, that when we took
that step, there would be no turning back.

I suppose we moved for a while in a dream, not fully accepting the significance of what was happening. When Gordon told me
he was from North Carolina and that his home was at Lake Lure,
I was thoroughly shaken. The hand of some mysterious destiny
seemed to be at work and it was too strong to be ignored. I told
him who my grandparents were and we marveled together. He

had actually met Roger Brandt, though he didn't know him well.

I couldn't bear to remember what had happened next. When Jim came home, reality had to be faced. Gordon, who was going home to North Carolina shortly, wanted me to break up with Jim and go with him. He insisted that we tell Jim what had happened and ask him to understand that I couldn't possibly marry him now.

This frightened me, woke me up to my safe, everyday world—to what my mother had instilled in me. I was too young and confused to accept such ruthlessness. It seemed impossible to wound someone so deeply whom I'd thought I loved. What Gordon saw in a future together was surely an illusion, to be dispelled by reality and good sense. And never mind a broken heart or two along the way. At that point, I didn't know what a broken heart was going to feel like. I hadn't lived long enough to find out who I was.

For the first time, Gordon was cruel, and I saw a side to him that I hadn't known and that frightened me further. I still remember his words. "What you mean, Lauren, is that you lack the courage to tell Jim. Hard for me to say and probably harder for you to hear, but right nevertheless. Neither of us meant for this to happen, but it has, and we need to tell Jim and get on with our lives."

"I can't," I said miserably.

"I expected more of you; you haven't discovered your own strength yet."

"You don't know me—not really!"

I never forgot the cool gray of his eyes at that moment. "I'm beginning to and I don't think I like what I see," he said, and walked away.

He went back to Lake Lure the next day, abandoning his classes and leaving Jim puzzled but ignorant. Though he wrote to my husband now and then, I never heard from him again—until the letter came informing me of Jim's death.

I'd been sure that Jim was my best friend and that marrying him would keep me safe forever. At nineteen, one could use foolish words like *forever.*

Of course I didn't know Jim Castle any better than I knew myself. He had seemed to dote on me and all that affection had even lasted for a year or two after we married. But it was his nature to love other women with equal enthusiasm, while still wanting to keep me as his wife and friend. This was the way he was, he told me, and I was foolish to think one woman was enough for any man.

I'd hate it that Jim's interest in Roger Brandt had grown since our marriage and was leading him toward Lake Lure. North Carolina had come to mean Gordon Heath to me and that felt like very dangerous ground indeed. Jim had entertained a fantasy of my going there with him and meeting my grandfather. I refused point-blank, and when he decided to go ahead with his documentary, having already won Roger Brandt's consent, I made him promise not to reveal my identity. All my mother's prejudice against her father had been instilled in me. It was my grandmother I wanted to know more about, but I never expected to have an opportunity to learn.

Jim might never have come here if it hadn't been for me. The guilt I had felt ever since his death never left me. Afterward, there had been no point at all in coming to this place—not until the cryptic note from *N* forced my hand.

The sun was climbing higher now, warming me where I sat on the log above the open space that looked out toward the waterfall. Later, when I saw the movie, I realized that this was the very log on which the chief had sat near the end of the picture.

I roused myself and turned from the view to examine the dusty make-believe Indian village where Jim had died. Had I expected that being there would tell me something—help me understand in some way? I only knew that I was glad to be here alone on my first visit. There would be other times, of course, when I would come here with Gordon and he would tell me exactly what had happened, though this was something I'd begun to dread.

All around me were small indications of the movie that had been made here. A multitude of extras must have swarmed about this place, springing to life at the call for "action." The remnants of cigarette butts lay in the white dirt, never to appear on the screen. A discarded twist of faded red and green cloth might have been a headband. A scrap of aluminum foil caught the sun—a definite reminder of the twentieth century.

A sound startled me, quickly bringing me out of my reverie. I stiffened, listening in disbelief to the faint thumping of a drum. This was not my imagination. The sound was real, and it grew in volume as I listened, insistent in its beat, pervasive as it rose from beyond the farthest longhouse.

A drum sounding in this very real Indian village! The curtain *had* gone up and the play had begun.

T ⋆ H ⋆ R ⋆ E ⋆ E

I SWUNG about, listening, suddenly lost again in my own imagining. For a moment, the village around me belonged to a real past, so that the sound I heard came down to me from another century.

But my common sense told me these were not ghostly hands playing a drum. I listened intently. The first beat came down hard, followed by two lighter taps on a different note—the whole repeated over and over, as though it might go on forever. I slipped from my perch and started along the path of white dust that led past the stake and on among the huts.

As I moved, the drumbeat changed to a steady booming—first on a low note, then shifting gradually up the scale to something higher. I had never heard a drum as versatile as this and I wanted a glimpse of the player before he saw me. Somehow, I knew it was a man playing the drum, though a woman could have held those sticks just as well.

The sounds seemed to come from one of the smaller huts at the far end of the village. As I drew near, I noticed that part of the bark had been stripped away, or perhaps had disintegrated, from this hut, so that I could stand outside and look through open basketwork to the interior. A man sat cross-legged before the drum, which was a large oblong wooden box. Thick gray hair, shaggy as a mop, tumbled over his forehead, joining eyebrows equally thick and shaggy. A beard so tangled that it was almost neat in its matting started below a full lower lip and hid his chin. His eyes were closed and brown gnarled hands held the drumsticks with loose wrists, so that they seemed to move of their own volition.

Since he didn't see me, I had time to examine this strange spectacle. He wore corduroy pants, colorless from many washings, and his brown shirt had seen a good many mendings. Though he was unkempt, he didn't seem dirty, and I suspected that he bathed in mountain streams.

Increasingly curious, I moved around to stand below the open space of the door, where I could view him without the interference of basketwork squares.

The drumbeat grew more monotonous now. While he couldn't have seen or heard me, he knew that I was there. Suddenly, he paused with both drumsticks in the air and tilted his head back so that he could see beneath a fall of hair that was as rough as the gray bark outside the hut. I found myself staring into sharp blue eyes that didn't welcome the sight of me.

After the drum, the ensuing silence seemed to reverberate with accusation, and I broke it hesitantly. "Hello. Your playing is wonderful."

His two drumsticks had round orange plastic heads, and he

dropped the sticks into holes at the front corners of the drum. Then he jumped up and rushed toward me so swiftly and unexpectedly that I might have been knocked over if I hadn't jumped out of his way. I watched in astonishment as he dashed off between huts and disappeared into the woods—a scarecrow figure with extraordinarily long arms and legs. The forest wall looked solid as he hurled himself into the green barrier, but he must have known where a path lay, for in a moment it was as though hardly a leaf had stirred. He simply disappeared, leaving his drum behind.

"You frightened him," said a voice behind me, a voice I had never been able to forget.

I turned to face the man who watched me. All the defenses I had built up against a first meeting with Gordon vanished. I felt as though someone had wiped away the years and I was nineteen again—with no sense at all and my wounds out in the open for anyone to see.

"Hello, Lauren," he said. "I didn't know you'd arrived."

"I—I was suddenly able to get away, so I just booked a flight and came. I stopped in at your mother's shop, but she didn't know where to find you." As I spoke, I was trying to get myself in hand. I hadn't dreamed that I would be so shaken by the sight of him.

This was an older Gordon, and I sensed an inner stillness about him that hadn't been there before—a stillness that seemed to wait and listen.

I found myself almost chattering to conceal my reaction. "A few minutes ago, I thought I was the only inhabitant of this movie set. Now it appears to be populated. Who is the wild man who was playing the drum?"

He accepted my lead. "That's Grandpa Ty. He's what folks used to call a mountain man, though he hasn't always been one.

Nobody knows exactly where he lives now—probably in one of the many caves around here. He's harmless unless you upset him. Which you seem to have done."

"He almost knocked me down."

"*Almost* is the key word. He didn't even graze you. He's probably developed almost an animal sense about the physical world."

This conversation seemed totally unreal. I wasn't even thinking about the old man anymore. Suddenly, we both stopped talking and stared at each other. I didn't know what either of us was looking for, but I was the one to drop my eyes first. Neither of us was the same person we'd been in San Francisco. We were strangers all over again—people who didn't know each other at all. Or could we ever really be strangers?

He was smiling, though I didn't understand the source of his amusement until he spoke.

"Ty was Victoria Frazer's younger brother. Which makes him—what?—your great-uncle?"

I tried to hide my surprise at this information. "Then Gretchen Frazer, who runs the lodge, is also his sister?"

Gordon nodded, losing interest in the Frazers. "What took you so long to come here after Jim died?"

Gordon was the main reason I'd never come, but I could hardly tell him that, so I went off on a tangent. "Your wild man left his drum behind."

"It's not his drum—it's mine. I keep it up here for him to play, since the sound seems to belong to the mountains."

He stepped past me into the hut, picked up a large canvas square, and started to cover the drum.

An impulse seized me. "I've never seen a drum like this before. Do you mind if I try?"

I didn't give him time to mind, but joined him inside the hut and picked up the two sticks with their round orange heads. When I bounced these lightly, the sounds were dissonant. I stopped to study the surface of the wood more carefully.

"The drum is hollow," Gordon told me. "The top—all those small sections—have been carved from a single piece of wood and then fitted to the rest. Each one carries its own tone."

He took the drumsticks from me. "Let me show you," he said, and tapped the wood more lightly than the old man had done. The sound was almost hypnotic in its repetition. Now he seemed aware only of the drum, so I was able to watch him openly.

His faded blue jeans and gray work shirt, unbuttoned at the throat, were outdoor clothing. His rather square face with its determined chin had never fitted any obvious category of male good looks. To me, he had always seemed individual—different—a complete contrast to Jim Castle. His hair was straight and thick and slightly reddish—an inheritance from his mother, undoubtedly.

Watching him, I felt increasingly shaken, far more disturbed by this meeting than I cared to be. Needing to be farther away from him, I stepped down outside the hut and looked around.

"This is such a beautiful spot—peaceful," I said when he stopped playing.

"It wasn't quiet while the movie company was here." He dropped the sticks into their slots and covered the drum. Then he lifted the large block of wood and stepped down beside me.

"Why did you come *now?*" he asked.

I didn't answer for a moment. "You wrote me that Jim's death was an accident. Please tell me what happened."

That air of inner calm was still there and his movements seemed unhurried as he turned toward another part of the village, speaking to me over his shoulder.

"I'll need to put this out of the weather. The wood is sensitive to temperature changes."

He hadn't answered my question, and I followed him to the longhouse that had been used to serve the movie company. Inside, he went directly to the abandoned refrigerator and opened the big door, storing the drum inside. An ingenious solution.

"I'll show you where Jim died," he said as he rejoined me, and we started across the village.

"Why *did* you come here now?" he repeated.

"I didn't mean to come at all. It always seemed too painful after Jim died. Perhaps I never would have, but someone wrote me a note asking me to come. The note implied that Jim had been murdered. After talking with your mother and learning about Natalie Brandt, I began to suspect that this had come from her. The person who wrote me signed the letter with the initial N. But why wouldn't she have suspected foul play sooner?"

We walked on toward an unfinished longhouse and I found myself all too aware of his nearness, of wanting to look and yet not daring to. "You may be right about Natalie," he said. "She didn't know what *I* suspected until recently. From the first, I've had a strange feeling about what happened, but I had no proof."

"Why didn't you write to me about this?"

"What good would that have done? I don't know what Natalie thinks you can do now. A short time ago, she came up here with me and I sounded out my suspicions because they were troubling me. Natalie can be pretty emotional, so she must have embellished what I said in her own imaginative way and then written to you."

"If Jim's death wasn't an accident, I need to know what happened."

We walked past the ominous stake, which gave me the

creeps, even though it was only make-believe. White dust spurted from beneath our feet and I wondered how long it would take for green growth to reclaim its own right to the land.

Gordon stopped and I stood beside him. "That's where the log that killed him fell." He spoke quietly, sadly.

Slender saplings curved over the unfinished roof of the longhouse. I puzzled aloud: "Nothing here seems heavy enough to do any damage."

"Look around at the finished longhouses and you'll see that they're all propped up by strong tree trunks. There's one missing here—the one that fell."

"But if it wasn't an accident—how could anything like that be planned?" None of this seemed real to me—especially not my husband's death in this place. Or that I should be standing here beside a man I'd once loved—and given up.

"It couldn't have been planned, but perhaps someone simply waited for an opportunity. If a tree that formed a support was pried loose from its lashing and Jim happened to be standing beneath it, someone could have pushed it down easily. Someone who came here with him and whom he trusted. But who? That's the part that stumps me; I can't think of anyone who didn't like Jim Castle."

"I don't understand why he was up here in the first place. An Indian village wouldn't belong in a documentary about Roger Brandt, would it?"

"I think Jim was trying to think of a logical way to lure Roger up here. The village fascinated him and he wanted to find a way to use it in his film."

"That would have been like Jim. When did you begin to suspect that it wasn't an accident?"

"Ty figured it out. His instincts run deep and he was obsessed by Jim's death. They'd struck up a friendship because Jim accepted the old guy as he is, warts and all. So Ty is the one who finally made me believe that what happened was deliberate."

I was still questioning, reluctant to believe. "Perhaps the wood rotted and it was Jim's bad luck to be in the wrong place at the wrong time?"

"Ty thinks that log wouldn't have come down on its own for years—that it had to have had help. But what he believed and my gut feelings aren't any sort of proof. The police were satisfied at the time that it was an accident. Somehow, though, it wouldn't let me be. Finally, I had to talk to somebody about Ty's claim. Natalie was deeply troubled by Jim's death, so I brought her here to talk it all out with me. I wanted to show her what might have happened, see if we could both believe it. What I told her put her into high gear, apparently, though I think it was foolish of her to get you involved in this."

Natalie and Jim, I thought. Logical, of course—that was the way Jim had been with pretty women. The movie village seemed to close in around me with its sense of a wilder, more primitive time. Or had it been, really? Today, violence was an everyday affair in many places. So why not here?

"Natalie has done some sketches of this place—pretty haunting stuff," Gordon said, watching me. "She's tried to sell them, but she doesn't have much luck. I think they scare people."

I remembered the painting of the spaceship coming down in the vivid lightning of a storm. Natalie Brandt would have even more to tell me.

Gordon moved off away from me, walking the length of the nearest longhouse. I watched him, wishing I could rid myself of my memories, my old feelings. We had both married other people. *I* had been the first to make that choice. Since then, he had been divorced and my husband had died. Whatever attraction he had felt for me was surely over long ago. I must remember that.

Suddenly, Gordon turned to look at me. "Natalie had a feeling that Jim wanted *you* to come here. She thinks he's been trying to reach her since his death and that you might be a catalyst."

This startled me. "Do you believe that?"

"I don't disbelieve." He looked off toward distant mountains, and I was reminded again that he'd sometimes revealed a mystical side in the past.

He came back to me abruptly. "Anyway, you're here, and Natalie seems to have brought this about."

A deepening sadness filled me. A sadness that a woman I had never met had felt my husband's death more profoundly than I. Sadness for Jim's lost gifts. Sadness, too, for the love Gordon and I had allowed to slip out of our hands, a lost love that would never come again. If I had chosen a different fork in the road—what then? But that didn't bear thinking about.

I walked to where a big tree trunk, stripped of its limbs, lay on the ground. It was one that might have supported a side of the longhouse that was beginning to sag.

"Is this the log that killed Jim?"

He nodded, not wanting to tell me. "Lauren, I'm sorry—"

"What can *I* do?" I spoke the words aloud, but they were addressed only to me. I didn't expect him to know.

He spoke abruptly. "Let's get out of here. This isn't a good place for us to talk." He looked around as though the trees themselves might be listening, and I wondered whether Ty Frazer still lingered out there. "It's nearly noon, so let's go down to Chimney

Rock for lunch. Then we can try to sort things out. Natalie should never have brought you here, and perhaps you shouldn't stay. I don't think there is anything you can do, and as Jim's wife you may not be entirely safe."

I didn't want to accept that idea and I didn't want to leave; there was still my connection with Victoria Frazer to hold me here. I didn't mean to be frightened away, whether I could do anything about Jim or not. And there was still the matter of a grandfather I couldn't help being curious about. I needed more time.

"Lunch will be fine," I told him.

"Good. Then let's get back to our cars and you can follow me down the mountain."

I went with him, turning my back on the ghostly Indian village. I didn't think I would come here again—which is an example of how little we can ever foretell the future.

Once I was behind the wheel, Gordon loped down the road ahead in a long-legged stride that I remembered. By the time I drew up beside his Jeep, he was ready to lead the way.

The bumpy road seemed shorter going down. When we reached the open area around the tiny chamber of commerce building, he parked nearby and I left my Ford beside his Jeep. Below us, the highway narrowed, forming the bottleneck for which there was no cure.

On foot, we followed the narrow verge at the side of the road for a short distance and then crossed to a small restaurant where Gordon was greeted as a friend. We took the one remaining booth and were given flatware wrapped in paper napkins. When the waitress had taken our orders and gone, I asked a question that had been troubling me since I'd seen the place in the village where Jim had died.

"Are you sure Jim didn't make any enemies while he was

here? I know he could be pretty pushy in order to get what he wanted, so I wondered—"

"Not *enemies*—as I told you, everyone seemed to like him. Of course there were a lot of people who were curious about what he would do with the Roger Brandt story—especially when it came to Victoria Frazer. But I don't think he stirred up any real resentment. Natalie told me that Roger actually relaxed and talked to him. And even Camilla Brandt, Roger's wife, seemed to accept what Jim was doing, though she was against it at first. She guards her husband's well-being carefully."

I sensed an uneasiness—something Gordon wasn't saying. When the waitress arrived with a sizzling hamburger for him, along with my chef's salad and two glasses of iced tea, I changed the subject.

"What do you do, Gordon? Jim said you were connected with Chimney Rock, but I don't know much about your work."

"I manage the park. With a lot of help. It's a spectacular place and the work keeps me outdoors a lot of the time. I've been sharing a house on Lake Lure with my mother since my divorce, and it seems to work out well for both of us. Though all this is probably temporary. I like what I'm doing, but who knows what the future holds?"

So he was still unsettled? A quality in a man that my mother had abhorred. Somehow I no longer minded. I felt unsettled myself.

I wanted to ask about his ex-wife but didn't dare.

He smiled at me—rather a fierce smile that challenged me to comment—as he answered what I hadn't put into words. "Betty deserved better than I could give her. She's happily remarried now."

For a little while, we concentrated on our food, perhaps both

43

of us too unsure of ourselves to speak. Then Gordon returned to the subject of Jim Castle. "Did you notice anything unusual in Jim's last letters? I had a feeling that he was keyed up about something—like a firecracker getting ready to go off."

"He didn't say anything specific, but the last time we talked on the phone he hinted that he was onto something important, perhaps even newsworthy. Is there any way to find out what it was? Do you think Roger Brandt would know?"

"Brandt isn't an easy man to talk to. Besides, all his contacts with Jim were at his house, and usually Camilla was present, so I doubt that Roger knew about Jim's interest in the Indian village or that he'd struck up an acquaintance with Ty Frazer."

"Would it be possible for me to meet Roger Brandt, do you suppose?"

Gordon's smile was pointed. "You don't plan to tell him you're his granddaughter?"

"I don't think so. That might put him on guard. I can't imagine that Camilla Brandt would welcome the appearance of Victoria's granddaughter. What is she like?"

"They were married out in California two years before he made the film with your grandmother. He was only twenty-one, but he'd been a big star since his late teens. In a way, Camilla's fitted in here better than he has. She's a very grand and beautiful lady who looks years younger than her age. Perhaps by now she's forgotten that Victoria Frazer ever existed. Though I'm not sure about Roger. Rumor has it that he keeps a secret collection of Victoria's films."

All this caught my imagination. It might be interesting to meet Roger Brandt without his knowing that I was related to him.

We finished our meal and walked back to our cars. Gordon

opened the door for me and held out his hand. He wasn't mocking me now and some of the stiffness I'd sensed in him earlier had fallen away—as though he had begun to accept me without reference to the past. But could I accept him as casually?

"Where are you going now, Lauren?" he asked.

"Back to your mother's shop. I want to see her again and explore that fascinating place."

"Good. I'll try to get in touch with Natalie. If you aren't busy tonight, would you mind if the three of us got together for dinner?"

"Of course not. I'd welcome the chance to meet her—and to see you again." I had meant to sound casual and friendly, but more feeling had come through than I intended, and he seemed to withdraw a little.

"Fine. If I can reach Natalie, I'll phone you at my mother's. Otherwise, I'll leave a message at the lodge."

I watched as he drove down into traffic, but I made no move to start my car. How did I feel about Gordon Heath now? He was no longer that young man I'd fallen in love with out in San Francisco. Neither was I the same young woman who had made a choice. The wrong choice, but that was over and done with. So why was I sitting here shaking?

Impatient with myself, I started the car and followed the road Gordon had taken toward Lake Lure.

F ★ O ★ U ★ R

WHEN I reached Finella's shop, I found her busy with a customer, so I wandered back to the kudzu room to discover just how friendly the ubiquitous vine might be.

The room was small, with a two-burner electric stove at one end, shelves where books tilted against one another—mostly cookbooks—rows of glass jars, and an oak table with a chopping-block surface. Obviously, cooking with kudzu was done in this room.

A large poster asked whether I knew that

Kudzu makes wonderful nonbloating forage for cattle?
Kudzu is a healthy and tasty food for humans?
Kudzu powder can be used in hundreds of recipes?
*Fresh kudzu shoots, picked right off the vine, are delicious
   in a salad?*

Kudzu flowers can be pickled in vinegar?
Kudzu roots can be steamed?
Kudzu can be used as treatment for many bodily
    ailments?
Cloth can be woven from kudzu fibers?

I was beginning to see why kudzu was considered friendly. A stack of books and pamphlets, including *The Book of Kudzu: A Culinary and Healing Guide,* stood on a display table.

When her customer had gone, Finella found me leafing through the kudzu material and her eyes brightened. "If you like to cook, you must try some of those recipes."

I smiled at such missionary fervor. "I can tell from your enthusiasm that it must be delicious."

"You can buy the flour in health-food and specialty shops and have a ball. It's such an inexpensive way to feed people *and* animals and it's the best way to stop the vine's needless encroachment where it isn't wanted. Some of us are trying to spread the word. Harvesting would be so easy in the South and kudzu is free!"

Finella's red hair moved with its own grace as her animation grew, and I warmed to her all over again. "I'll take some flour home with me," I promised.

"Did you find the Indian village?"

"I not only found the village but I saw your son. It doesn't seem possible that you're old enough to be his mother."

Her smile rewarded me. "I like that! He was born when I was seventeen and didn't have much sense. Neither did his father, and we didn't last long together. I'm glad he's turned out as well as he has. In a way, we grew up together, so we're good friends. What do you think of him?"

So she really had no idea that he'd known me eleven years ago in San Francisco. The subject of my feelings about her son was something I didn't want to get into, so I was relieved when the bell on the shop door sounded.

Finella looked out toward the door. "That's Ty now with my new batch of kudzu. He keeps me supplied. You'll have to come meet this remarkable mountain man."

Obviously, Finella didn't know of my relationship to the Frazers, either, and I was glad that Gordon had been discreet.

"We've already met—in a way," I told her, following her across the shop. "He was playing a drum up in the village, but he rushed off before I could talk to him. Gordon told me a little about him."

As she went to greet Ty, Finella waved me toward a table. "Those are some of Gordon's drums over there."

I walked over to the area she'd designated. The drums were so big and heavy that they'd been arranged on the floor. Gordon hadn't mentioned that he'd made the drum I'd seen, and now I could admire more of his meticulous work. Each drum was different, each beautiful in its own way. I tapped my fingers lightly across a sectioned surface, catching the faint musical echo.

Ty had come into the shop with his burlap bag of kudzu vines. He heard the sound and looked over at me. "What's she doing here?"

"Mrs. Castle is a friend—she's Jim Castle's wife. You remember Jim, don't you?"

His eyes widened as he looked at me from beneath his bush of eyebrows and hair. "She shouldn't have come here."

I walked toward him cautiously, not wanting to alarm him again. "Why is that?" I asked quietly.

He seemed to dismiss me and spoke directly to Finella. "I thought I'd bring you another batch before there's a nip in the air and it goes to sleep for the winter."

"Thanks, Ty. Will you put it in the bottom of the refrigerator back there so it won't wilt before I can get to it. The flour is beginning to sell pretty well."

Now that I knew of my relationship to this wild-looking character, I watched him with all the more interest. It hardly seemed possible that he was related to the legendary Victoria. My mother had come to Lake Lure just once. It was when I was about ten, and when she returned she had only harsh things to say about the place. She'd said nothing about Ty and little about Gretchen, the one relative she'd seen when she was here.

I wondered what Ty's reaction would be if he knew that I was not only Jim Castle's wife but also his own great-niece.

On his way to the kudzu room, something caught Ty's eye and he dropped the bag to give his full attention to the painting by Natalie Brandt that Finella had been framing when I walked in that morning.

"Hmph!" It was both grunt and comment. *"She* paint that?"

"You mean Natalie?" Finella said. "Yes—it's pretty good, isn't it?"

Ty stared fixedly at the painting with its storm blues and midnight purple overcast, through which the glowing elliptical shape slanted toward the top of Rumbling Bald Mountain.

"Sure is," he said. "Looks just like I saw it when those space people came down. Too bad they disappeared. I'd like to've had a closer look."

Finella spoke softly. "I didn't know you saw the ship, Ty."

"Sure—I was on the mountain. I was keeping an eye on

Justyn and Roger. Brandt-watching! So I saw it come down in the storm."

"Finella was telling me that no trace of the ship was ever found," I said, cautiously entering the conversation.

"Who knows what those army fellas found—or didn't find. Maybe they missed a thing or two."

Something in Ty's voice seemed to alert Finella. "Would you know where to look, Ty? Was something left up there on the mountain?"

He waved his long arms, startling us both. "Don't *you* go poking into stuff like this. That's what that young fella from California did. And look what happened to him!"

I spoke softly, to not excite him further. "Gordon told me what you believe, Ty. I'd like to know more about my husband's death. That's why I've come here."

He ignored me, studying the painting again. "How come she could do it like that?" he asked Finella. "*She* wasn't even born when it happened."

"Imagination," Finella said. "And perhaps Natalie's extrasensitivity. Artists can see things in their own minds. Besides, I'm sure Roger and Justyn have talked a lot about what happened. I must ask Justyn what he thinks, now that I've seen his daughter's painting."

The old man turned a sudden close scrutiny upon me, coming closer, so that I could smell the aura that floated around him—of pine needles and forest growth, with perhaps a hint of moonshine thrown in.

"You were the one up in the village. When I was playing the drum. You look like *her*."

This was startling—did he mean Victoria? "Who do you think I look like?"

50

He had a way of not answering direct questions. "You better go home real soon—before something happens to you, the way it happened to young Jim."

"Please tell me about that."

His mouth seemed to clamp shut in the mat of shaggy whiskers and he picked up his sack and walked past me toward the kudzu room.

Finella shrugged and rolled her eyes graphically. Just as Ty returned, clearly in a hurry to get away, a man came into the shop. For an instant, the two stared at each other, and I could sense the tension, the animosity that leapt between them.

The newcomer scrunched up his face and waved a hand in the air as if to clear the room of a bad aroma. He wore a billed nautical cap and his face had the weathered look of an outdoorsman. Ty seemed to have caused his grim expression, for he smiled cheerfully enough at Finella as Ty went out the door, muttering to himself.

Finella shook her head despairingly. "Hello, Justyn. Is the old feud still on?"

Justyn? So this was another relative on the Brandt side—Roger's son and Natalie's father.

"It's not likely to end," he told Finella. "Not as long as there's a Brandt or Frazer alive."

And what, I wondered, if there was someone alive who was both Brandt *and* Frazer?

Finella introduced us. "Justyn, this is Jim Castle's wife, Lauren. Justyn Brandt."

As he took my hand, he gave me a look that I couldn't fathom. A look of suspicion, of distrust?

"What brings you here now?" he asked abruptly.

I didn't tell him that a note from his daughter had summoned me. "I suppose it was time to come."

Clearly, he considered this no answer. He continued to study me, his eyes hidden beneath the bill of the cap he hadn't bothered to remove. His scrutiny made me uneasy, but now he seemed to make up his mind about something.

"While you're here, you ought to see the lake," he said as abruptly as before. "There's a boat leaving in twenty minutes. Would you like to come?"

This invitation out of the blue seemed puzzling. I looked at Finella, but she appeared to see nothing unusual.

"Go ahead, Lauren. Justyn conducts tours of the lake, so you'll be in good hands."

Perhaps this was a way of getting closer to the Brandt establishment. "I'd like that," I said.

"Good." He sounded somehow unenthusiastic. "I'll take you over to the boat. Finella, my mother wanted me to stop in and see if you can be available when it comes to supervising the decorating of the old barn. Lake Lure Inn has been using it for storage for years, but now it's all to be cleared out so we can hold our big party there."

"Of course I'll help," Finella agreed. "I'll give her a call and see what I can do. Lauren, let me get you a sweater and scarf before you leave. It can be cool and windy on the water."

She went to a closet and came back with a white sweater and flowered scarf, and I thanked her.

"We can walk across to the dock," Justyn told me when we were outside. "Just leave your car here."

I had a feeling that he was on the verge of disliking me—yet wanted contact at the same time.

"What is this party you mentioned?" I asked as we crossed the highway together.

"It's a fund-raising affair for the Lake Lure area," he told me. "A costume ball that my mother's been cooking up. The barn behind the inn used to be used for square dances way back, but this will be more spectacular. It's less than a week away, so all the invitations have gone out. Will you be here, Mrs. Castle?" He gave me a sidelong look as he asked, and I wondered about his odd, not-altogether-friendly interest in me.

I said I wasn't sure. But I was thinking it might be fun, if Gordon was still my friend.

Near a strip of water where the *Showboat* was moored, several blue-haired ladies sat on a bench, watching ducks on the water as they waited to board the boat.

"I'm Captain Matt now," Justyn warned me. "Otherwise, the Brandt name causes too many questions."

"Are people still interested in Victoria Frazer?" I ventured.

"Yeah, I reckon they are. Of course all sorts of stories are told around here. Just don't believe everything you hear. I always point out the place where she's supposed to have drowned. My passengers expect that." He sounded dismissive, as though this was something he did reluctantly.

"I'm staying at Rumbling Mountain Lodge," I told him, "so I've met Gretchen Frazer. It's strange to think of her and that peculiar old man who brings the kudzu to Finella as the sister and brother of Victoria Frazer."

Justyn didn't comment—he was busily greeting the women and two men who waited to come aboard. A green carpet along the dock contrasted with a band of red paint at water level on the boat. Railings and seats were a sparkling white and a yellow awning spanned the central section's rows of seats.

I heard my name called and looked toward the road. Finella

was hurrying across as I went to meet her.

"Gordon asked me to catch you if I could. He wanted you to know that dinner's all planned. Natalie and you and he will meet at the Lake Lure Inn at eight. Is that still good for you?"

"Oh, yes. Thank you for coming to tell me. I'm looking forward to meeting Natalie."

"Well, have fun," she said as she dashed off with a quick wave.

Justyn handed me aboard and I went to sit on a wide, upholstered sofa set in the stern, above the outboard motor. Two women sat down next to me, one explaining to the other what we could see from the boat. I listened unobtrusively.

"That's the Lake Lure Inn over there," one told her friend, pointing. "You can see the red roof just above those willow trees. In the old days, all sorts of celebrities used to stay there. There's new management now and it's waking up again."

I looked with interest at the great white building with a red tile roof that suggested Spanish architecture. It had been built imposingly in the old, grand hotel style. I would be dining there tonight with Gordon and Natalie, and a small stirring of excitement ran through me. A great deal might hang on whatever happened at the inn this evening.

Having seen everyone aboard, Justyn continued his Captain Matt role—cheerful and garrulous. Clearly, this was something he enjoyed doing, and his rather morose manner had disappeared.

Once the motor was running, he told us, no one would be able to hear him, so he would point out a few things to watch for now. There would be other pauses on the way, when he'd turn off the motor and explain a bit more.

The ducks paddled away on rippled water as we started off,

apparently familiar with human antics and not alarmed. In a moment, we were out on the lake, and I was glad to slip into Finella's sweater and tie the scarf over my head. Except where our wake stretched white and frothy beneath where I sat, the water was calm, reflecting the greenish cast of trees that grew thickly down to the lake's edge. At the far end toward the gorge, where I'd been this morning, high peaks cut into the sky. A scene of dramatic beauty.

Old Rumbling Bald was closer now, directly across a narrowing strip of water, its reflection in the lake doubling its ominous strength. I looked up at the rock-scarred face and felt again its strange spell. Perhaps Natalie's painting had added to my sense that the mountain had something to tell me—an urgent something that might be frightening. I could imagine a sky lighted by a purplish overcast, out of which an elliptical form slanted toward unfamiliar territory—our planet earth. *Star Flight*, she'd called her painting.

While the boat moved smoothly on its pontoons, I began to notice interesting irregularities along the shoreline. The original valley, as Justyn had told us, was very deep, carved out eons ago by the Rocky Broad River and formed roughly in the shape of a cross, with two coves cutting into either shore to form the arms. There were numerous other small indentations, as well—sheltered inlets where boats were moored, and homes had been built on the banks above.

The lake shimmered with color from the sky, the richness of dark evergreens along the shore tinting otherwise murky water. No roads were visible from here, no cars, only the dots of rooftops among the trees. Coves and boathouses became mere trimming along the water's edge, and when Justyn turned off the motor, a sense of the lake's beauty and peace possessed me.

The boat rocked gently and I began to relax. The haunting vision of Natalie's painting faded and the long, narrow lake held me gently. I needn't think of death. I needn't think of Jim, or Victoria Frazer. I could let everything go and give myself up to this entrancing scene. Autumn was becoming evident where mountains cast their reflections across the mirror of the lake, lending color to its surface.

By the time Justyn turned to speak to us, I was lost in reverie. "Some old-timers claim that down there in a deep part of the lake a little Baptist church is still standing," Justyn said, warming to his story. "When the valley was flooded, the church was left to receive the waters through its open doors and windows. I'm told that if you're out in a boat above that spot on a Sunday morning, you can hear the ghostly echo of a church bell tolling. Though the only congregation down there these days consists of fish—of which Lake Lure has plenty."

I liked the story and I stared into the water, wishing I could see into its mysterious depths and glimpse the little church. Justyn's next words spoiled my new contentment.

"Over there on the bank just below the mountain," he told us, "is where Victoria Frazer, the famous young movie actress from the thirties, is supposed to have drowned." This time he seemed to speak by rote, without feeling, performing a duty.

Even though I'd known this might happen, I felt shaken. In spite of buzzing voices around me, I found nothing romantic about Victoria Frazer's death—or in the part Roger Brandt might have played in whatever had happened. My mother had come home from her single visit to Lake Lure believing that *her* mother had not committed suicide and that somehow my grandfather was more to blame for her death than anyone realized. This idea seemed to have come from a conversation she'd had with someone during her visit. The one relative she'd seen when she had come here—her aunt, Gretchen Frazer—had refused to discuss her sister's death. My mother had told me this much but no more. I never learned who had made her think my grandmother hadn't taken her own life. So now I hated to hear Roger's son pandering to the idle curiosity of his passengers. When one of the women asked whether we would see Roger Brandt's house, I stiffened.

Accustomed to the question, Justyn waved an arm in a broad gesture toward thick forest growth at this end of Rumbling Bald. When I turned my head, I could see a big white house set high among the trees. It had two chimneys and decks at three levels, looking as though it had grown there over many years, not all of its additions architecturally compatible. I could feel no sense of connection to the house where my grandfather lived. It meant less to me than that vague spot near the shore where Victoria Frazer was supposed to have drowned.

Cameras were out now, pointing toward the house. One woman asked whether we could get a little closer, but Justyn shook his head.

"Mr. Brandt asks that all boats keep away from his dock. He values his privacy and doesn't welcome visitors. We respect that."

One blue-haired lady rejected this discouragement and spoke to her husband. "Maybe we could drive around by the road and get closer?"

Justyn stepped on this notion at once. "The road doesn't go all the way around the lake. Mr. Brandt has a private access road with a gate across and warning signs for trespassers."

He cut off any further questions by starting the motor. I

watched the shore as we glided past the Brandt house. At water level, it boasted two boathouses. A tower with glass all around rose from one corner, offering a tremendous view down the lake. As we moved on, the rocky face of Rumbling Bald reduced the house to a miniature set high among the trees.

Now Justyn gestured toward what lay ahead. We were approaching the long white dam that had made Lake Lure possible. A road crossed over the top and I could see a car moving above the spill of water. While I felt no emotion about it, I turned in curiosity to watch the Brandt house as we slipped past.

There would be no opportunity for me to set foot on those grounds unless I made my identity known, and I didn't think I would do that, so I wanted a last look. Because I was the only one still watching, I saw the woman who came running out along a dock that reached into the water. She was waving something white—a sweater, perhaps. Waving it urgently at the boat.

I called to Justyn over the din of the motor, waving my own hands to catch his attention. "Someone's trying to signal you from the Brandt house," I shouted.

He looked toward the dock in surprise and then grinned at his passengers as he cut the motor for a moment. "You're in luck. It seems we're wanted over there. Maybe for an emergency."

Everyone aboard buzzed eagerly as Justyn restarted the motor. As we approached the shore, cameras clicked and people got visibly excited as Justyn pulled in beside the dock and tossed a rope ashore. The woman caught it and wound it expertly around a post as Justyn used a boat hook to pull us to the dock.

"What's up, Natalie?" he shouted.

"Is Lauren Castle aboard?" she called.

Justyn nodded toward me, and Natalie Brandt spoke to me directly. "Would you care to come ashore, Mrs. Castle?"

This was an interesting surprise. Meeting Natalie Brandt in her own setting would be far better than waiting until the formality of dinner tonight. Besides, I might even catch a glimpse of my grandfather. I was unexpectedly excited.

"Of course," I said, while my fellow passengers stared at a possible celebrity in their midst.

"I'll drive her back," she told Justyn, "so you won't need to pick her up."

I looked at Justyn and saw a surprising anger in his eyes.

Natalie reached out a hand to help me ashore. Justyn touched a finger to his cap in a mocking salute before pulling off into the middle of the lake. He hadn't spoken to his daughter at all after his initial inquiry.

When I stood on the boards of the dock, I was aware, first of all, of the great white house rising high on the hill above, with all its many windows like curious, staring eyes. Nothing moved up there, but I wondered who might be watching. Of course, I would be no one exceptional to anyone here, just Jim Castle's wife.

Natalie's scrutiny was open and searching, so that I felt wary and a little suspicious. She might very well have responded to Jim's easy appeal, and he would have found her attractive and interesting. This other granddaughter of Roger Brandt's was distinctive-looking in her own way. Her oval face and long black hair, left free to float down her back, could be a heritage from Spanish ancestors on her grandmother's side. Black eyebrows with an upward tilt accented dark eyes. Her only makeup was the touch of crimson burnishing her unsmiling mouth. She wore well-faded jeans and an outsized blue shirt, its sleeves rolled up.

I studied her as intently as she was studying me, and the coolness between us was evident.

"Finella phoned me to say that she'd confirmed our dinner

plans with you," Natalie said. "When she told me you were on Dad's boat, I thought it might be easier if we met before tonight— on our own."

"Your father didn't seem pleased," I ventured. She shrugged and gestured toward the walk that climbed to the house.

"Let's go up to my studio, where we can talk. My grandfather and grandmother stay in their own part of the house, so we won't be interrupted."

I felt cautious and uncertain as I followed her up the walk. *She* had planned this meeting. She had brought me to Lake Lure in the first place and I wanted to know more about why.

A flight of rustic steps led from the walk to a stretch of porch at the lower end of the house. Natalie climbed the steps and I followed her.

"We can go in here," she said, opening a door into the wide, light-filled room that was her studio. I looked around with interest. Paintings stood everywhere—some leaning against the wall, some mounted, some in frames. One rested on an easel, though I didn't focus on it until later. I remembered what Finella had said about Natalie's paintings being hard to sell and I could see why.

Many were of the lake, but it was never depicted in bright sunlight. Eerie moonlight or grayish mists of early morning were often shown. One painting in particular held me. Under a lowering sky, mist gathered near the lake shore beneath the rocky face of Rumbling Bald—mist that seemed to drift into the form of a woman even as I stared.

"Our local legend," Natalie said carelessly. "It's a good thing my grandparents never come here—they'd hate that picture. Come and sit down, Lauren." She used my name easily, probably having heard it from Jim.

I went to a cushion-heaped sofa facing the windows, where

I could look out at lake and mountains. I had arrived here all too suddenly and I still had a sense of unreality about where I was and whom I was with. This was my *grandfather's* house. This woman was my cousin. Yet blood didn't speak to blood and I could feel no kinship. I was Victoria's granddaughter before I was Roger Brandt's.

"Coffee?" Natalie asked. "I have a little kitchen back here."

I shook my head. "No, thank you." Shared coffee seemed too intimate for my detached mood. It was time to make the plunge, so I asked a direct question.

"Why did you send me that strange note?"

She made no denial. "It brought you here, didn't it? An ordinary letter might not have worked."

"Why did you want me to come?"

A faint spark came into her eyes. "I thought you might bring things to a head. Gordon Heath told me what he suspects, what Ty Frazer believes. I didn't know any of this until recently. When Gordon told me that they thought Jim had been murdered, I felt I had to take some sort of action to bring you here. Your presence might attract the truth about Jim's death."

"I don't see how you can possibly expect that to happen."

Natalie had been staring off toward the opposite shore—a more serene vista than this wilder side. Now she looked at me directly, challenging.

"Don't you care about what happened to Jim? Don't you want to know?"

The depth of her feelings for Jim became obvious. If there'd been any doubt in my mind about their relationship, it was gone. She and Jim had undoubtedly been lovers and I could only feel sorry for her.

When I didn't respond, she went on, sounding defensive.

"Jim said you were breaking up, that things had been bad for a long time. He said he wasn't tied to anyone."

"Then why bring me here now? If Jim's death was no accident, the trail has been cold for nearly two years."

"It was probably cold in the first place. I think the murderer was very clever. Any indications must have been carefully removed, or hidden. But once Gordon told me his conclusions, I began to see the possibilities if you came here."

"What conclusions? What game are you playing?"

She jumped up, her long black hair swinging across her back—a lithe figure, with nervous hands that were seldom still. I began to sense that she knew more than she was admitting; there was something she wasn't yet ready to tell me. I didn't trust her, but she fascinated me. I waited silently for whatever course she would choose next.

She stopped before a window that looked out toward Rumbling Bald and rested her forehead against the glass, as though she welcomed the cool touch.

When she didn't answer me, I challenged her further. "There's something else you want from me, isn't there? Something that has nothing to do with Jim's death—at least directly?"

She turned back to me, her expression calmer, and she almost smiled. "You're as perceptive as Jim said you were. There *is* something else. Something you may say no to at first. That's the other reason I took the dramatic course to catch your attention and bring you here. It's why I snatched you off Dad's boat today. Dad never liked Jim, and I know he wasn't pleased that I did. I want you to think about what I'm going to say before you dismiss it. Give the idea time to settle in."

She hesitated, as though unsure of how to win me over to whatever she wanted me to do.

"I'll listen," I said quietly.

"All right. What I want is for you to finish what Jim Castle began—the documentary about Roger Brandt. Jim told me that you're a good writer. You know how to tell a story, and he said you'd done some fine scripts for TV movies. So I think you're the right person to do this. You can carry on where Jim left off."

I was already shaking my head. "I couldn't possibly! I'm no good at all with a camera, and besides, this would need a director with experience."

"But you know what works on a screen. I'm pretty good at the camera part. I've even had a show or two of my photographs, and I've done several videos that Jim thought were good. For this work, we'd need a written script—at least an outline to follow, questions to be asked. We'd need some sort of plan that would give us form before interviews ever started. Jim wanted to use me to interview my grandfather, though I was never sure that was a good idea. You could be more objective. I'd rather stay behind the camera."

What she was suggesting came as a total surprise, but suddenly the possibilities began to seem exciting. If I interviewed Roger Brandt, all sorts of opportunities to know this family might open for me. It was a way to get a toe in the door. I might even be able to question Roger Brandt about Victoria Frazer—and open up a source of information unavailable to me otherwise. Still, I owed nothing to the Brandt side of the family, and I was puzzled by Natalie's request.

"Why do you want to do this?" I asked.

Emotion deepened her voice and I sensed her sincerity. "I *care* about my grandfather. He means more to me than anyone else. What happened to him when his career was destroyed by gossip and all the false stories was unfair—wicked."

Wicked seemed a strong word. What about Roger Brandt's treatment of Victoria? In what direction did wickedness lie?

Natalie continued more quietly. "Jim Castle gave my grandfather a new hope that his side of what had happened would be honestly told. Since Jim's death, he's become depressed. He has a foolish notion these days that anything he touches is sure to be doomed."

I didn't want to feel sympathy for Roger Brandt. "How do you think the Victoria Frazer part of the story should be handled? Your grandfather can't have come out of that completely free of blame."

Natalie sighed. "I don't think we've ever heard the whole story. Of course that was the big romance of the day, as far as the press was concerned, but I'm not sure it was that important to my grandfather. I suspect that he'd had other affairs that my grandmother had to put up with—she's a strong woman. Victoria must have been weak—to drown herself like that. She must have known that he would never leave his wife."

Clearly, more than Roger Brandt's story needed to be told. Whether there was ever a documentary or not, perhaps I owed it to my grandmother to take this on. Someday I might write a book about *her* story—if ever I knew enough about what had happened. This might be a way to learn one side at least.

I pushed Natalie with another question. "How does your grandfather feel about Victoria Frazer now?"

"He won't talk about her. Jim was just beginning to get past his guard when he died. You won't have an easy time." She paused, studying me thoughtfully. "Still, Grandfather likes pretty women, and he just might be willing to see Jim's wife. Gran may be dead set against this, of course, and she won't trust you. She distrusted what Jim was doing at first. Often she can seem as modern as tomorrow, then in the next minute she's an old-fashioned, very proper lady." A spark of amusement came into Natalie's eyes. "It's possible that her opposition may make Grandfather all the more willing to do this. They love each other and sometimes hate each other at the same time. First, of course, he has to meet you. He liked Jim, so that's a start. And if you can get Gran to trust you, this will be even easier."

I drew back a little. I didn't like the aspect of playacting. "I don't want to stir up old feuds. If your grandmother doesn't approve . . ."

Natalie laughed, an unexpectedly harsh sound. "What lies between my grandparents is no feud. I'd call it a gentlemen's war. I've often wondered why they stayed together over the years, or why on earth they came here to live in the first place. That's something he won't discuss any more than Gran will. She must have been hurt by his affair with Victoria. Apparently, it was a bit more than one of his casual flings, though I don't think my grandmother ever considered leaving him, any more than he'd have left her."

"What about your father?" I asked. "Will he approve of this?"

"Probably not. But he's often at odds with my grandfather. I don't think he'll try to stop it."

"There are other aspects of the story I'd want to look into," I warned.

"Like what?"

"I'd want to talk with Victoria's sister, Gretchen. I met her last night. How will your grandfather feel about that?"

"Jim asked the same question. He knew Gretchen and liked her. He'd talked to Ty Frazer, thanks to Gordon, and he'd even gotten him on tape. Finella told me on the phone that you've already met our local character. Of course you'd have to persuade Ty not to run off in fright, if you decided to interview him, too. But as far as I'm concerned, you can explore in any direction you choose. We can always edit later."

So there would be censorship? Not that this would matter, since there might never be a finished script, anyway. My own purpose in doing this was not the same as Natalie's.

"Will you think about this, Lauren?"

"I'll think about it, and if you can set it up, I'd like to meet Roger Brandt."

"Yes, of course. Before anything else will work, we must get Grandfather's agreement to see you. If you can't win him over, it's hopeless. Let me talk to him. Perhaps I'll have some ideas for you tonight at dinner. Gordon can help, too. He liked what Jim was doing—and my grandfather likes Gordon."

I decided to bring up something that had troubled me. "When Jim's things were sent to me, I didn't receive his notes on this project or any of the film he'd shot. There should have been film at least."

"I pulled everything out myself," Natalie admitted. "I didn't want what had been completed to be lost. Jim had a lot of plans, but he only got around to filming one interview. You can see that, if you like. And I'll give you his notes."

I wasn't sure I wanted this to happen. There seemed something terribly unsettling about watching a film Jim had started so shortly before his death.

Natalie must have registered my concern, for she spoke abruptly. "You're looking tired, Lauren. I'll drive you back to the other side so you can rest before dinner."

I quickly accepted. I had a lot to think about and I wanted to be alone.

As we started down the long studio, I stopped before the painting on the easel, my attention suddenly riveted. This was one of Natalie's Indian village scenes that Gordon had mentioned.

She had chosen a chilling subject—the stake I'd seen planted in the center of the approach to the village. As always, Natalie had let her imagination soar. A figure, his arms secured by an overhead pole, was already obscured by a veil of gray smoke rising from wood where low flames were beginning to burn.

Pale green moonlight permeated the scene, with the darker forest rising on one side, the trees bending a little as though some high wind touched them. All around the stake, ghostly figures moved in a circling dance. My focus was upon that central figure—whether man or woman, I couldn't tell, though agonized facial features were visible, the most arresting being the haunted eyes turned toward the sky. For an eerie moment, it was as though I had exchanged places with that figure so soon to die. I shook myself impatiently. What an odd thought for me to have.

Natalie came to stand beside me. "A bit weird, isn't it? Sometimes what I paint has very little to do with my own will. Something takes control of my brush and then a scene *just happens.* I was painting like that when I did the *Star Flight* watercolor Finella has in her shop. Sometimes it's as if I've painted something out of a past I've never seen. Though other times the subject seems prophetic—as if the occurrence is yet to happen. With this one, I was probably seeing what had already taken place for the movie."

I didn't know how the scene in the film was managed, but it

was unlikely that flames and smoke of this magnitude would have been started around an actor. I was glad to turn away from that agonized face whose pain and fear reached out to touch me.

Natalie led the way to the door, and, as we stepped outside, a woman appeared, coming down the walk from a higher part of the house. I knew at once who she must be. Though she was over seventy, her back was straight and she was arrestingly beautiful. Natalie's resemblance to her grandmother was clear, but Natalie's beauty was sharp and young and a little edgy. Camilla's had grown more controlled and seemingly serene. She carried herself with a dignity that I suspected would never be easily ruffled. Taller than her granddaughter, she looked tan and fit, as though she must spend effort and time to keep herself in good physical condition.

There must have been face-lifts to preserve the integrity of chin line and neck. Only one flaw detracted from her almost-perfect beauty—a scar on her right cheek. As far as possible, it had been hidden with skillful makeup, but nothing could conceal a puckering of flesh where something had cut in a deep diagonal slash.

She paused at the sight of us. "I'm sorry, Natalie. I didn't realize you had company."

"It's all right, Gran. We're just leaving. This is Lauren Castle, Jim's wife. Lauren, my grandmother, Camilla Brandt."

The cool look she gave me was intimidating. She wore, like a garment, a manner that seemed almost royal. Her pale violet silk dress flowed around her, revealing a perfection of figure that would have been the envy of women half her age. I wondered whether pride was mainly what had held Camilla Brandt together for all these years.

Natalie went on to explain my presence. "I kidnapped Lauren

from Dad's boat, since I wanted to meet her. Now I'll drive her back to her car."

Camilla Brandt held out her hand to me with a natural courtesy that I suspected nothing could ever shake. "We were all grieved about Jim's death, Mrs. Castle." Her speech had a cultivated ring; her voice must have aged little, since there was no quaver in her tones, no faltering.

I thanked her for her sympathy and she bowed slightly before turning back to her own part of the house, moving with a natural grace that was timeless.

Feeling a little stunned, I followed Natalie to the garage on the upper level, where she'd left her car.

"You resemble your grandmother," I remarked.

"I only wish! You should see pictures of her when she was young and a great beauty. If only I could have known her before all that legendary wildfire went out of her. I think Grandfather was always a little intimidated by her. There are stories about her when she was young. They must have been madly in love."

She opened the door of the Mercedes and I got in, lost in my own sober thoughts. Madly in love for a time, perhaps? But then there had been Victoria Frazer. How much, or how little, had she meant to Roger Brandt? His career had ended because of Victoria, but not his marriage. For the first time, I wondered whether Victoria's death could have been a relief to him. If he had turned away from her when she was pregnant, she might well have committed suicide in despair. There was a great deal I wanted to know, and working on this film, even if nothing came of it, might help me answer those questions.

"Your grandmother should be part of the film, if we do pick up Jim's work," I said. "It would be interesting to talk with her."

Natalie shook her head. "That wouldn't be allowed."

"Who would oppose it?"

"If Grandfather didn't allow Jim to talk with her, he certainly wouldn't permit you to do so."

In that case, I thought, I must find a way to talk with Camilla Brandt on my own.

As Natalie backed the car out of the garage, she turned her head to look at me. "You *are* working on a script in your mind, aren't you? The writer in you is taking over. I can tell by the way you look."

I smiled vaguely, impressed by her perceptiveness but promising nothing.

We wound through the woods on the Brandts' private road and came out upon an open stretch that offered a view of the lake. Rumbling Bald was behind us now, and when we descended to the level of the dam and started across, I could look straight up the gorge to where it narrowed near Chimney Rock. The Indian village that I'd visited this morning, and that Natalie had painted so disturbingly, was somewhere up there.

"Have you lived here all your life?" I asked Natalie.

She drove easily, relaxed at the wheel. "Yes, except for four years at the University of Virginia."

There was another story here—the story of Natalie Brandt. For just a moment, I wanted to tell her who I was and claim our relationship. But I didn't know her well enough yet to guess what the result of such a revelation might be. It was better to wait and go slowly. So for now I would continue to play my hand as Jim's wife. I'd already been given more glimpses of the Brandts than I'd ever thought possible.

Natalie spoke quietly as we neared Finella's, where I'd left my car. "You're a deep one, Lauren. There's something *you're* holding back, but you'll tell me eventually."

I had nothing to say to that, so I left the car with a brief "See you tonight." When I reached my own car and looked back, I saw that she still sat there with her hands on the wheel, looking after me, her expression not altogether friendly.

F ★ I ★ V ★ E

WHEN I entered the lobby of the lodge, Mrs. Adrian spoke to me from the desk. "If you have time, Mrs. Castle, Miss Frazer would like you to come down to see her. She said you would know the way."

Tired as I was beginning to feel, this was an invitation I couldn't refuse. I went out to the walkway that led toward the water and stood there for a moment, the view holding me all over again. In afternoon sunlight, Rumbling Bald looked more serene, less frightening. Across the lake in the direction of the dam, I could now recognize the roof of Roger Brandt's house. How remarkable, I thought, that I might have access to that house and to Roger Brandt. Providing, of course, that he agreed to see Jim Castle's wife.

As I reached the level of Gretchen's small house, I heard voices and paused on the walk. The big room she'd taken me into last night was farther along, but these sounds came from nearby, where a door stood open. I went to look in at a surprising scene.

The small room was square, with white plastered walls and very little furniture. Its central focus was a white bed, upon which lay a child—a little girl of about ten, dressed in pajamas. Gretchen Frazer sat in a chair drawn up to the opposite side of the bed from where I stood. Her eyes were closed and she wore a beatific expression, as though held by some inner rapture. The deep lines of her face had lifted and she almost glowed with a peaceful radiance. This was a different woman from the one I'd met last night—a woman who had been a little rough-edged and curt. I watched, fascinated.

She sat with her hands straight out before her, held an inch or two above the child's chest. Her lips moved as though she uttered some whispered prayer. In contrast, Siggy von Hogg sat on his haunches on my side of the bed, observing the ritual with complete attention.

Someone stirred in a corner to my right and I became aware of a woman who sat on a straight chair, her coloring as fair as that of the child on the bed. When she caught my eye, she raised a finger to her lips, warning me to be quiet. The little girl's mother, undoubtedly.

Like Gretchen's, the child's eyes were closed, and she was breathing harshly. But even as I watched, the rasping breaths lessened and color began to return to her small face. Gretchen rested a light hand on her forehead.

"The fever's gone. She doesn't need it anymore, and her coughing will stop now," she told the woman as she bent over the child, brushing the girl's hair away from her face. "Let me get you some herbs to give her in a drink and leaves that you can use to

73

make into a poultice to put on her chest tonight."

She started to rise and saw me. For just an instant, she looked startled. Then, without speaking, she went to busy herself at a cabinet and put a small parcel into the mother's hands. The woman began to fumble with her purse, but Gretchen stopped her.

"There isn't any charge. *This* is my reward." She touched the little girl's head again as the child sat up and smiled.

When they went out of the room, Siggy came to snuffle at my ankles, seeming to smile up at me when I bent to scratch between his ears.

Gretchen shooed him away. "Manners, Siggy," she said, and the pig ambled away. "I'm glad to see you, Lauren. Come into the other room, please. I have something to show you."

I was still under the spell of what I'd just witnessed. There seemed to be a goodness at the core of this woman that she tried to hide with her brusque manner.

I spoke warmly. "How wonderful to have a healing gift like that!"

We'd entered the kitchen area, where I'd sat last night. She waved me to a chair and flicked a hand, dismissing my words.

"It's not always wonderful. Sometimes nothing happens and I blame myself for not knowing enough."

"Have you always been able to help the sick?"

She answered openly. "Whatever gift I possess seems to have come to me after my sister, Victoria, died. That was a difficult time for me spiritually and I was reaching out for—for anything that would help me. When I found out what I could sometimes do, it frightened me at first. It seemed to happen serendipitously, until I began to understand that *this* was why I was here on earth. I couldn't help my sister, but I could use my powers for others." She broke off for a moment and then went on abruptly. "We need to talk, Lauren."

I'd always found that phrase ominous: It usually meant that something would be said that I didn't want to hear. I sidetracked her with a question, postponing.

"What were the leaves you gave the little girl's mother for a poultice?"

"Kudzu. The Japanese have used it in healing for centuries. I'm afraid I'm only a beginner when it comes to understanding its virtues."

"I saw the kudzu room at Finella Heath's shop today."

Gretchen looked pleased. "I introduced Finella to the miracle of kudzu. She's taken off like a crusader. How did your day go, Lauren?"

Perhaps she, too, was postponing the need to talk to me.

"I've covered some unexpected ground," I said, and gave her a brief account of my adventures. My visit to Roger Brandt's house caught her attention.

"Did you actually see him?"

"Not even a glimpse. Though I was introduced to Mrs. Brandt."

"The formidable Camilla! What did you think of her?"

"We barely met. She's an impressive lady, but I had a sense of coolness toward me."

I decided to tell her about Natalie's request. "I may pick up the work Jim started. Only the writing part, of course. Natalie Brandt said she could handle a video camera, if I would do the interviewing. As Jim's wife, there's a chance that Mr. Brandt might talk to me now. I would have to come up with questions, of course, and an overall plan that would give me a framework."

Gretchen regarded me somberly. "Don't let the Brandts twist you around to their own purposes. I don't think this is a good idea. Who cares about Roger Brandt these days?"

"There's been a revival of interest in his films around the country. Why does the idea upset you?" I could guess, but I wanted to challenge Victoria's sister.

"Because it would all be done to glorify *his* career. After what happened to my sister, I can hardly be enthusiastic."

I wasn't ready yet to tell her that I might be a lot more partisan to Victoria's story than that of the Brandts, though I touched on this lightly. "I've always been fascinated by Victoria Frazer—so her life will be part of whatever is covered. That is, if you are willing to help me."

She closed her eyes and seemed to go far away in her thoughts. When she looked at me again, I knew that she'd rejected the idea. "It's better to let the past go, Lauren, and get on with your own life. I have a feeling that you've been marking time since your husband died."

Gretchen had a quick, blunt perception that disconcerted me. She saw too much too clearly. But perhaps I could be perceptive, too.

"Is there something about your sister that you don't want to see published?"

"A great deal," she said. "An artist's *work* should be judged— not her life."

I let that go, though I was all the more curious. "I met your brother, Ty, this morning," I told her.

"Tyronne? Did he bring Finella a bag of kudzu? He keeps me supplied through her."

Tyronne? It was difficult to connect so romantic a name to that rough old man with his quick-moving nervousness.

"He came in while I was in the shop," I told her. "But I'd also seen him earlier up in the Indian village where the movie was made. He was playing a drum—wonderful, eerie sounds!"

"Poor Ty. Perhaps he suffered more than anyone else after Victoria died."

"Oh?" I waited, and she went on sadly.

"When he was young, his ambition was to become a doctor, and Victoria was helping him. She easily earned enough to send him through medical school. He was bright and eager for life, and he had the healing gift, too—though not in the same way it developed for me. In the early days, Victoria was good to everyone."

"What happened?"

"After she fell in love with Roger Brandt, she changed. She lost interest in everything and everyone else. Maybe she wouldn't have withdrawn her support for Ty, but he thought that was what she meant to do. We all lived together in this house in those days. That was long before the lodge was built. I remember when Tyronne sat right here in this kitchen, and he was angrier than I'd ever seen him. He called Roger Brandt a seducer. After Victoria died, he forgave her, but by that time he'd gone off the deep end and become the way he is now. At first, I was afraid he might try to kill Roger. But the Brandt house was a fortress in those days—Camilla saw to that—and he'd never have gotten past the guards."

"It didn't seem to be guarded when I was there this morning."

"Nobody bothers anymore. Celebrity seekers are after younger prey and many of his old fans don't know he's here. Though if you go through with this documentary, that may change. How did you happen to get into the place?"

"I was on Justyn Brandt's boat and Natalie invited me ashore. But tell me about Tyronne."

"He lives in the mountains. I think he knows every cave on Rumbling Bald, and he likes wild animals better than he does people. That's where his healing gifts come in." Gretchen's words seemed heavy with an underlying sadness. "Everything would have been different if Victoria and Roger hadn't fallen in love."

"I liked Ty, even though he shied away from me."

"I suppose he's happy as he is, and we let him alone. He doesn't miss what we call civilization. Gordon Heath is one of the few he's made friends with. And, of course, Finella. She's a free soul in her own way. You know, I suspect he believes that Victoria's spirit still haunts the lake out there, but I don't talk with him about it. Although I do know that he thinks she wants him to do something now—something that will make up for all that happened."

"What did happen?"

"She died," Gretchen said simply. I had the feeling that she knew more than she was willing to tell me, but I didn't press her.

"It was all such a long time ago, Lauren. When she died, it was a terrible thing for Tyronne and me. We've both learned to live our own lives, but it was hard for us to welcome Jim's efforts to dredge everything up again. He's still doing that, in a sense. But you can stop it if you just let everything alone."

I wasn't sure I could do that. If Jim hadn't died by accident, I *owed* him. Because of Gordon and San Francisco and too many years of a less-than-ideal marriage. And because Jim had been my friend, even though our marriage hadn't worked out. I owed him a great deal.

Gretchen went on, rambling a little. Mental and emotional

exhaustion seized me as I listened, and she saw this.

"You're about out on your feet, Lauren." She reached out to take both my hands in hers. Her touch was light. It sent warmth flowing up my arms to envelop me, and for the first time I experienced the energizing force of Gretchen's power.

"You needed this," she said with satisfaction. She released my hands. "Go and rest now. You'll wake up refreshed and ready for the evening."

I hadn't told her that I was meeting Gordon and Natalie, and I wondered whether her talents ran to clairvoyance. In any case, I felt better, and I seemed to float toward the door without effort, completely relaxed. As I went up the walk toward the lodge, she stood outside, watching me go. A curious thought came to comfort me. Gretchen was my family. She was my grandmother's sister, and I had a feeling that she wanted me to know that she was on my side, even though she might only think of me as Jim's wife. I realized that she hadn't told me why she wanted to see me, but perhaps she'd accomplished what she wanted indirectly.

I didn't want to think ahead to the coming meeting with Gordon, since that might upset me all over again. In fact, I didn't want anything to interfere with the sense of serenity that Gretchen's hands had induced.

In my room, I slipped on a robe, drew draperies across glass doors, and lay down on the bed. Gretchen's spell held me and I fell asleep instantly.

When I began to dream, the experience seemed very real. Someone had come into my room from the lakeside—a woman in a white dress. Fair hair stirred on her shoulders as she moved to the foot of my bed. My eyes were closed, but I could see every detail of the room clearly, including the shimmering, ethereal vision who raised her hands toward me as though entreating.

Let me go, she whispered. The sound was in my mind, but the words were clear. *Please let me go.*

In the dream, I spoke to her, though I made no sound. "I'm not holding you—so how can I let you go?"

The whispering voice pleaded. *Find me and let me go.*

Even as I answered her, part of me rejected what seemed to be happening. "You're at the bottom of the lake. How can anyone find you?"

Outside, a dog bayed mournfully. Immediately, I was awake and sitting up in bed. No shimmering vision hovered in the room and no voice whispered through my mind. But the dream had been disturbingly real, brought on, no doubt, by all that had just happened, but with no connection to reality. I didn't need to worry about fulfilling the request of a figure in a dream. So why did this strong connection with Victoria Frazer persist now that I was awake?

I tried to make peace with the dream. If in some fantastic way I should be given the opportunity to free Victoria Frazer from whatever bonds still held her to an earth where she no longer belonged, I would do everything in my power to succeed. My wide-awake self promised her that.

I had a bond with Victoria that my mother had never known about. In my early teens, I'd gone into a secondhand bookstore that specialized in old movie magazines. There I had found an issue printed a month after her death and devoted to her. It contained several photographs. She had been impossibly beautiful. I studied her delicate face with its huge, expressive eyes.

No man could have resisted falling in love with a face like that—not only because of her enchanting appearance but also because of a vulnerability that showed in her softly rounded chin and full, voluptuous mouth. It was a face that waited to be kissed and that invited protection. But Roger Brandt had not protected her.

The magazine writers romanticized that Victoria and Roger had fallen in love during the making of *Blue Ridge Cowboy.* There was even a photo of them together—a publicity still for that picture. It showed a tall, handsome man with an amused, slightly wicked look in his eyes—something that had appealed to a nation of newly born moviegoers and to my grandmother.

In the photograph, the beautiful young woman looked up at her hero with love and adoration. And the entire country swallowed the fantasy. In reality, it must have been very different. There had been a wild, uncontrollable passion, suffering, scandal, and death. And I was the child of the baby that had been born of that less-than-ideal union. Was I, perhaps, more like my grandmother than I'd ever been like my mother?

I wondered what Camilla Brandt had thought of that photograph. She must have seen it when it appeared. But perhaps she had known even then that Roger would never leave her for some movie actress.

My dream still haunted me and I tried to shrug it off. I didn't subscribe to the legend of a great romance, and I found there was an indignant part of me that wanted to meet Roger Brandt in order to tell him just what I thought of him.

Suddenly aware of the lateness of the hour, I took a shower that was cool and bracing and put on a white cotton peasant blouse with a round neck. A smoky blue chambray skirt flared out from a wide blue leather belt, and I liked the effect. I was dressing in self-defense, needing to give myself confidence and courage. I didn't have to look like Victoria Frazer—only like a woman far removed from that foolish young girl in San Francisco. The full-length mirror on the bathroom wall seemed to approve of me and I gave it my best smile.

When I went down to the lobby, I found Gordon waiting for me. I managed to be friendly but casual, discounting the way his eyes lighted when he saw me.

"I thought perhaps we could go together. Natalie will meet us at the inn," he told me as we went out to his car. Not a Jeep this time, but a small, sleek sports car, midnight blue. On the way, he told me that he'd given Natalie a call before he left home. "She said she'd had you up to the Brandt house and that you'd met her mother. What do you think of Camilla?"

My reaction to Roger's wife had been mixed. "She's beautiful and she carries her years well. But she chilled me a little."

"She can do that. Jim never got very far with her, though he felt she should be part of his project."

"Natalie wants me to pick up Jim's work and continue with the writing. Perhaps even do the interviewing on-camera. She would handle the photography part."

My news surprised him. "That's a switch! When Jim died, she said she'd never want anyone to finish his work. I wonder why she's changed her mind. Will you take her up on it?"

"I don't know. Roger Brandt would have to be convinced, and I doubt if he'd accept me for the job."

"You're still not telling anyone about your relationship to Victoria and Roger, are you?"

"No, I'd rather keep that quiet for now. A sort of ace up my sleeve, though I don't know how I'll use it."

He seemed intrigued by the possibilities, though he didn't comment.

The Lake Lure Inn was so close that the drive took only a few minutes. There was no time to tell him about other matters that disturbed me.

We drew up before the long white stucco building that I had seen earlier from the boat. Its Spanish-flavored architecture had been popular in the early years of the century, though its style was more likely to appear in California than North Carolina. The inn's great resort days had ended in the forties, but now all of Hickory Nut Gorge, with Lake Lure at this end and Chimney Rock at the other, had become popular with tourists once more and the inn was coming to life.

We climbed wide cement steps under a green canopy. Once, carriages and early motorcars must have drawn up to this entrance. Just inside the door, a round walnut table held a massive fresh flower arrangement in charming pastels, the polished wood gleaming beneath. Beyond rose an impressive staircase that climbed to a landing and branched on either side to the floor above. To my right and left, the lobby was furnished with dignified sofas and a variety of comfortable-looking chairs.

Natalie Brandt rose to meet us—a colorful, rather surprising figure. She had changed from her artist's work clothes to indigo blue trousers banded in silver at the ankles. The plain silver top was hung with long strands of shells and bright beads. Even her dangling earrings dripped with tiny shells. Altogether, she looked stunning and exotic, and I could imagine that her appeal for Jim Castle would have been immediate. Jim had liked and enjoyed women, and I was just as glad that I hadn't been desperately in love with him. We'd done better as friends.

Natalie seemed a bit more wary toward me than she had been earlier, and I wondered whether her grandmother's seeming disapproval of me had succeeded in turning her against me.

We went out to a long, enclosed porch, where well-spaced tables and a wall of windows created an attractive dining area. Heavy white tablecloths were overlaid with squares of pale peach and chairs were upholstered in the same color.

A waitress seated us beside a window and provided us with menus. Feeling uncomfortable about Natalie's manner, I absorbed myself in listening to a recitation of the specialties of the evening. We ordered rather quickly, and as soon as the waitress had gone, Natalie spoke to me, putting my suspicion into words.

"I must tell you right away, Lauren, that my grandmother is absolutely opposed to your continuing Jim's work. I should never have suggested this without consulting her first."

"Perhaps your grandfather is the one to consult," I said. "However, I'm more relieved than anything else. I never really thought I'd be right for this." I kept out of my voice any regret I might feel for the loss of this access I could have had to our mutual grandfather.

Gordon had little to say, watching Natalie and me but leaving the exchange mostly to us.

I asked a direct question. "Have you seen the film that your grandfather made with Victoria Frazer?"

"No one is supposed to see it. Grandfather owns what I believe to be the only print in existence and he keeps it locked in a safe. He's never run it for me, though he's shown me *his* earlier pictures."

"Why won't he show it to you?" I asked bluntly.

A spark flared in Natalie's dark eyes. "Maybe he's afraid that if he takes it out, my grandmother will get her hands on it and destroy it. She still has enough temper to do that."

"Does she feel that strongly about Victoria Frazer after all these years?" I asked.

"I expect that she was forced to put up with a great deal. She has a right to feel any way she wants. I admire her tremendously."

I noted the use of the word *admire* rather than *love*.

Gordon said, "I've heard some of the story—that Camilla was the one who held everything together when the going got rough."

Natalie spoke more quietly, her annoyance with me subsiding. "That's the way it must have been. My father was born the following year, but he's told me stories he heard from Great-grandmother Brandt. She told him that when the scandal broke, the house was in a state of siege from reporters and the curious public. Audiences can be unforgiving toward an idol with clay feet. That was when my grandmother engineered a trip to Switzerland and took the family out of the country. They didn't come home until everything quieted down. Then they returned secretly and Gran made the house a fortress."

"Home was really California, wasn't it?" Gordon asked.

Even as I listened intently to Natalie, I was still all too aware of Gordon across the table. Everything about him had changed—and nothing had. I seemed to be two women—the one putting on a front and pretending she didn't care, the other much more involved than I wanted to be.

Natalie answered him. "My grandfather couldn't bear to stay in Hollywood after all that happened. It can't be easy to suddenly become a fallen star after so many years of fame. His supposed friends were cutting him off, and suddenly no work was available. I expect there was enough money to live wherever he wanted—between what he'd been earning and my grandmother's private wealth. But he'd become attached to the house they occupied here and the beautiful Lake Lure area. He's told me that much."

Perhaps not even Natalie Brandt knew the real reason why

Roger Brandt had stayed here and I wondered whether it might be something more sinister than she suspected.

Natalie puzzled out loud. "For me, Gran has always seemed a much bigger mystery than my grandfather. She must have loved him a great deal to forgive him for Victoria and stay with him in this place where one of the biggest scandals of their day happened. She certainly wasn't sympathetic when Grandfather first agreed to let Jim Castle do a documentary. Though I must admit that when Grandfather puts his foot down, she gives in, and I think it's Grandfather who would oppose any plan to finish Jim's film."

"Why was he willing to talk to Jim in the first place?" Gordon asked.

"Perhaps because then he could have told his own side of what happened for the first time. No one with Jim's obvious integrity had ever wanted to listen. The press and his studio simply leapt to conclusions. But when Jim died, I think he must have soured on the project."

"Would he have addressed the mystery of Victoria Frazer's death if Jim had been able to continue working with him?" I asked.

For just an instant, Natalie seemed uneasy. Then she took up the challenge. "How could he? How could anyone? Who knows what state she may have been in? It didn't help that her body was never found, but part of the lake is a hundred feet deep. Divers searched for days without any success. There was only her scarf, caught on a dock piling, to show what might have happened. And she left an unfinished letter to her baby daughter that was taken to be a suicide note."

I knew about that. "Roger Brandt could hardly do a documentary about his career and leave Victoria out."

"Of course not. He'd have had to face up to that. Jim meant to interview Victoria's side of the family—those who are left—

Gretchen and Ty. Grandfather didn't want that, but Jim was beginning to win his trust, and perhaps a few secrets might have
surfaced. *If* there'd been enough time. If Jim hadn't died."

Natalie stared at me challenging and then continued with
a bite of scorn in her words—perhaps to hide the pain she
might feel.

"The great romance between Roger and Victoria that the
papers went overboard about lasted for a little over a year. Their
affair began in California, months before they were both cast in
Blue Ridge Cowboy. After the movie was finished, the infatuation
must have been over for Grandfather. Now I suspect that Gran
wants to pretend that it never happened."

"But it wasn't over for Victoria Frazer, who had a baby," I
said dryly.

Natalie bristled. "Victoria must have been a silly fool, and she
probably got what was coming to her. I think that woman was a
born seductress! The parts she'd played in her own movies weren't
all that innocent. That's what made her acting in a film with a folk
hero like Roger Brandt all the more dramatic. She was a woman
who had no scruples about taking another woman's husband. *If* she
could. In this case, she hadn't a chance against my grandmother."

I simply looked at her, and was glad to see her flush. I
suppose she regarded herself in quite a different category from
Victoria Frazer, and her affair with *my* husband didn't seem to
trouble her. Now, more than ever, I wanted to search out Victoria's
side of the story and find out who had really done the seducing.

Our meal had been served and the food was good, but I was
hardly paying attention to what I put in my mouth.

"I have something to give you—something from Jim," Natalie said abruptly.

While I waited in surprise, she reached into her purse and

handed me a sealed white envelope. My name was written on it in Jim's familiar scrawl.

"I don't understand. If there was a letter from my husband, why wasn't it mailed to me?" I asked.

"When I saw him that last evening, he was pretty keyed up. He hinted that he'd learned something that would blow everything sky-high. Whatever that meant. He didn't show me what he'd written or what he'd put into that envelope before he sealed it. Your husband and I had become close friends, Lauren, and he said I was the only person he could trust to give this to you—other than Gordon, of course. But Gordon was away that week, so Jim said that I should give you the letter *only* if you came to Lake Lure. He seemed to imply that he might not be here to give it to you himself."

She stopped and stared out the window for a few moments. "After he died and it was considered an accident, I didn't know what to think or do. You didn't come to Lake Lure, so I waited."

She thrust the envelope into my hands as though she wanted to be rid of it. I felt something slightly thicker than a sheet of paper at its center, and I knew that once I opened this envelope, I would never be able to turn back from whatever course lay ahead.

"Do you think Jim had a premonition that something would happen to him?" I asked.

She shook her head and tears came to her eyes. "I don't know. I wish I did."

I slit the flap with my finger and took out a folded sheet of paper. Inside was a rough circle of green material about three inches across that looked as though it had probably been cut from some larger piece. Its edges seemed to indicate the clean cut of a knife. It was apparently made of some synthetic that I'd never seen before—too tough to tear and strangely luminous—almost unearthly! Or perhaps radioactive?

Jim's handwriting scrawled across the page. He had always written as though he was short of time and in a breathless hurry, but this was ragged, even for him.

Dear Lauren:

It will probably be better if this never comes into your hands. I don't expect that it will, because the puzzle is almost clear, and I'll handle it myself. That is, as soon as the last piece clicks into place.

Gordon Heath is away, or I would leave this with him, but I know Natalie will follow my instructions. Talk to Ty Frazer, since he knows where this fabric came from. If he takes you to the source, as he did me, everything will become clear.

Be careful. Victoria Frazer didn't drown herself—she was murdered.

I hope there'll never be a reason for you to receive this letter.

Love,

Jim

I sat for a moment with Jim's letter and the scrap of green material in my hands, feeling shocked and deeply shaken by this confirmation of my fears—both about Victoria's death and Jim's. The letter hinted too much without saying enough.

Silently, I handed it to Gordon and watched as he read it.

"What is it?" Natalie cried. "What has he said?"

As he read Jim's words, Gordon looked as disturbed as I felt. This was support for what Ty believed. Gordon gave the letter to

Natalie and when he covered my hand with his own, I tried to take some comfort from his touch.

"So Jim's death wasn't an accident and neither was Victoria's," he said quietly, picking up the piece of fabric.

Tears filled Natalie's eyes again as she watched.

The green iridescence shone in the lamplight as Gordon turned the scrap about in his hands. It looked as though it would glow in the dark.

"It's almost as thin as paper," he said, "but very tough. And it doesn't crumple. I have no idea what it is. Maybe some new sort of synthetic?" He handed it to Natalie, who examined it silently and gave it back without comment, along with the letter.

"Maybe I should send this piece away to have it tested, Lauren," Gordon said.

I didn't want to wait for tests. "I'd rather show it to your friend Ty and ask him about it, as Jim suggested in his letter. Could you set up a meeting with him, Gordon? He has a tendency to duck when he sees me."

"I'll see what I can manage," Gordon promised.

Natalie appeared to be studying the dessert offerings on the menu from which we had ordered earlier, as though it absorbed her full attention. I noticed that her hands were trembling. Gordon stared suddenly in the direction of the door, and I saw his look of surprise. He pushed back his chair and stood up as the hostess led Finella to our table. She still wore her blue denim jacket with the patches of color at the shoulders, but she had lost the poise I'd sensed in her at the shop. She was agitated now.

"I'm sorry to interrupt, Gordon," she told him the moment she reached our table. "Something has just happened that you'd better know about." She glanced at Natalie and me. "All of you."

Gordon pulled out a chair and she sat down, waving away a menu and asking only for coffee.

"I've just had a surprising visitor in my shop," she said. "It was your grandfather, Natalie. I hadn't seen him in years, and he still looks as handsome and distinguished as ever."

"Why on earth—" Natalie began, but Gordon motioned for her to wait, and she was quiet.

"He came into the shop like a storm cloud," Finella continued. "I remember how dramatic he used to be, and he hasn't lost his touch. He wanted to know if I'd seen Jim Castle's wife, and I said you'd gone to dinner with my son and his granddaughter. That seemed to upset him still more. He strode around vigorously— you'd never guess his age!—and stopped before your *Star Flight* watercolor, Natalie. Apparently, he hadn't seen it before, and he appeared even more disturbed."

"I don't see why," Natalie said. "He and my father were on the mountain when that—whatever it was—came down. I painted from his own description."

"Well, he didn't like it, and he turned away as though he couldn't bear to look at it. He wants to talk with you, Lauren, as soon as possible."

This didn't bode well for my first meeting with Roger Brandt, and I began to feel alarmed. "Did he say why he wants to see me?"

"Not a hint. He just went off in the same dark cloud. So I thought I'd better come over here and warn you right away. He really scared me."

"Before I met you for dinner tonight, Camilla told him you might continue with the documentary, Lauren," Natalie said. "He was against it. He said you couldn't possibly pick up Jim's work—

no one could. But I didn't think he'd go running around trying to find you. At least he hasn't come here."

Looking a little guilty, Finella said, "I'm afraid I told him where you're staying, Lauren."

Natalie pushed back her chair. "I'd better get back to the house and talk to him—get him calmed down. Sometimes he listens to me."

I tried to reassure her. "Just tell him that I could never fill Jim's shoes, so he needn't worry. Though I would like to meet him before I leave, if it's possible. Perhaps he could tell me more about what Jim was doing."

"I still think you should finish the film, whether he approves or not," Natalie said. "I wonder if I could win him around, in spite of my grandmother."

She left us rather abruptly and rushed off with her shells and beads clashing.

I didn't want any dessert, but I drank my coffee, feeling tired and scared, and I told Finella that I might be leaving Lake Lure soon. I would stop in to see her before I went home. All the while, I was aware of Gordon listening quietly, though he'd made no comment about all this drama. When we left the dining room, we walked Finella to her car and then Gordon drove me back to the lodge, with hardly a word between us. What was there to say? When we reached the driveway and he stopped the car, he kept me for a moment longer, and his words surprised me.

"I wonder if you should leave so soon, Lauren? Are you being frightened away?"

"Perhaps I am," I told him, though one of the things I was most afraid of was my confused feeling about Gordon himself.

"If you leave," he said, "I suspect that everything will stop.

All the questions will fade away and no answers will ever be found. That's the safe and easy course." His tone hardened. "You're pretty good at taking the easy course, as I remember."

Perhaps the sudden anger that shook me came from the fact that he was speaking the truth. But that young girl who had loved him and been afraid to act didn't exist anymore. I might be afraid of a lot of things, but I wouldn't run away from Gordon now if there was a *real* reason to stay.

"You don't know anything about me," I said sharply. I opened the door on my side and got out to run up the steps and get away from him as quickly as I could.

By the time I reached the lobby, I felt tired all over again. I wanted only to go up to my room and do nothing for the rest of the evening. The last thing I wanted was to think about Gordon, either in the past or the present, and I wasn't sure that was something I could turn off.

When Mrs. Adrian spoke to me from the desk, I paused unwillingly.

"Mrs. Castle—there's someone here to see you." She nodded toward the far end of the lobby, where a sitting area had been arranged. She looked so excited that I knew at once who must be here.

"It's Mr. Brandt, Mrs. Castle. Mr. Roger Brandt! He's waiting for you."

There was nothing else to do but face him. I took a long, deep breath and went to meet my grandfather.

S ⋆ I ⋆ X

HE ROSE as I approached, and I would have recognized him anywhere. His hair was white but still thick, and lines had deepened in his face. Yet the look of the young man was there. His bearing, as erect as ever, indicated a man who kept his body in shape.

Until now, I'd seen him only in black and white. He seemed far more impressive in color and he still had a presence that was part of Roger Brandt's film mystique. His skin was well tanned and a patterned red silk scarf—his signature in the old days—was tied jauntily at his throat. His corduroy jacket appeared to have been tailored to fit him and corduroy pants ended in expensive, well-worn leather boots that had undoubtedly been made to order. Added to the charisma that had belonged to the young man was an intimidating assurance. He looked both angry and for some reason surprised at the sight of me. I had to stiffen my inner resolve and stand up to him. I raised my chin—a chin cleft as deeply as his own—and gave him look for look.

"Mr. Brandt?" I said before he could attack. "I'm Lauren Castle, Jim's wife."

He didn't trouble to acknowledge this. "Sit down," he said curtly, gesturing toward the far end of the sofa where he'd been sitting.

I stayed where I was. "I prefer to stand, since this will take only a few moments. Your granddaughter has suggested that I pick up my husband's work on the documentary about you. But of course that's out of the question. I haven't the skills or the interest to carry on Jim's work. So if you've come here to tell me not to, you needn't have troubled."

He blinked, and I suspected that his vanity would reject an excuse that indicated a lack of interest—in him. But before he could dismiss me and stride out of the lobby, I continued.

"Perhaps you'd like to know why I don't want to touch this project. I have a strong feeling that the real story concerns Victoria Frazer. But to learn about her life would be much more difficult than to learn about yours. So I won't even try."

I expected his anger to explode around me. Bristling white eyebrows, more unruly than when he was young, seemed to climb his forehead above eyes that had widened as he stared at me. Then a faint quirk appeared at one side of his mouth, creasing up one cheek—not a smile, but possible amusement because someone so insignificant would dare to mention Victoria's name in his presence.

"Please sit down," he said. "We can talk more comfortably if you'll stop looking like a firecracker about to go off."

So much for what I'd considered defiant dignity. I sat down

in the farthest corner of the sofa from him, my feet close together and my hands clasped like a schoolgirl's on the knees of my blue skirt. At once, I unclasped them and folded my arms—the body language of defiance. I would *not* allow him either to intimidate or ridicule me.

His own relaxing into the opposite end of the sofa seemed casual enough—but then, he was an actor. "I'm sorry, Mrs. Castle. I seem to have misunderstood what my wife told me. I liked your husband, and his death was a shock and a great loss. But now you've made me curious. I want to know why you think Victoria Frazer's story is so important. Her career was hardly more than a flash in the pan."

"Through no fault of her own," I told him. "There was a revival in Los Angeles of all your films that have survived. I've seen most of them. But never the one picture you made with her. Years ago, I found in a secondhand bookstore an old movie magazine that carried Victoria's picture on the cover. When I bought it and read the article, I could see why men must have fallen in love with her."

He didn't seem to care for that conclusion. "You're young and romantic. Almost any female face can be given extraordinary beauty with makeup and lighting and the right camera angle. On the street, you might not have noticed her."

I tried not to rise to the bait. "I don't believe that. I don't think *you* believe that."

He looked away as though I'd touched him in some way. "This is a very strange experience, Mrs. Castle. I haven't talked with anyone about Victoria Frazer in a good many years. What is it that appeals to you about an actress who is mostly forgotten, except here at Lake Lure, where she has become part of a sentimental legend?"

I tried not to sound indignant at such a dismissal coming from *him*. "I suppose the mystery of her death is part of the appeal for me. Why was her body never found? What really happened?"

He showed his impatience clearly. "Do you think every effort wasn't made at the time to find her?"

"Not *every* effort. Haven't *you* wanted to know what happened to her?"

This time, I'd really gotten through to him, and he looked uncomfortable. "I think you'd better go back to California, young lady. Your decision not to try what Natalie has suggested is the correct one."

He was an arrogant man, and I disliked arrogance. "You shouldn't allow yourself to become antique, Mr. Brandt. *Young lady* is a patronizing term, and as old-fashioned as all those cowboy movies you used to make." If he was arrogant, I was rude, but I didn't care.

Once more, I thought he would rise and stalk out of the lobby. Instead, he surprised me by laughing. "Touché! You remind me of my granddaughter. She never lets me get away with anything. Just the same, there would be no point in opening up that old tragedy again. The only reason I was seeing your husband was because he stayed away from all reference to Victoria Frazer, except when it came to the one movie I made with her."

Of course Jim would have touched on all that later, as he won Roger Brandt's confidence, but I let that go.

"Did you ever really care about her?" I asked bluntly, holding my breath.

He looked at me and then away—a look more sad than angry.

Now it was I who baited him. "Jim wrote me that all this was a closed book—so far."

"And it would have stayed closed. Now, if you'll excuse me . . ." He rose, ending our discussion.

I stood up beside him, aware of how tall he was—over six feet. There'd been no shrinking of his spine with age.

I made one last attempt to pierce the armor he wore. "Natalie told me you may have the only existing print of *Blue Ridge Cowboy*. I'm going away soon and I won't try to do anything about your story—or Victoria Frazer's. But I would give anything to see that film. I would love to know how she looked and moved and spoke."

He asked me the same question he'd asked before, phrasing it in a different way. "Why are you so drawn to an actress who lived before you were born?"

For just a moment, I was tempted. I wanted to say, *Because she is my grandmother.* But I held back the words. Once he knew, he might shut me out altogether. As Jim Castle's wife, I would seem more harmless. For a moment, I looked at him as my grandfather—not as an intimidating and famous actor but as someone I might get to know, someone from whom I had inherited part of myself.

I smiled for the first time since we'd met, and he looked startled, peering at me a bit myopically.

"You remind me of someone. What did you say your first name is? Lauren? A beautiful name." He paused and then seemed to make up his mind suddenly. "If you will call Natalie tomorrow, she will bring you across the lake to my house. Set a time with her and I will show you the film."

Taken by surprise, I found myself stammering as I thanked him, and he looked pleased to have reduced me to shaky gratitude. He probably still fancied himself as having a way with women.

"Good-bye, Lauren," he said, holding out his hand. When I put my own into his, he clasped it warmly for an instant. "I'll see you soon," he added, and started across the lobby. As he neared the door, he turned and looked at me over his shoulder. The gesture was deliberate and exactly the way he had done it so often in his films, his look amusing, captivating, engagingly mischievous.

I was not captivated, and I knew the dueling between us had not ended, even though I was now, so surprisingly, to see the movie he'd made with Victoria Frazer. It was as though a ghost out of the past had winked at me. Then he was gone, and I shook myself back to reality and started upstairs. A flirtatious grandfather was not part of my plan.

At least I no longer felt tired, but surprisingly elated and alive. I saw Mrs. Adrian watching me curiously from the desk. The town would probably buzz tomorrow with the story of the reclusive Roger Brandt actually turning up at Rumbling Mountain Lodge to see Jim Castle's wife. I wondered what Gretchen Frazer would think about this.

As I went upstairs, my exuberance lessened. The meeting with Roger Brandt had been too sudden, too unexpected. I began to think of all I had said to him and what I hadn't said. At least I was to see him again, and I was to learn what my grandmother Victoria had been like on the screen. I would actually see her as she had been when the world loved her—forever young.

The moment I unlocked the door of my room, I knew someone had been there. The sliding glass door to the balcony stood open and a breeze from the lake swept through my room. Perhaps one of the maids had come in and forgotten to close the door.

I crossed to take care of this, then became aware that someone stood outside, looking toward the water, his back to me. After an instant's shock, I relaxed. My visitor was only a small boy.

"Hello," I said. "How did you get up here?"

He turned to face me without alarm—a child of about ten in jeans and a plaid shirt. "Over there," he said, pointing.

Below the railing, the hill dropped away steeply. However, at the far end a thick branch of an oak tree reached toward the balcony that ran past all the rooms on this side. Obviously, it had been no trick for my visitor to climb out along the limb and drop onto the deck. Since I hadn't locked the glass door, he had been in and out easily.

"Do you mind telling me who you are and why you're here?" I spoke quietly, not wanting to frighten him off before I had a few answers.

"I'm Zach," he said. "Grandpa Ty sent me."

This was even more surprising. "Ty Frazer is your grandfather?"

"Not really. But all us kids call him that. He teaches us about mountain things. Stuff our dads and moms don't know."

"I see. And why did Grandpa Ty send you here?"

"He said I should give you this and tell you to take it and go away."

Zach fumbled in a jacket pocket and brought out a small, somewhat battered jewel box. When I'd accepted it from him, he ran along the deck, swung himself onto the tree branch, and disappeared before I could ask him anything more.

I took the little box into my room and sat down at the desk to open it. Packed into grubby cotton was a slim bracelet of silver links. Every few links along, a tiny silver bell was attached. When I held the bracelet up, the bells tinkled musically. It was a beautiful trinket, but I wondered why Ty had sent it to me. However, I had a very good suspicion about the woman it might have belonged to.

Ty was Victoria's brother, and who else could this lovely bracelet have belonged to but Victoria? And if I was right, even more questions were opening up. Some of these could be answered only by Ty himself. Did *he* know who I was?

I picked up a phone book of the Lake Lure area and looked for Finella and Gordon's number. In a moment, I was dialing their home. Finella answered, sounding cheerful and warm, welcoming whoever called. I told her that something had come up and I needed to talk with Ty Frazer.

She showed no surprise. "He's not easy to reach. Mostly, we just wait until he turns up. Gordon's out back feeding our two cats, but I'll let him know you want to see Ty, in case he runs into him."

When I'd thanked her and hung up, I went back outside and stood at the rail, once more looking out at that great crouching mountain that always drew my eyes.

Movement on the walk to the boathouse caught my attention. Gretchen Frazer was climbing toward the inn. She saw me at the railing and stopped below me.

"Mind if I come up?" she asked.

I didn't feel like talking to anyone else tonight, but I suspected that her request was more like a command, so I invited her up cheerfully enough. If the grapevine had been busy, she would know about Roger Brandt's visit.

I waited for her at my open door and she strode in, bristling with indignation. "That actor isn't welcome on these premises," she told me.

I explained at once that I'd had nothing to do with bringing about his visit. She slumped into the room's one armchair while I sat in the straight desk chair and waited for her to go on.

"What did he want?" she demanded.

"I suppose he intended to tell me off."

"About what?"

"Remember, I told you that Natalie Brandt had asked me to continue with my husband's documentary about Roger Brandt. He came here to make sure I wouldn't touch Jim's project."

"And will you?"

I shook my head. "No, probably not."

Her indignation faded a little. "Of course he'd be afraid that you wouldn't be as sensitive to his story as Jim had been. He likes to control people and events. He was slowing Jim down, setting limits. I heard about this from Jim himself."

"Do you suppose that Jim uncovered something the Brandts don't want to see exposed?"

She hesitated, and I wondered whether Gretchen knew more than she was willing to tell me.

"Who knows? They're strange people, the Brandts. What does it matter now, if the whole thing's being dropped?" She dismissed my question with a wave of her hand.

"It might matter if it had something to do with how Jim died."

She considered this somberly. "I suppose that's a possibility. Ty thinks—" She broke off, shrugging.

"Gordon has told me what Ty thinks," I said.

She shook her head wearily. "It never does any good to count on what Ty thinks. He's been confused for a long time about a number of things."

"Natalie would really like me to pick up this work. She feels her grandfather should be remembered."

"Hah! Don't talk to Natalie. Talk to Camilla—*if* they'll let you. Roger wouldn't let Jim Castle interview his wife. So of course Jim was all the more eager to ask her questions he knew he couldn't ask Roger."

"You talked to my husband quite a lot, it seems."

"We'd become friends to some extent, since I can be a good listener. I know he wanted me to talk about Victoria, and maybe I would have eventually, if only to spite the whole Brandt clan. Of course, Jim was a romantic. He built up the Victoria Frazer–Roger Brandt legend into something bigger than it really was. I suspected that he'd sensationalize the story—in a dignified way, of course. I liked your husband very much, Mrs. Castle. He was what my mother used to call a 'gentleman,' back when the word had meaning."

"Thank you," I said, and then abruptly changed the subject. "Did you see your sister's baby before it was sent away?"

Gretchen stared at me for a moment and I saw her sadness. "Of course I saw her. I wanted to keep her, but Victoria didn't want her to grow up around here. Even though I promised to move away if I could keep her, she chose to send her to friends in California."

"Couldn't Victoria have kept the baby?"

"How could she in that day? The scandal would have made it impossible, much as she loved her baby. Besides, Victoria must have had other plans for herself by that time."

"You mean suicide?"

"What else?"

But Gretchen didn't look at me now, and I sensed that there might be more that she wouldn't tell me. After a moment, she continued.

"I tried to keep in touch with Margaret after Victoria died. But she wrote only occasionally. When she grew up, she came to see me just once. The visit didn't go well, since we were strangers. I don't know now whether she's dead or alive."

Her sadness and loss ran deep, and my feelings toward Gretchen softened. I knew about my mother's one disturbing visit to Lake Lure.

"What was she like—Margaret?" I spoke softly. Now I was getting close to old mysteries my mother would never talk about.

"She was afraid of this place. She hated the lake and that mountain out there. She didn't try to meet her father, and he never knew she was here. That was just as well. No matter what he pretends, I can't believe that he ever forgot Victoria or forgave himself for what he'd done to her. He might even have tried to claim his daughter."

"That wouldn't have pleased Camilla."

"Of course not. But Roger usually does as he pleases."

I asked the same question I'd heard before. "Why would he live here, after all those terrible things had happened?"

Gretchen looked out at the dark lake. "He is the Keeper of the Legend."

"What does that mean?"

"Anything you like. Perhaps the real reason why he stayed was to punish Camilla."

"Why? Wasn't she the injured one?"

"He loved my sister. He couldn't imagine losing her. That's why he insisted on staying at Lake Lure after *Blue Ridge Cowboy* was finished. The studio was trying to avoid scandal, so they came up with another movie for him set in these mountains. He wouldn't leave Victoria, you see, and she was in seclusion about ten miles from here, waiting for the baby to be born. Camilla would never have permitted a divorce. Oh my, no! And laws were pretty strict in those days. I could never understand Roger's appeal, but I think Camilla loved him. And she would never have given him up. So when he decided to stay here, and bought the house he'd rented, he forced her to choose—either live here with him or go back to California alone."

None of this quite satisfied me. "Have there been other women?"

"Who knows? He doesn't stay here every month of the year. He was a young man—he had to do something with his life. Now and then, he leaves his family and goes off on his own."

"He doesn't sound like a very lovable person."

"Lovable!" The word rang with derision.

"If I could have kept Margaret—such a sweet little baby!—everything would have been different."

Again sadness touched her voice, and I could guess how empty the years must have been for her—with the sister she'd loved gone, her brother lost to the strange life he'd chosen, and the baby out of her reach.

She pulled herself back to the present and stood up abruptly. "It's better not to poke into all that unhappiness, Lauren."

She went to the door without further ado. "Good night, Mrs. Castle." She'd turned formal again. "I just wanted to tell you to stay away from *all* the Brandts. Don't let Roger beguile you with that actor's role he plays. And be especially careful with Ty. These days, he lives in his own fantasy world."

I assured her that I would be careful—whatever that meant—and closed the door.

When I went to bed, I slept soundly, with no vision from the lake to disturb my peaceful dreaming. Breakfast arrived early, as I'd requested, and when I'd eaten, I phoned Natalie to set up the date for the meeting with Roger. Apparently, she had already been told that I was to come over. Though she sounded puzzled, she asked no questions. She would pick me up in the early afternoon—around two o'clock.

So now I had a free morning on my hands. My primary mission at the moment was to locate Ty Frazer, since I wanted to know more about the bracelet he had sent me.

Around nine, I got into my car and drove down to the little cluster of buildings near the landing that was Lake Lure's business center. There I found Justyn Brandt walking along the dock where the *Showboat* was moored. I hadn't seen him since Natalie had taken me off his boat yesterday. Though his look didn't seem to approve of me, I had something to ask him, so I ventured over.

"When I was in Finella's shop yesterday, I saw the painting your daughter made of a spaceship that seemed to be crashing on top of Rumbling Bald. Finella said that you and your father were actually on the mountain when this happened."

He lighted up with an animation I had seen in him only when he was talking to his passengers on the lake tour. The story was one he had probably told many times before and he seemed willing to repeat it again.

"I was only a teenager when it happened, but that was the most exciting experience of my life. Dad and I were climbing Rumbling Bald that afternoon, when a fierce storm broke. A strong wind came up and the sky turned dark as midnight. But before we could take shelter in a cave, lightning flashes showed us some strange sort of aircraft just above the summit. We were free of trees there and we could see it clearly. It was like nothing I'd ever seen before. It looked as though it was about to crash, but we couldn't hear anything because of wind and thunder. With the next flash, the sky was empty, and we were pretty sure it had gone down."

He stopped, lost for a moment in his own vivid memories, and then continued.

"We tried to fight our way to the top, but it took us another half hour just to go five hundred yards. It was rough going because of all the debris from the storm and the mud. I'd never thought much about UFOs, but I'll never question their existence again. I know that's what we saw; it couldn't have been anything else. But we couldn't get to the top that night to verify what we'd seen.

"Afterward, of course, nobody believed us. That was back in the fifties and our own government was telling us there wasn't any such thing as a UFO. By the time we got back—in the middle of the next day—army intelligence had soldiers up there restricting access to the area. They claimed they were on maneuvers and that's why the area was off-limits, but Dad and I suspected a cover-up was going on. Two days later, they were gone and so was every trace of whatever we saw. There was still a scorch mark on the ground where something had slid along, but that was it. Even today, that same hush-hush policy is in effect—though the public is waking up to what's going on."

We had been walking along the boards of the landing, but now Justyn turned back toward the boat, where passengers had begun to gather.

I stopped beside him. "Did you talk to Jim about this?"

He hesitated, as though wondering how much he should tell me.

"My father doesn't like me to discuss what we saw—which wasn't much, really. You have to remember that the whole thing was pretty scary at the time, with the sky filled with black rain and rolling thunder. I was seventeen, but, believe me, I was pretty frightened. Dad said people would make fun of us, and we needn't look like fools."

Justyn stared off toward Rumbling Bald. "We searched the woods all around, but we never found any other trace, and we never knew for sure what had happened. It was as though the whole thing had been a dream."

We had been walking slowly toward the boat as we talked, and now there was more I wanted to ask him. I searched my handbag for Jim's letter and drew out the scrap of green material. Justyn took it from me, seemingly puzzled.

"What is this?"

"Jim left it for me in a letter he gave to Natalie. I think it was cut from something larger. He wrote that I could trust Gretchen and Ty, but no one else. He had come to believe that Victoria was murdered."

Justyn spoke sharply. "I doubt that. And I'm not sure your husband's views could be trusted."

"You didn't like Jim, did you?"

"I had no reason to," he said coldly, and I remembered that he was Natalie's father, and Natalie had been all too interested in Jim.

He was still examining the scrap I'd given him. "Will you let me have this piece of material?"

I didn't mean to give it up, and I took it back. "First I want to find out what it means."

"I wish you luck," he told me dryly, his manner dismissive. I watched as he herded his passengers aboard the *Showboat* and started the motor for the noisy trip around the lake.

Finella's shop was just across the highway, and I walked over to see whether she had heard from Ty.

S * E * V * E * N

WHEN I stepped into Finella's shop, she was waiting on a customer who was examining woven wall hangings. Today a mint
green jumpsuit seemed to complement her cheerful manner. She
brushed a strand of red hair from her cheek and smiled at me.

I waited until she was free and then told her about Natalie's
request that I continue with Jim's work.

"And will you?" she asked.

"That's what Roger Brandt was upset about, but I've said I
wouldn't. The only reason I would go ahead is because it's a
project that would give me access to more people I'd like to talk
to. About Victoria Frazer, especially."

Another customer came in and I wandered off idly among
display tables. I still wanted to ask when she expected to see Ty.
As I rounded the display of Gordon's drums, I saw a woman sitting
on a couch at the back of the store. It took a second glance to
recognize Camilla Brandt. This morning, she looked trim in white

twill trousers topped by a navy shirt. Her black hair was covered by a wide-brimmed straw hat with a navy band. Again she seemed completely assured and just as intimidating as I remembered.

I wasn't anxious to talk with her and I would have disappeared into the kudzu room, but she looked up and saw me. Instead of the polite mask she'd worn yesterday, her face lighted, her smile surprisingly friendly.

"Mrs. Castle! I've been wanting to see you again ever since my granddaughter told me that she had asked you to continue your husband's work. Can we talk about it? I do hope you will consider doing this."

Her words astonished me, after everything Natalie had told me.

When she gestured to a place on the couch, I went to sit beside her, feeling hesitant and a bit wary.

"I'm glad to have this opportunity to talk with you away from the house, Mrs. Castle. Can you tell me about your plan for this film?"

I had no idea whether she knew that her husband had come to the lodge to see me last evening or that I was to visit their house this afternoon, and her very friendliness made me uneasy and uncertain. She seemed to be a complex woman, whose motives might be difficult to read.

"Nothing is decided yet," I told her evasively. "I'm not at all sure I have the ability or even the wish to pick up Jim's work. Your granddaughter's suggestion came as a surprise." I said nothing about her husband's opposition to any such plan.

"What you have," she assured me calmly, "is an intimate understanding of the subject because your husband cared so deeply about this project. You would bring a certain sympathy to it, and you're not an outsider."

110

Her interest mystified me. "Did you like what Jim was doing?" I asked.

"I was against it at first, since I thought it might create problems. Along with all his success and national popularity, my husband endured a certain amount of—shall we say—adversity."

To put it mildly, I thought. "I'm not sure my approach—if I tried to do this—would be the same as Jim's. From what Natalie has told me, his focus was on Roger Brandt. But I might want to take a different approach."

Finella was free again and had come near us, listening with interest.

"What do you mean?" Camilla asked.

I answered quietly, watching for her reaction. "I would want to include Victoria Frazer. After all, the actress made an important picture with Roger Brandt. I would talk with Gretchen Frazer, Victoria's sister, if she was willing to help me. And perhaps to her brother, Ty. Though of course this may be futile even to think about."

Camilla Brandt crossed her knees and swung a long, aristocratic foot in its white pump. The movement seemed to give her time to consider. Beneath the brim of her shadowing hat, I could see again the puckering of the scar on her cheek.

"It might be interesting if you could accomplish this," she mused. "Something of Victoria Frazer's true nature might even emerge with such an effort."

I nodded, but I suspected that Camilla Brandt's prejudiced viewpoint would not be mine.

"Since I'm staying at the lodge, I've already spoken to Gretchen Frazer a couple of times," I said.

"Does she know what you intend to do?"

"Not *intend*," I insisted. "I haven't made up my mind yet."

"Of course Gretchen would have an idealized memory of her sister, and that would hardly help you to present the truth. The old man is completely unbalanced and would be useless for your purposes. Interviewing him would be like trying to interview a squirrel."

I knew what she was doing. Her real purpose, no matter how friendly she seemed, was probably to put barriers in my path and discourage me from finding out more—which made me all the more interested.

Although Finella had overheard Camilla's remarks, she didn't appear to sense any undercurrents. As though a thought had just occurred to her, Finella clapped her hands and said, "I know just the person who could tell you about Victoria, Lauren. Her name is Betsey Harlan. She was Victoria's dresser and a good friend. Talking to her might help you make up your mind."

"Where can I find her?"

The look Finella turned on Camilla was speculative. "Perhaps you could drive Lauren out to see her?"

The request surprised me. Finella must realize very well what she was asking, and of whom. I full expected Camilla to back away from such a suggestion, and she was already shaking her head.

"I don't think that's a good idea. Betsey's very old now, and an invalid. She wouldn't want to be disturbed."

Finella further surprised me, and I wondered whether she was baiting Camilla just a little. "She's not much older than you are, Camilla. But if you don't want to do this, I'll ask Gordon."

The other woman remained serene in her manner. Perhaps it occurred to her that it would be better to be present during any conversation I had with Betsey Harlan.

"I'll take you," she decided. "If you're free, we might as well do it now. I'll be busy this afternoon."

I accepted readily and we went out to Camilla's Lincoln. The Brandt family's taste apparently ran to expensive cars. We drove away from the mountains and into wide, rolling valley land.

"This is apple country," Camilla told me. "Wonderful fruits and vegetables grow in the area because of the thermal belt."

"Thermal belt?"

"It's a narrow strip that runs through this part of North Carolina; it exists because of the topography. Our temperature never gets as cold or as hot as the surrounding mountains and countryside. So the growing season is long. Of course this makes Lake Lure ideal for a resort and this valley ideal for farming. We're going to an apple farm now."

Though she spoke easily of the countryside and her manner remained cool and assured, I still had the feeling that taking me to see Betsey Harlan was the last thing Camilla wanted to do.

"Can you tell me something about the woman you're taking me to see?" I asked.

"She lives with her grandson's family. Of course, she may refuse to talk with us, you realize."

"Did you dislike her in the old days, Mrs. Brandt?"

"I've had little reason to like anyone connected with Victoria Frazer."

I felt chided and put in my place. "Of course," I said. "I'm sorry."

"Don't be. While Betsey and I had our problems, a lot of time has passed, and neither of us is the same woman she was when Victoria was alive. I must warn you, however, that Betsey can be sharp and spiteful. She doesn't mince words, and you may not hear flattering things about any of us. Though she's confined to a wheelchair, she's still lively and independent. Unpredictable."

"You've seen her recently?"

"Natalie's seen her—she painted a picture of her not long ago—and she's reported to me."

"How did Betsey happen to become Victoria Frazer's dresser?"

"Victoria was from this area originally, so she and Betsey were childhood friends. When *Blue Ridge Cowboy* was being made, Victoria brought her to help with her makeup, her hair, her costumes, and I understand she was very good with a needle. I think she made some of the things Victoria wore in that picture. Everything about making a movie was simpler in those days. Now a battery of professionals works on the stars. I imagine that Victoria picked Betsey not only for her natural skills but because she was young and impressionable and devoted. She would do exactly as Victoria wished. She was certainly a friend and confidante."

All this sounded promising. There might be a great deal that Betsey Harlan could tell me—if Camilla's presence didn't silence her.

"Were you ever on the set while the film was being made?"

The tilt of Camilla's hat brim was away from me and I could see her lovely profile, which lost none of its clean line until it reached her throat. In the bright light that came through the windshield, the scar on her cheek looked white. The pause before she answered me might have been because she was remembering something.

"I wasn't often on the set. Roger didn't like to have me there when he was filming. Of course, since many of his scenes involved outdoor action, I couldn't possibly watch."

"But you met Betsey on the set?"

She didn't answer immediately. We had turned into a side road and I saw signs for apples along the way. The mountains had receded and the land rolled with small hills. When she finally spoke, her voice seemed casual enough, almost as though she were telling me of everyday matters.

"I knew her, of course. And she also came to see me after Victoria drowned herself."

This was a surprise, but I had no time to question her because we'd turned through a gate set in a rail fence. Camilla pulled into an open space where several cars were parked.

"We're here," Camilla said. "Perhaps you can ask Betsey to tell you the rest. She came to see me for a curious reason."

Across the open yard, a large farmhouse painted sunflower yellow stretched its hospitable width in a long porch with low steps. Several families were purchasing apples and carrying loaded baskets out to their cars. A boy in his early teens came toward us when Camilla beckoned.

"We've come to see Betsey Harlan," she told him. "I am Camilla Brandt."

He regarded us doubtfully. "She don't hardly see people these days, but I'll go ask."

In a few moments, he was back, looking surprised. "My great-grammaw says you kin come in. I'll take you to her room, if you want."

We followed our guide up the steps to the low porch that ran the width of the house, then through a big sitting room filled with furniture not yet old enough to be antiques. He motioned us toward an open door at the rear.

We stepped into a room that was immediately cheerful with

color. A bright homemade quilt covered the bed and several served as wall hangings, as well. A crocheted throw that picked up the colors of the quilts covered the knees of the woman who sat watching us from her wheelchair. Though Camilla Brandt must have been only a few years younger, Betsey Harlan seemed decades more ancient—a small, wizened figure wrapped in a fringed gray shawl that was the only drab spot in the room. Brown eyes that looked out of a face mapped in wrinkles were bright with intelligence and curiosity.

Camilla quickly went to the wheelchair and took Betsey's small, bony fingers into her own well-cared-for hands. Hands more than faces give age away, and in spite of care, Camilla's were touched with veins and brown spots. She bent to kiss Betsey's cheek, surprising me. I hadn't thought of her as especially gentle or kind, and I wondered whether the gesture was genuine.

When Camilla introduced me, Betsey turned her sharp, bright look on me, searching for something. "I remember your husband, Mrs. Castle. He came to see me two years ago. But I wouldn't talk to him." Her look snapped back to Camilla. "I never told him anything about Roger."

"That was probably wise," Camilla said calmly. "But Mrs. Castle is especially interested in Victoria Frazer. She may pick up her husband's work and I thought you might like to tell her something about the past. No one else knew Victoria as you did."

The shrunken shoulders beneath the shawl seemed to straighten and her small, pointed chin came up. "Your husband only wanted to know what I thought about Roger, Mrs. Castle. I never liked Roger." She threw a quick glance at Camilla. "Miss Victoria was too good for him!"

She motioned for us to sit and we drew two chairs closer to the wheelchair.

116

"Tell Mrs. Castle whatever you care to," Camilla said. "I don't mind. You know that, don't you?"

Though she spoke to Camilla, Betsey's eyes remained fixed on me with a sharp intensity. "Yes, Miss Camilla. I understood that when I went to see you after Miss Victoria died."

Her light, whispery voice filled with loving praise as she told me of Victoria's beauty, of her kindness, her goodness. Later Betsey had worked on other films made in the South, starring other actresses, but she'd liked none of them as well.

"Miss Victoria trusted me. She knew I wanted what was best for her when I did her face and hair and helped with her wardrobe. I was handy with a needle, and that was useful to her. I made her dress and that beautiful turban she wore in her last picture. But when it came to that wicked man, she wouldn't listen to me at all." As she spoke, she seemed to forget Camilla's presence. "She thought he would leave his wife and marry her. I tried to tell her he couldn't be trusted, but she went her own way—and look what happened to her."

I didn't dare to look at Camilla and I spoke softly. "What *did* happen to her, Betsey?"

"He killed her, of course. He done the deed so's she'd never be found."

I had to look at Camilla now, but her expression remained calm, as though she'd heard all this before and discounted it.

Betsey ran on, wandering a bit. "I remember Miss Victoria's darling baby. Miss Gretchen would have kept that li'l ol' baby and raised her, but maybe it was better to send her away and do it quickly. Out of that man's reach."

I asked a direct question. "Betsey, did you have any evidence at the time that Victoria's death wasn't suicide?"

"I *knew* Miss Victoria better than all of 'em." Her voice

strengthened with new vehemence. "When she was strong again, she meant to follow her baby out to California, where she had friends because of her movie work."

Camilla spoke quietly, calling her back. "I think Mrs. Castle would like to know why you came to see me after Victoria was gone."

Betsey's eyes brightened, as though this was something she might relish. She didn't answer at once, however, because she was staring fixedly at Camilla. Camilla casually covered the scar on her cheek with one hand, as though all too aware of what Betsey saw. For the first time, she seemed ruffled. "Betsey, tell Mrs. Castle why you came to see me."

The old woman lowered her eyes to the crocheted throw over her knees. "I thought you ought to know about your husband. That's why I came."

"It's all right to tell Mrs. Castle what you believe."

Betsey looked up at me with tears in her faded brown eyes. "I think he wanted to be rid of Miss Victoria before she could tell too much and ruin his career. That's what I wanted Miss Camilla to know."

"Of course I didn't agree with you. My husband would never have hurt anyone."

Betsey turned away, wheeling her chair over to her dresser to take out a tissue before answering. "She should have stayed here where she was born and bred. But if she had gone out to California, maybe I'd have gone with her for good, even if it meant leaving Ty."

"Ty?" I asked, startled, as she wheeled back toward us.

"Tyronne—Miss Victoria's brother. In those days, he fancied me. I reckon I fancied him, too, for a while."

Camilla looked amused at my expression. "You should have seen us all when we were young, Mrs. Castle. Betsey was the prettiest girl to come out of North Carolina. And Ty was a handsome boy. He loved the mountains even then—but he might have loved Betsey more. Who knows what might have been if his sister Victoria hadn't disappeared—died. That was what destroyed him and turned him into the caricature you see now."

"Ty came to see me once after we were old." Betsey's voice dropped to a whisper. "He brought me honeysuckle. Imagine! When that stuff grows like a weed everywhere. We didn't talk much. He took a look at me, and I took a look at him, and we knew those two young kids were long gone and that we wouldn't even like each other anymore. I felt a little sad about that, but I've had another romance or two since Ty, and I've been married." She stopped and looked at Camilla. "You didn't do so well with your marriage, did you? My man may have died, but at least he never wandered in the years we were together."

A faint irritation touched Camilla's voice. "Suppose we talk about Victoria. What else can you tell Mrs. Castle that might be useful if she decides to go on with her husband's work?"

Betsey paid no attention to this. "Roger Brandt came to see me once after Miss Victoria died. Bet he never told you that, Miss Camilla."

Camilla looked surprised. "What did he want, Betsey?"

"He wanted me to stop talking about him. He told me he would send a lawyer to see me if I went on telling the things I knew."

"What are the things you know?" I urged.

Betsey hesitated, her bright, faded eyes sweeping my face. In the pause, I had a sense of Camilla's stillness—as though she had braced herself against whatever might come.

Betsey, however, was following her own side road. "I don't want no truck with lawyers. I don't want him sending some city fellas to see me, making threats."

"That was a long time ago," I assured her. "I don't think anything you might tell me now would get you into trouble."

But Betsey had mixed up her many decades and was wandering. I knew by Camilla's expression that she wanted to get away. Since talking with Betsey now would be hopeless, I thanked her and asked if I might come again sometime. She looked past us, through us, without answering. Nevertheless, as we went toward the door, she called after us, her voice strong again.

"Of course there was that fight Miss Victoria had with Ty. But you know about that, don't you?"

Camilla turned back quickly, surprised. "No, Betsey, we don't know. Will you tell us?"

Now she stayed with her subject. "Ty loved his sister a lot. And he went kinda crazy when he knew she was going to have that man's baby. He threatened to kill Roger Brandt—he was talking real wild. I was there, so I saw what happened when Miss Victoria slapped him. Ty went off crazy mad. Miss Gretchen was there, too. She was the youngest, but she always sort of looked after Ty, and she was the only one who could calm him down when he went outta control."

"Did Ty ever try to carry out his threat?" I asked.

"Not so far." Betsey drifted off again and Camilla touched my arm.

"We'd better go. Thank you for seeing us, Betsey. Is there anything I can do for you?"

Unexpectedly, Betsey nodded. "Yes, Miss Camilla—you can

go on out and wait in the car for Mrs. Castle. I got to talk to her for a minute."

Clearly, this didn't suit Camilla and I knew that the last thing she wanted was to leave me alone with Betsey.

"I'll only be a moment," I told her, and she could do nothing but give in and return to her car.

"What's your name?" Betsey asked me when Camilla had gone.

At first, I thought she was wandering again. "I'm Jim Castle's wife," I reminded her.

"I mean your real name. What's your first name—what do they call you?"

"I'm Lauren Castle."

She shook her head. "Get me that Bible over there."

Her request sounded urgent, so I went to a nearby table and picked up the black leather-covered book she'd indicated. It wasn't a big family Bible, but of ordinary book size, with shiny gold on the edges of the thin India paper. She took it from me with hands that shook a little.

"Sometimes I have the sight, though not always when I want it. I knew right away when you walked in who you are. But I didn't want to say anything while *she* was here. She doesn't know, does she? Victoria was your grandmother. You're that little baby's baby. I always knew you would come and that you'd be the right one, even if your mama wasn't."

For a moment, I couldn't speak. Then I dropped to my knees beside her chair and looked into eyes that seemed suddenly clear. An unexpected sense of relief poured through me.

"No one else knows," I told her, deciding not to mention Gordon. "No one else must know—not yet. I'm not ready."

She patted my hand. "We won't tell anyone. There are bad feelings out there, though I don't know from where. Anyway, I'm real proud that you come to see me. I got something for you I been saving all these years." She flipped the Bible open to the place she wanted and I saw a spray of dried flowers pressed between the pages. There was also a piece of something hard wrapped in tissue. It had formed a depression that made the place easy to find.

"Ty gave me those flowers when he was young and knew better than to bring honeysuckle. Violets and forget-me-nots. Hah! Never mind the flowers—this is what I been waiting to give my pretty lady's granddaughter."

She picked up the bit of yellowed tissue and opened it, holding it out to me. It contained a tiny stone—something that looked like a bit of gravel.

"Take it," she ordered.

Mystified, I did as I was told. The grayish bit of stone felt rough in my fingers and I had no idea what it was.

"Hold it up to the light," Betsey said.

Now I saw that a tiny cap of dull green emerged from the socket of gray rock. When I held it toward a window, the cap gleamed translucent with green light.

I wondered out loud. "It's an emerald?"

"That's what it is. Uncut. Not worth anything because it's too small. Cutting would make it just about disappear. Miss Victoria gave it to me for fun. There's an emerald mine hereabouts, and she and that man dug some of those little stones right out of the earth for a scene in the movie. You're the one who should have it now."

"I'll treasure this," I told her, and bent to kiss her crumpled cheek. "May I come and see you again before I leave?"

"You sure can. But first maybe you'd like to see something

else. Something I hid away and kept when they packed off all your gramma's things for charity. Look behind that door over there."

I opened the door of a small closet and found a clear plastic garment bag—a zippered bag of more recent vintage than the dress it protected. I took out the long gown and held it up on its padded hanger. Yards of white cloth had been used and it frothed out over my hands, released from the restriction of years.

"She wore that dress in the movie she made here," Betsey said softly. "It was a funny scene because she wore an evening dress and he wore cowboy clothes. She tore it once—" She broke off, as though she'd stopped herself from saying something more. "It was a bad tear, but I mended it so you can hardly tell."

The gown was made of some filmy material that had been popular at the time. It was sleeveless, with a scooped neck and a softly full torso that would cling around the bust and then float out in an ageless style that fell to the floor.

As I held up the gown that had once been worn by Victoria Frazer, I felt again a strange enchantment. It was as though my grandmother touched me—as though, through the dress, she could reach out to me.

"You're about the same size," Betsey said. "You could wear that dress."

I smiled at her. "Hardly. But thank you for letting me see it." I returned the gown carefully to its protective bag and touched it gently—almost a caress—as I hung it back in the closet.

"Nobody ever knew I kept that dress," she told me. "Nobody missed it. All those strangers picking over her things. She was six months pregnant with your mama when she last wore that dress, but I made it so cleverly that no one could tell."

Suddenly, I knew what I must show her. I dropped the

tissue-wrapped emerald into my bag and drew out the silver bracelet. Tiny bells chimed as I held it out to her.

"Do you recognize this?"

She put her hands in her lap so they wouldn't touch the bracelet. "*He* gave her that. I hated everything he gave her because I knew how false he was. How come you've got it now?"

"Ty sent it to me by a small boy. But I don't know why."

Her face crumpled into even more lines and I thought she was going to cry. "Put it away. Get rid of it. He is a wicked man."

I knew she didn't mean Ty.

Suddenly, all the energy faded out of her and she looked tired and very old. It was time to leave.

"Thank you for seeing me, Betsey. And for recognizing *me*."

She roused herself for a few more words. "Don't show *her* that bracelet. Or the emerald. After all, she's *his* wife."

"Roger Brandt is my grandfather," I reminded her. "And I can't help that."

"So long as you don't do anything about it. It's not your fault. My beautiful, magic lady was young and foolish and too much in love. *I* can still remember what that's like. I'm sorry about your husband. He seemed like a nice man."

She closed her eyes, looking even more ancient, and appeared to doze off gently. I went out to where Camilla waited for me in the car.

"That took a while," she said as I got in beside her. "What did she want?"

I couldn't tell her all of it. "She wandered a bit, but I think she wanted to tell me how sorry she was about Jim."

"Yes—she can wander, poor old thing."

As Finella had pointed out, not all that many years stretched between Betsey and Camilla Brandt and I smiled to myself. This woman would never think that *old* applied to her. And in a way, it really didn't.

We were driving away from the apple farm when she spoke again. "I'd hoped that Betsey might give you something you could use for the documentary. Did she?"

I had a feeling that she was simply probing. "I'm not sure. Why do you want to see Jim's work continued, when your husband doesn't?"

Her attention was fixed on the road ahead and her patrician profile told me nothing. It took her a little while to answer me.

"Roger deserves to be remembered, whether he appreciates that fact or not."

Somehow I doubted that this was her true motive. She might simply be quoting Natalie.

"What if something comes to light that you don't expect? Something that might hurt him? Betsey seems to think she might be able to damage him."

Camilla turned her head to look at me and I saw a flash of excitement in her eyes—quickly hidden. "Perhaps it's time for all that's been concealed for too long to come out. The terrible, as well as the good."

The intensity in her voice shocked me more than her words. Had I detected a vindictive quality in Camilla Brandt, directed toward her husband, that the passing years had never erased? Perhaps she had even *wanted* Betsey to say those things about Roger Brandt. Yet Camilla had stayed with him all these years. Natalie had said that they loved and hated each other.

I could find nothing to say, and if Camilla sensed that she had shocked me, she gave no sign. We spoke very little until we reached Lake Lure. Then I asked her to drop me at Finella's. She left me there with a careless wave of her hand and drove away. It might even be that she wanted to use me in some way against her husband—so she hadn't minded *what* Betsey might say.

When she heard the bell at the shop door, Finella came out from the back room. "You're just in time, Lauren. Gordon and I are about to have lunch. I hope you'll join us."

I thanked her and followed her into a small sitting room pleasantly furnished with informal odds and ends. A gateleg table had been set with woven yellow place mats and china in soft delft blue. A tiny vase of asters celebrated the season.

Gordon was setting out cold ham and potato salad while Finella brought hot rolls and a pot of coffee to the table. Without warning, the shock of seeing him struck me all over again—even more piercingly than when I'd met him in the Indian village. When we sat down to eat, I said hardly anything. Luckily, Finella filled in the gap with a story about a customer she'd met that morning in the shop.

I said nothing because I wasn't really present. Some treacherous, long-buried emotion had pulled me back to San Francisco. I stood all over again with Gordon on a hilltop and watched the fog roll across the bay. That day, I had been totally aware of everything about him—as I was now. There had been such sweetness for me in those few days, and a sharpening of my senses. I had never felt as much alive since then.

There'd been only a handful of days, yet they had seemed timeless. Nothing existed for us except each other. All that mattered were the moments we shared. Underneath the tremulous sweetness, I was aware as well of a new lacing of excitement and anticipation as we moved toward a new closeness that now seemed inevitable.

I had not hesitated when the time came. Nothing could ever take the memory of our loving away from me. Now, when I looked at Gordon, I knew how the crisp texture of his hair would feel to my touch. I knew the tracing of his fingers down the line of my chin and throat. I knew so much more, and something in me shattered into little pieces of pain.

Gordon was watching me and I dared not look at him. I must remember that he had become someone I no longer knew as I'd known that man in California. Finella saved me when she asked about Camilla's and my visit to Betsey Harlan. I steadied myself and told her how much I'd liked Betsey and about my surprise that Ty had once courted her. Gordon listened but remained silent, remote. He had distanced himself from me, and my heart, already cracked, felt about to break.

Now and then customers came into the shop and Finella went out to wait on them, leaving us alone.

Somehow I had to reach him, and I spoke quietly. "We both loved Jim. Can we accept that and find some common ground?"

He listened coolly. "I can understand why you wouldn't let Jim talk about his wife's real identity. But why are you playing out this deception here in Lake Lure now? Don't you think you could at least tell Natalie?"

I tried to explain the way I felt. "I know I can learn more if no one is aware that Victoria Frazer was my grandmother. I'm sure Camilla would never have taken me to see Betsey if she'd known who my grandparents were. I don't think she'd want to have anything to do with me at all. So I'm sorry if you think this is a cheap deception, but I feel it's necessary."

He didn't seem impressed, though he made no comment.

I went on. "This afternoon, Roger Brandt is going to show me the film he and Victoria made together. I expressed an interest and he made the offer. But I wonder if he would have done so if he knew that I was his—his illegitimate granddaughter."

"How did that happen?"

I was explaining about Roger Brandt's visit to the lodge when Finella returned, and she listened with delight when she heard what I planned.

"That's exciting. He never shows that film to anyone."

"Why don't you tell my mother about your connection with the Brandts?" Gordon asked.

I felt betrayed. I didn't mind having Finella know, but not in a way that forced my hand. Now I had no choice.

"Victoria Frazer was my grandmother and Roger Brandt is my grandfather. When Victoria sent my mother to California friends, she told them that the baby's father was Roger Brandt. There was no reason to doubt this, considering the way the fan magazines had carried on in print."

Finella was delighted. "How dramatic! Gordon—you knew about this?"

"I've known for a long time. Lauren and I first met at the university in Berkeley years ago. I've gone along with Lauren's playacting, but it's begun to wear on me. I don't know that her reasoning for this is justified."

Finella ignored the impatience in his voice, but I could not, and it cut through me.

"Will you tell Roger this afternoon, Lauren?" she asked.

"I don't think so. I'm not enthusiastic about telling either Roger or Camilla. What would be the point? I'd like to see that film and know what my grandmother was like. Then I'll just go home."

"In spite of what happened to Jim?" Gordon asked. "Not that there's much *you* could do about that."

His words stung, and he'd meant them to. What had happened to Jim was the one thing that held me here. *Someone* knew what had happened to him. Someone knew what had happened to Victoria, and perhaps these two deeds were connected—because of whatever Jim had discovered. Something I might still discover. But there was nothing more I could say to Gordon Heath. He had set himself against me—for reasons that probably went deeply into the past. And how could I blame him? I was the one who had lacked the courage to take a different road from the one I'd so comfortably planned.

If I stayed now, Gordon would go on hurting me—perhaps punishing me for the past. And, worst of all, enjoying it. I wanted none of that.

I glanced at my watch. "Thank you for lunch, Finella. I'd better get back to the lodge, since Natalie will be picking me up."

She came to the door with me and Gordon followed me outside. When we reached my car, he was still with me, a bit doggedly. I got behind the wheel and when he leaned in the open window, his words surprised me.

"Maybe I owe you an apology."

"You don't owe me anything," I said.

He changed the subject abruptly. "Would you be willing to get up before dawn tomorrow morning, Lauren?"

I stared at him blankly and he continued.

"There's something I'd like to show you, but we'd need to make it by sunrise."

I couldn't follow this change in him. It was too sudden. Unless—during our recent lunch—he, too, had remembered San Francisco? A pulse of excitement beat in me—but I must be careful, very careful.

"Where are you taking me?" I asked.

Small lines that I remembered crinkled at the outer corners of his eyes. "Let's make it a surprise. It will be more fun that way. Just be ready by four-thirty. I'll wait for you in the lobby of the lodge."

He turned away, as though I might change my mind, and went back to his mother's shop. I drove up to the lodge feeling light-headed. I was afraid of anticipating more than might be offered, but that was what I was beginning to feel. Now, however, I must get ready for the visit to my grandfather. Much as I wanted to go, I knew an ordeal lay ahead.

Back in my room, I considered the few clothes I'd brought along. My turquoise blouse was fresh and my full blue skirt would serve again, but this afternoon I would wear white coral instead of lapis.

While I waited for Natalie, I took out the tiny emerald that Victoria Frazer had dug from the earth so long ago. A million years might be nothing in the life of this stone, but it was only the time since Victoria had dug it out of the earth that interested me.

I held it on my palm, closing my fingers around it, and willed it to "speak" to me. Something light as a feather seemed to touch my cheek and a sense of well-being I could think of only as loving breathed through me. *Her* presence—as I'd felt it when I held her gown in my hands?

The jarring ring of the telephone broke the spell. Natalie was waiting for me in the lobby and I hurried down to meet her.

This afternoon, she wore jeans again and a man's shirt, so I felt dressed up and aware of the way she looked at me when I got into her car.

"Would you mind explaining what this is all about?" she asked as we turned onto the road that wound high above this end of the lake. "Why does my grandfather want to see you?"

There seemed no reason not to tell her, though apparently Roger had not. "When I returned to the lodge last night, your grandfather was waiting for me. He wanted me to know how opposed he is to my picking up Jim's work. But when I asked about the film he'd made with Victoria Frazer and showed an interest in seeing it, he offered to screen it for me." That wasn't all, but it was enough to tell her for now.

Natalie braked the car and turned abruptly into a parking space beside a house set high above the lake. It was closed and shuttered—probably occupied by summer people who had left when the season ended. Now it offered a private spot to sit and talk without interruption.

She plunged in at once. "My grandfather has never shown *me* that picture. So why you?"

"I'm not sure. I told him about finding an old magazine with pictures and an article about Victoria Frazer. I said I wished I could have seen her in *Blue Ridge Cowboy*, so I would know what she really looked like at that time, and he invited me to see his print of the movie. That's all there is to it."

So simple an explanation didn't satisfy Natalie, but before she could push me further, I asked a question of my own. "Yesterday, when you took me off the boat, you were the one who wanted me to go on with Jim's work. Then, last night at dinner, you'd changed. I could sense your edginess toward me, and it's there again now. Why?"

Her sigh had a rueful sound. "I'm sorry. It really has nothing to do with you. Jim said I would like you, and I do. But my grandfather's reaction turned me in a different direction. So I backed away. After all, I wanted the film finished for his sake— and Jim's."

"But your grandmother seems to want this. I met her at

Finella's shop and she took me to see Betsey Harlan—a fascinating experience."

Natalie sat with her hands on the wheel and I saw the way her fingers tightened. When she spoke, her voice was tense. "If *Gran* wants this enough to try to catch your interest, then perhaps my grandfather will change his mind."

I had wondered about any possible vindictiveness on Camilla's part. It must have been very difficult to live with the scandal of Roger Brandt's betrayal. I could only imagine the toll Victoria's life and death had taken on Camilla's marriage.

She backed the car away from the empty house and drove down to the road that ran across the top of the dam. "Theirs is a complicated relationship, Lauren. Sometimes I've even wondered if he thought he might be rid of her by moving here permanently—that she'd go back to California. But she stayed with him in spite of everything. Still, I don't think she's ever let him forget what he owes her because of Victoria."

"What a terrible way to live."

"I know. Either love or hate is bad enough. But when you mix them, the results can be explosive. Sometimes I think he's protecting her—or maybe she's protecting him. I keep waiting for the spark that will set off a fire storm."

She watched me speculatively, as though she wondered whether I might furnish such a spark. Of course she couldn't know how large a conflagration I might create once those two knew that I was Victoria Frazer's granddaughter. Suddenly, the matter of revealing my identity became a little frightening—no longer a simple choice for me to make.

When I didn't respond, Natalie said, "No matter what anyone says, I hope you won't pick up my foolish suggestion about Jim's work. If I had dreamed what Grandpa's reaction would be, I would never have written to you in the first place."

"There's still the matter of how Jim died," I reminded her.

"I think about it all the time, but maybe it was just an accident. I don't know what I think anymore."

We were nearly there; I braced myself for the coming encounter with Roger Brandt. By this time, I was feeling far more uneasy than I'd expected to. Natalie's change of attitude raised all sorts of questions in my mind and I didn't think she had told me all her reasons for trying to dissuade me from following through on her suggestion.

I knew one thing: I must step carefully and cautiously with every member of this family.

E ⋆ I ⋆ G ⋆ H ⋆ T

WHEN WE reached the house, Natalie took me into her grandparents' wing on the upper level.

An entryway led into a large open area that contained a sunken living room; a higher level formed the dining room and kitchen.

Across the living room, sliding glass doors opened onto a stunning view down the lake to hazy blue peaks at the far end. The colors of this entire space were warm and strong, complementing both the view through the glass and the green and gold of two Japanese screens that had been used to partition off the far end of the room.

"He's waiting for you," Natalie said, and led the way toward the screens.

There was a space between them where she could step through into Roger Brandt's own wide living room. He sat in a well-worn green leather armchair, his feet up on an ottoman and a book in his hands. I had time for a quick glance around at a desk, a wall of pictures—from his movies, no doubt—and many shelves that held books and objects he might have collected in his travels. Then my entire focus was on the man.

He stood up to greet me and I had the immediate sense of an actor performing. He meant to charm me—for whatever reason—and I stiffened to resist his easy attraction. There was nothing I wanted to like about Roger Brandt.

His handclasp was cordial. "Thank you for coming, Mrs. Castle," he said as though he was indebted to me.

I murmured something polite and noncommittal, aware of Natalie's skeptical look.

"We might as well start right away. Natalie has things to do, I'm sure." He gave his granddaughter a glance of dismissal.

Natalie stood her ground. "I'd like to see this picture, too, Grandfather."

His smile showed a brittle edge. "Not this time, my dear. I want you to watch for your grandmother and keep her away while I'm showing Mrs. Castle this film."

This, Natalie would accept, however grudgingly. "I don't expect her home soon, but I'll keep her away if she shows up."

He thanked her and she went off, giving me a look I couldn't interpret. I was aware again of his striking appearance—gracefully worn—perhaps more seasoned and impressive because of his years. The silk scarf at his throat might hide the damage of age, but it also gave him a jaunty air that I remembered from the screen. Vertical lines creased his cheeks when he smiled and gave his face more character than the young man had possessed.

Roger Brandt touched a button and a movie screen was

revealed on the side of the room away from the view. Two armchairs were set before it and he motioned me into one of them. When he'd turned off the lights and drawn the draperies across the glass, he came to sit beside me. The projector stood on a table before him and he turned it on.

The black-and-white picture began to run and my attention was wholly absorbed. Roger Brandt was immediately on-screen in full cowboy regalia. He'd skipped the movie titles and gone straight to the action, where he seemed to be riding to the rescue of a beautiful society girl who had been kidnapped by the villains. His handsome palomino was climbing a wooded trail above a river that tumbled across black rocks. Undoubtedly, the Rocky Broad, since this was no western landscape. When he dismounted before a tumbledown mountain shack, a rough-looking character came to the door. There was a heated verbal exchange and then the cowboy thrust the bigger man aside and strode into the shack. How well he knew how much the camera loved him!

But now Victoria Frazer was on the screen and I had eyes for no one else. There were no close-ups at first, but she looked utterly beautiful in the careful disarray of torn shirt and well-cut jodhpurs, dirty at the knees. At once, Roger released her from her bonds. There was no talk between them—it was straight action as he carried her from the shack in strong young arms.

Obviously, the character he played in the film was not in awe of her patrician elegance, and her half-amused response to this high-handed rescue reminded me of later actresses who had played such roles with less sophistication than Victoria Frazer. She was like no one I had ever seen on a movie screen. If she had lived, she would have been one of the greats, and my own emotional response surprised me.

"This is a picture that should be revived," I whispered to the man beside me.

He stared at me, then looked away, nodding toward the screen, so I watched again. The first real close-up showed Victoria's enormous eyes, which could express every nuance of emotion, even though their green was lost in black and white. Only in the eyes did we resemble each other. I couldn't imagine anyone would ever take me to be related to Victoria Frazer, and I sighed with a certain regret. Again Roger glanced at me and then back at the screen.

The slightly foolish story ran on and I didn't try to follow it. I simply watched those two whenever they were on, watched the electricity that sprang between them. *This* wasn't acting and I could understand why Roger had no wish to have his wife know that he owned a print of *Blue Ridge Cowboy*.

The scene changed and I missed the transition. The cowboy and the lady were dining together in a lavish private room that I guessed to be at the Lake Lure Inn. A room apparently engaged by the wealthy young woman—much to the comic embarrassment of the cowboy, unused to such surroundings. It was obvious to the audience that their love affair was doomed from the first, since they were totally unsuited to each other. After some awkward conversation, the cowboy brought out a gift for the lady. He handed her the crudely wrapped box across the table.

"It's something that belonged to my mother," the cowboy said. I heard the ardor beneath his words and knew that it was real.

Victoria's voice was low, throaty, filled with tears as she expressed delight, unwrapping the tissue to reveal a satin box. If cameras whirred around them and booms moved, with the whole movie crew watching, to say nothing of the director—one would never know. I'd often wondered how movie actors could lose themselves so completely in a scene, carrying an audience with them into the story, in spite of the mechanics of moviemaking that surrounded them.

The camera moved in for a close-up as Victoria held up a silver bracelet decorated with tiny silver bells. She gasped with delight, and the camera caught the shine of tears on her cheeks.

Roger Brandt whispered in my ear. "I really gave that brace-let to her when we played the scene. She was happy then—her tears were real."

I heard the catch in his voice, the sadness. Though all this was long ago, the record of a living moment between them was still there in the film—and he had not forgotten.

How strange to consider that we, the audience who watched old movies, knew so much more than the actors on the screen ever could. We knew what hand fate had dealt them—who had lived and who had died. We knew what the future held for them, and that made such films all the more poignant.

The bracelet shone with its own silver light and the tiny bells, silent now in my purse, chimed from the screen. Victoria held out her hand and Roger clasped the bracelet about her wrist.

I wanted to take out my treasure and show it to him, but I didn't dare. I had no idea what the consequence of such a move would be and I wasn't ready. Not yet. One day soon, perhaps, I would show it to him and tell him who I was. Not because I felt affectionate or sentimental but because I wanted—rather fiercely at that moment—to hurt him, punish him for what he had done to my grandmother. Now, however, I simply watched in silence.

The story on the screen continued to unfold rapidly. The villains showed up again and there was the usual fistfight. The cowboy and the meanest assailant did a dive through breakaway

138

glass in a prepared window frame, sailing out into space and then dropping to the ground, where they finished the fight.

Beside me, Roger Brandt laughed softly. "That fellow didn't like me, and he punched pretty hard, though I gave as good as I got. It was a fine fight. You did your own stunts in those days— that was really me flying through the window. Not like the easy course actors take today."

I nodded politely and then looked back to the screen, where there was another scene that held my rapt attention. The cowboy and the lady were scrambling around in the dirt, digging for gems. I missed how this tied in to the story, not that it mattered. My grandmother held out her hand to show the cowboy her assorted treasures. He picked out one small stone and swept the rest from her hand. Then he kissed her palm warmly.

I knew this, too, was real. The love scenes were all real—and, of course, even more passionate offscreen, since a baby had re-sulted. On impulse, I reached into my bag for the scrap of tissue that held the tiny emerald Betsey had given me. This I could show him. Like Victoria on the screen, I held it out on my palm for him to see. Even uncut, the green end that emerged from its sheath of stone caught a gleam from the screen.

"Is this the emerald she gave you?" I asked.

He took it from me and for the moment we both forgot actors and screen as the projector wound on.

"Where did you get that?" he demanded.

"It really is the same emerald," I told him. "Your wife took me to visit Betsey Harlan this morning. Before we left, Betsey sent your wife out to her car so we could talk privately about Victoria. She gave me this and she showed me a beautiful white gown she said Victoria wore in the picture."

Whatever Roger's reaction might have been, he revealed

nothing. He held the stone in his fingers and watched the screen. "Look," he said, "you'll see the dress."

Time had passed while we were talking and a ball was in progress far from the small mountain town where the earlier scenes had taken place. Victoria wore the white dress Betsey had shown me, her beautifully shaped head bound in the gracefully folded white turban Betsey had probably made for her.

Waltzing in the arms of an officer in uniform, she looked so sad that it broke my heart. I knew this sadness, too, was real, since she could never have her cowboy for keeps either in the story or in real life.

But then—dramatically—the palomino mare, with Roger Brandt in the saddle, stepped onto the polished floor of the ballroom, with silver chandeliers glowing overhead. Alarmed and indignant, dancers scrambled out of his way. When he reached Victoria and her partner, he dismounted and took her from the officer's arms to whirl her down the room in a waltz so beautiful that the other dancers stood apart and watched. The dress flared out as the camera followed them and then came in for a close-up of Victoria's face as she watched her partner with her heart in her eyes. One might wonder where a cowboy had learned to waltz like that, but this, of course, was Hollywood.

The mare, well trained not to take alarm, stood still, waiting. Suddenly, Roger Brandt swept his partner down the room and then left her as he vaulted into the saddle. The camera showed the agony in Victoria's face as she looked up at him. Then, in a sudden graceful move, Roger leaned down to her. She took his hand and sprang with skill and ease into the saddle in front of him, hooking a knee over the western pommel. His strong arms around her, they rode away into a staged sunset. At the last minute, Roger turned his head and glanced back at the camera, speaking worlds in that familiar look. Strangely, Victoria never looked back for the camera to catch a final close-up of her.

Startling me, Roger left his chair abruptly to turn off the projector before the credits ran. He made a great business of opening the draperies and flooding the room with trembling light from the lake. Perhaps he didn't want me to see whatever emotion had touched him and might show in his face.

When he returned to the chair beside me, he had himself in hand. "So there you are." He spoke with a deliberate lightness, as though he discounted any earlier feeling he might have shown. "I haven't watched that in years. I ought to burn it, really—it's not my best picture."

"But you won't," I said softly. "Why did you let her go? Why did you let the baby go?"

Anger sprang to light—not in the actor but in the man. "That is nobody's business. Now that you've seen what she was like, Mrs. Castle, what will you do with this remarkable knowledge?"

His cold fury frightened me, but I managed to answer quietly. "I'll feel it—savor it. I'll remember. How graceful she was, flying up into that saddle in front of you. What riding skill that must have required."

"Hah!" he said, irony evident in his voice. "Such great skill!" Whatever momentary mood the movie had roused in him was gone. He was an old man—impatient, and perhaps a little put off by young love.

"Why are you so interested?" he demanded. "Your husband didn't care in the least about Victoria's side of the story."

"He wouldn't have let you know if he did." For a moment, I was almost ready to tell him the truth. But once taken, the step would be irrevocable, and I had no idea what the result might be. Roger Brandt was unlikely to open his arms to a granddaughter whose mother he had long ago rejected.

"How did she die? How did she really die?" I asked.

He turned away from the light, so that whatever he felt about the question was hidden. His next words astonished me.

"Will you have dinner with me tonight, Lauren?" It was the first time he had used my first name. "I would like to take you to the Esmeralda Inn, where we all stayed while that picture was being made."

Perhaps I'd been wrong. Perhaps remembrance of how the young man felt had remained. I tried to keep too much eagerness from my voice. "I would enjoy that."

"Fine. Then you can tell me about your visit with Betsey Harlan and why Camilla took you to see her."

So, as I suspected, he'd had no knowledge of what his wife had done.

"I'll pick you up at the lodge at seven," he continued. "Though I don't advise letting Gretchen Frazer know that you're meeting me. I'm not a favorite of hers."

"I've already discovered that. But I don't consult with Miss Frazer about anything I do."

This time, his smile once more belonged to the actor—warm and approving. He still held the tiny emerald and I didn't ask for it back.

"I'll be waiting for you," I promised. "Thank you for the privilege of seeing *Blue Ridge Cowboy*."

Whatever emotion had shaken him after the picture ended was now under control. Suddenly, he looked very tired, and I took my leave quickly.

When I reached the door by which I'd entered, Natalie was waiting for me. "Let's go out another way. Gran has just driven in, and it's better if she doesn't know that you were with my grandfather. She has an uncanny ability to figure things out, and it would be disastrous if she got wind of this screening."

She led the way to the lower part of the house, where I had visited her yesterday, and then went out on the walk that ran down to the boathouse.

"I'll take you back to the lodge by boat," she said, hurrying ahead of me. "I just hope Gran doesn't look out a window and see us."

All this secrecy and caution disturbed me. "Does everyone in this family keep secrets from everyone else?" I asked as we reached the stretch of dock that ran beside the boathouse.

Natalie didn't answer. A small pontoon boat was tethered to the dock. I noted its name wryly: *The Jolly Roger.* Natalie held it steady while I stepped down to sit in one of the four seats. But before she could cast off, Justyn came running down from the main house, looking upset. What a family at odds this seemed to be.

"I'd like to talk with you, Mrs. Castle," he said as soon as he reached us. "You seem to have caused my mother to act in an odd manner this morning. I came back to the house with her just now and I'm worried about her state of mind. We do try to protect her and my father."

This seemed surprising. Protect them from what? I'd seldom seen a lady more in control of herself than Camilla Brandt. I'd have thought she was always one to guard her emotions.

"Get in, Dad." Natalie sounded impatient. "Let's get away from the house. Grandfather has just shown Lauren his print of *Blue Ridge Cowboy.* If Gran should suspect he has that movie, much less that he's shown it to Lauren, she'll really be upset." Justyn took the seat opposite me. I suspected that he was the one who was upset.

As we chugged out of the little cove and reached the body of the lake, I tried to give myself up to savoring the beauty of this place. I mustn't allow these crosscurrents in the Brandt family to upset me. I had a lot to think about before my dinner with Roger Brandt. More than anything, I wanted to see Gordon and tell him all that had happened and find out what he thought about these developments. But that must wait until morning. For now, I looked down the lake to where distant high peaks stood in hazy blue contrast against the sky. Bright sunlight gave the lake a golden cast. All around, thick tree growth tapered down the banks to the water's edge, reflecting its deep green shade. At no point was the lake very wide, conforming as it did to the shape of the original valley that had been filled in. This made it possible to grasp a clear, lovely vista almost all at once. A luring lake indeed.

Along the route, I could look into little inlets where boats were moored and where houses showed through the trees. The houses sat at the water's edge and also high on the steep hills beyond.

When we were out of sight of the Brandt place, Natalie turned off the motor and we drifted on calm water.

Justyn was ready to explode. "Why did Dad show you that movie, Mrs. Castle? Nobody ever mentions Victoria Frazer around him—so *why?*"

I tried to answer quietly. "Your mother wants me to continue Jim's work that was left unfinished, so I felt I needed to know more about the Victoria Frazer side of the story. I mentioned to your father that I wished I could see the picture and he offered to show it to me. That's all."

Justyn looked more shocked than seemed justified. "Why is everyone so put out about this?" I asked. "It all happened so long ago—what can it matter now, except as an interesting story?"

Justyn and Natalie exchanged a look I couldn't read. He made an effort to control his temper and speak more quietly.

"I never approved of Jim's project in the first place, Mrs. Castle. It's pointless for you to try to pick up his work."

I rather agreed, but I wouldn't tell him that. "Your mother seems to think this is something that should be done."

"She's off on one of her enthusiastic notions," Natalie told her father. "She even took Lauren to see Betsy Harlan this morning. A prejudiced viewpoint if ever there was one. I wondered if Gran might want to stir things up."

"I'd better talk to her," Justyn said. "Not that she's likely to listen. Mrs. Castle, you can't possibly know all the ramifications involved, but, believe me, it's better to let this alone."

"Ty Frazer thinks my husband was murdered. Perhaps that brings everything into the present?" I suggested.

For a moment, Justyn looked disconcerted. "Ty's a crazy old coot, unbalanced and dangerous to himself and others. He should have been committed long ago. Both my parents put on a good show most of the time, but they're more fragile than you might think. I want to see them left alone."

"Even if they don't *want* to be left alone?" I said. "Your father invited me to dinner at the Esmeralda Inn tonight and I've accepted."

He looked so worried that I felt a little sorry for him. "I don't think you should be concerned about this. I'll probably go back to California soon and nothing will come of this documentary. I never did think I was the right person to carry this on."

"And Jim's death?" Natalie asked softly.

Justyn threw her a guarded look but said nothing.

"Unless I get some sort of lead besides Ty Frazer's suspicions, I don't see what I can do about that," I continued. Neither of us dared mention Jim's unsettling letter. Gordon had cautioned us not to let anyone else know about its contents.

"What happened when you visited Betsey?" Justyn asked.

He still seemed too intense, but I gave him part of the story. "She seems devoted to the memory of Victoria Frazer. She showed me a dress Victoria had worn in the film with your father. When I watched the movie just now, it was strange to see her wearing that very dress and the turban Betsey probably made for her. How sad that clothes outlast the people who wear them."

"What did you think of the movie?" Natalie asked.

A larger boat than ours went past and wide ripples spread, rocking us gently.

"I was more interested in the actors than the story," I said, and then ventured further, watching these two—father and daughter. "It seemed to me that Roger Brandt and Victoria Frazer were very much in love in those scenes they played together. They seemed too absorbed in each other to be acting."

Justyn snorted rudely, but before he could say anything, his daughter answered me.

"That was a passing thing. It happens sometimes when actors are thrown together, playing love scenes day after day. But when the moviemaking is over, so is the affair, *if* there really was one. I don't think my grandfather has ever truly loved anyone but his Camilla."

"And does she love him?" The question came from me unbidden, and Natalie looked away—off toward Rumbling Bald.

"What happened with Victoria must have hurt deeply," she said.

146

"Of course it did!" Justyn sounded angry again. "As it would any woman whose husband had an affair."

"I expect it upset Victoria, too," I pointed out, ignoring this last comment but noticing the embarrassment it caused Natalie. "Especially since she was carrying his child."

"What if that mysterious baby is just a part of the legend, too?" Natalie speculated aloud. "After all, who knows by this time what's fiction and what's fact—since neither my grandfather or grandmother is willing to talk."

I was proof that the baby, at least, wasn't fiction. "I've talked to Gretchen Frazer and I know about the baby. She wanted to keep it. And years later, when Victoria and Roger's child was a grown woman, she came here to see Gretchen."

Both Justyn and Natalie looked surprised, but Natalie shook her head at me. "Let it go, Lauren. Gretchen would say anything to hurt my grandfather. It's only a story to you, and dredging it up is hardly worth the hurt to those concerned. I'll take you back to the lodge now."

We were silenced by the motor, and I could sense the hostility that I seemed to have roused in both Justyn and his daughter. Yet, at the same time, I had a feeling that they were not wholly in sympathy with each other.

The little boat moved at a slow, steady pace down shining, land-enclosed waters. I could see the lodge set among tall trees high on the bank as we approached. When we turned in toward the boathouse near Gretchen's house, I saw that she was out on the dock, busy with her own pontoon boat and with Siggy, who was waiting eagerly, snout in air, to get aboard.

Gretchen was hardly pleased to see us and I was able to observe how strongly the old feud held. She completely ignored us as Natalie steered around to the opposite side of the boathouse, out of Gretchen's sight. There Justyn helped me, none too graciously, onto the narrow walk. Natalie said a hasty good-bye and they chugged away across the lake, apparently no more anxious to see Gretchen than she was to see them.

When I walked around the end of the boathouse, however, Gretchen was waiting for me. She spoke cheerfully enough, with no reference to the Brandts.

"Hello, Lauren. You're just in time to come with me, if you'd care to. I'm going to visit a patient across the lake."

My preference just then would have been to go straight to my room, but this woman was my great-aunt. She would know the details of what I'd begun to call the legend better than anyone else.

I got into the boat safely, in spite of Siggy's enthusiastic effort to assist me. Gretchen rapped him lightly on the snout and he quieted like a child whose feelings had been hurt. She heaved his hundred pounds into the boat and he settled down happily, poking his nose into the rushing air like a dog as we moved away from the dock.

These little pontoon boats with their noisy outboard motors seemed to be used by homeowners around the lake, both for fishing and as a means of getting about on the water.

We moved diagonally toward the opposite shore at the gorge end of the lake. When a long white building showed among the trees, Gretchen pointed and shouted, *"Dirty Dancing."* As we went past, I recognized the setting where part of that film had been made.

The farther shore of the lake was more sparsely settled than the side we'd left. Gretchen turned into a small inlet and headed toward a dilapidated dock that seemed about to fall into the water. When she'd cast a looped rope skillfully over a post and pulled us in, I looked up at the house above. Like the dock, it seemed ready to fall to pieces.

Siggy began to wriggle and make squealing sounds. With his short legs, he needed help again. Once he was happily ashore, grunting his pleasure, Gretchen spoke to me.

"Want to come in?"

"Does anyone live here?"

"My brother, Tyronne, is here now because he's had an accident. He got word to me—so I've come across to tend to him."

My quest to find Ty was to be solved more easily than I'd expected. I followed Gretchen onto the dock, watching as she tapped Siggy with her sturdy walking stick and he managed the rickety steps on his own.

"Your brother lives here?" I asked.

She snorted. "Tyronne doesn't tell anyone where he *lives*. This place is deserted and due to be taken down, so he takes shelter here sometimes when it's necessary to find a roof of sorts."

The front door hung open on broken hinges. Weather had done a good bit of damage inside, but the far reaches of the big room were mostly intact. It was furnished—if that was the word— with a three-legged kitchen table, a stool, and a broken-down couch with sagging springs. On one end of this couch, Ty Frazer sat, nursing his shoulder and obviously in pain. Siggy snorted with joy and rushed over to his friend.

Ty pushed him away with one foot. "Hold off, boy—this isn't the time to play."

The pig sat back on his haunches, sticking out the tip of his tongue.

"That's a smile," Gretchen explained to me as she set down the bag she'd brought and went to examine Ty's shoulder. He gave me an uneasy look that indicated no welcome and then paid attention only to his sister.

"Ouch! That hurts."

"Of course it hurts. It's lucky you could get a message to me. Hold still now—this will hurt even more."

I sat down on the stool and watched as she gave her brother's shoulder a quick wrench. Ty yelped and then put up a wondering hand.

"You did it! It's back in place."

"No big deal," Gretchen said. "I'll fix you a kudzu poultice you can renew yourself. But you can't do much for a few days— that shoulder needs time to heal."

He grinned at her, offering no argument, and she went to the back of a room where there'd once been a working kitchen.

I took the silver bracelet from my purse and spoke to Ty. "I received the package you sent by the small boy. This belonged to Victoria Frazer, didn't it? Why did you want me to have it?"

"Who else would I give it to? Jim Castle told me about you." For once, the eyes that looked out of his whiskery face met mine directly. "He told me *all* about you. We already had a secret between us, so he felt he could trust me. I don't talk to nobody about what I know. Of course the bracelet had to go to you."

Gretchen returned to her brother with the kudzu poultice. As she placed it on his shoulder, he grunted again, sounding like Siggy. "This will help, so I'll tape it in place. Hold still now."

When the poultice was arranged to her satisfaction, she turned to me and saw the bracelet in my hand. Her eyes widened and she looked completely shocked.

"Where did you get that?"

"Ty sent it to me. I understand that it belonged to Victoria."

She almost snapped at her brother. *"Why?* Why would you give it to *her?"*

Clearly, this wasn't something he wanted to discuss. "Maybe this isn't a good time to talk."

"It's as good a time as any—while I've got you under my thumb. So explain."

He shot me a look from beneath shaggy brows and scowled at his sister. "Who else should it go to? Maybe it's time you woke up. This here's Victoria's granddaughter. That's who she is—not just Jim Castle's wife."

Gretchen stared at me, and whatever she saw in my face appeared to confirm Ty's words. "I don't like being deceived," she told me, and held out her hand for the bracelet. "Give me that!"

I shook my head. "I'm sorry, but I want to keep it for now. There's someone I want to show it to."

She understood at once. *"Him?* Roger Brandt? Much good it will do you."

So I was to be accepted by Gretchen with no more pleasure than I'd been shown by Ty. Though at least he had claimed me as family.

She admonished him again about caring for his shoulder, asked whether there was anything she could bring him, and gathered up her medical equipment.

"Go on home," he said grumpily, "and take *her* with you."

Gretchen spoke over her shoulder to the pig, not looking at me. "Come along, Siggy. We're going now."

Siggy stopped rooting in a cobwebby corner and trotted after her as she went through the door.

I'd returned the bracelet to my purse, but I wanted to know a lot more about where it had come from. My questions, however, had to be postponed and I left my stool to follow Gretchen. She, however, was off and down the steps to the dock, while I was still telling Ty I hoped he'd feel better.

To my astonishment, I heard the boat start up, and when I looked out the door, it was heading for the entrance to the little cove.

"She's left me behind!" I cried. "How could she do that?"

He grunted again and put a hand to his shoulder. "I reckon you gave her a shock."

"How will I get back to the lodge?"

"Walk, I suppose. That's what I do. You know how, don't you?" His eyes noted my flimsy sandals and he shook his head in disgust. "You better get started. There's a sort of path not far from the water. The next house is only a couple of miles around this end of the lake. If they didn't leave at summer's end, they'll take you back. If nobody's there, just keep going. Walk far enough and you'll get around to the other side on your own."

I began to wonder whether I would reach the lodge in time to be ready when Roger Brandt came for me tonight, and I grew angrier with Gretchen Frazer by the moment. Nevertheless, before I left, I had to ask Ty the question to which I needed an answer.

I opened my handbag, took out the patch of luminous green "leather," and held it out to him. "Do you know what this is?"

He didn't touch it—he clearly didn't want to touch it. When he said nothing, I spoke again.

"Jim left this for me in a letter he gave to Natalie shortly before his death. Do you know where Jim got it?"

He seemed to rouse himself and his voice grew stronger. "I gave that to Jim."

"Why? What is it?"

"Never mind. Just throw it away and forget about it. Maybe if I hadn't taken him there, Jim Castle would be alive now."

"Ty, I don't know what you're talking about. Who would have wanted to hurt Jim? Everybody liked him."

"Not everybody. There was more than one person he scared. So you better go home now before somebody gets scared of *you*. There's some pretty powerful people around here—people who don't want to be interfered with."

"What about the bracelet you sent me?"

He closed his eyes. "*She* gave me that. She wanted you to have it. She knows you're here—she's watching."

"*Victoria?* A dead woman?" I said.

"You're stupid," he said. "Nobody really dies. She's still around, just the way Jim Castle is. They didn't want to stop living—neither of 'em."

"Ghosts don't hand out silver bracelets, Ty."

"You know a lot for somebody so young, don't ya?"

"What do you know about what happened to Victoria?"

"Everybody says she drowned," he muttered, turning his head to check the poultice on his shoulder.

"I don't think so. Not of her own accord. I think there's something else *you* know. Maybe something you never even told Gretchen."

He shifted his weight on the sagging couch. "Ask your grandfather if you want to know. He's the one to ask. Go away now—start walking."

I still hesitated, wishing there was some way to get him to open up to me. "You'll be all right alone?"

"I'm always alone. That's the way I like it." Then he added something he must have been turning over in his head. "Gordon said you saw Betsey today. I saw her once a few years ago. She's an old woman now."

I bristled. "As you are an old man. *I* thought she was beautiful. I expect we all carry the maps of our lives on our faces when we get older. Hers is an interesting one. Of course I can't tell anything about yours because you've buried it in whiskers."

I slung my bag over my shoulders and went through the door.

"Don't step on a copperhead!" he called after me. Hardly reassured, I went down toward the water to look for the "sort of path" that I must follow in my flimsy shoes. I could only pray there'd be someone home at the next house.

N ⋆ I ⋆ N ⋆ E

SOMEHOW I got through that long, stumbling walk, hating Gretchen every inch of the way. A blister started on my heel, but at least no snakes appeared. Most of the time, I felt buried in thick woods. Only glimpses of the lake appeared now and then, and treetops hid the mountains. The path was totally overgrown in places, but I managed at last to reach the house Ty had mentioned.

Fortunately, I was in time. The retired couple who summered there weren't leaving until the next week. They offered sympathy for my predicament and the man drove me back to the lodge in his station wagon. By the time I reached the lobby, there was just time to go up to my room to shower and change my clothes before Roger came for me.

As I reached the stairs, Gretchen came from behind the desk to hurry after me. She was the last person I wanted to see. I started up, turning my back on her.

"I need to talk to you," she told me.

"I don't think we have anything to say," I said curtly.

"Wait, Lauren." We'd reached the upper corridor and I didn't wait. She hurried on. "That was no way for me to act, going off and leaving you like that. I thought about driving back for you, but a car can't get through to where Ty's holed up, and I didn't think you'd stay put."

"I'm in a hurry now," I told her. "I don't understand why you left me, but I haven't time to talk about it. There's no point. I need to shower and dress before dinner, and there's a blister on my heel I need to fix."

"Please." She sounded surprisingly meek. "It's about Victoria that we need to talk."

This hooked me. If she wanted to talk about her sister, Roger would have to wait.

"All right," I said. "Just for a moment."

I opened the door of my room and she followed me in, taking over in her own way. "Let me see your foot, Lauren."

I didn't want her ministrations. "I'll do fine with a Band-Aid."

She motioned me toward the bed. "Take off your shoes and lie down."

When she spoke in that tone, one obeyed. Unwillingly, I slipped out of my sandals and lay down. She sat at the foot of the bed, where she could reach my foot.

"Just relax. Let everything go."

That wasn't easy, but I closed my eyes. Her hands were gentle as she touched me. I turned on my side so she could reach my heel and I showed her the place. When her hands hovered above my foot, I could feel a subtle current of warmth play over my leg. Tension fell away and I relaxed, though I opened my eyes so I could watch her.

She was quiet now, with her eyes closed—as though she'd gone away to some inner space. Her face seemed to glow with a light that came from within. I lay very still, and after a few moments she sat back and smiled at me—a smile that reminded me of one I'd seen only that morning—on Victoria Frazer's young face. Gretchen spoke to me in what was now a restrained manner, and I was compelled to listen.

"What Tyronne said was a shock to me, Lauren. I rejected it at first and only wanted to get away from you because I was terribly angry that the two of you would play such a mean trick on me. But when I had time to think, I realized that it must be true. I don't understand why I didn't sense who you were from the first. Your eyes are like Victoria's, but I refused to make the connection. *Now* I can feel who you are with my entire being. You *are* the child of my dear sister's baby. Oh, how I wanted to raise her. If Margaret had stayed with me, I would have fought the Brandts, if necessary, just to keep her."

She closed her eyes, lost in another time, and I wondered about her words. I couldn't imagine that the Brandts would have wanted the child. Certainly not Camilla, and probably not Roger.

When Gretchen opened her eyes and spoke to me, her words were startling. "Now *you* have come in her stead. Victoria's granddaughter—my own blood kin!"

Old emotion was welling up out of long suppression and I wasn't ready for the change. But before I could say anything, she continued.

"I want to warn you about your grandmother, Lauren. Don't open any doors that will let her in. She used to hurt people—she was very unkind to Tyronne."

"What do you mean, *warn* me? What doors could I open?"

"Just don't get caught up in what must seem like a romantic

157

story. It wasn't that. It was sordid and ugly—especially for Roger Brandt. So be careful about stirring up sleeping passions."

I wasn't sure what to make of any of this, and I spoke abruptly. "This afternoon, Roger Brandt showed me his copy of the movie he made with Victoria Frazer. There was a scene in it when he gave her that very bracelet Ty sent me."

Gretchen shivered. "You're already going too far. I remember that picture very well. It was released before she died—even before the baby was born. They made movies quickly in those days. I saw it in Asheville. A foolish picture—not worthy of the actress she had become. I never wanted her to make it. But she was attracted by Roger's fame. They had met at a party in Hollywood six months before they came to Lake Lure to make *Blue Ridge Cowboy.* They were almost inseparable from the first. She didn't know it when shooting began, but she was already three months pregnant with his child."

I could begin to understand the past a little better and it saddened me.

I told her that Camilla Brandt had taken me to see Betsey Harlan and that Betsey had shown me the white dress Victoria had worn in the picture.

Gretchen's mood changed at once. She didn't want to hear any of this. "Stand up," she ordered, "and tell me how your foot feels." Obviously, I was not to learn whatever she thought of my visit to Betsey. Were her memories of the past too painful to be resurrected?

I sat up on the edge of the bed and when I touched my heel to the floor, I found the soreness gone. The red mark was no longer a budding blister. By this time, I could almost take such miracles for granted.

"Thank you," I said.

She turned gruff again. "Hurry now and get ready for your date."

I watched her intently as I told her who I was planning to see. "I'm to have dinner tonight with Roger Brandt."

If I'd expected anger or indignation, she showed neither, only shaking her head sadly. "I suppose this had to happen. Just watch your back when you're with Roger, Lauren."

"I know. I've seen some of his little tricks, so I won't be taken in."

"Does he know who you are?"

"No, and I don't want him to until the right moment comes. Victoria belongs to the past, and for now I want him to see me in the present."

She turned as she reached the door. "*You* are part of his past and that may be pretty upsetting to him."

"I hope it will be," I said, "if he ever finds out." Gretchen nodded and went away.

Now I hurried to get out of my stained clothes and showered quickly. I'd brought one other dress that was suitable for dinner—a rosy mauve silk in a chemise style. Its high, round neck was right for my gold chain with a Japanese dragon pendant. The chain was a gift from Gordon in those San Francisco days I didn't want to think about, but it tied me to the present. I combed my hair carefully, twisting it into a chignon at the back, and slipped a tortoiseshell comb into the knot. Gold earrings were the last touch, and I was ready.

I stood before a long mirror and smiled at myself ruefully. I had dressed as carefully as if I was going to meet a lover—not an elderly grandfather—but this meeting might involve far more than

I could anticipate. Certainly more than Roger Brandt expected.

I assured myself that I didn't look in the least like Victoria. For tonight, I wanted to be only Lauren Castle. Tucked safely in my purse was the tissue-wrapped silver bracelet, though I had no idea when or if I might take it out.

The desk rang to tell me that Mr. Brandt had arrived. I heard the excitement in Mrs. Adrian's voice and I told her calmly that I'd be right down. Then I braced myself and went to meet my grandfather.

He watched as I came down the stairs, a look of approval in his eyes. When he came to meet me, his shoulders were straight under a dark blue jacket that was out of style, though it must have been expensive in its day. His gray flannel trousers were well creased, and again he wore his signature scarf twisted about his throat—blue and white in a geometric pattern. Tonight he was no cowboy, but a man well seasoned by the years, slightly heavier than he'd been when young, but still a man very sure of himself and his charm.

He'd brought the beautiful old Mercedes in which Natalie had driven me—a car that was probably valuable—but not as ostentatious as expensive California cars could be. He opened the door for me, seated me, and went around to the driver's side. One would never have guessed his age by his easy movements. Both he and Camilla clearly kept themselves in top shape.

"The Esmeralda is on the other side of Chimney Rock," he told me as we reached the highway beside Lake Lure. "It's only a few minutes' drive." He glanced at me and then back through the windshield. "You said earlier that you visited Betsey Harlan this morning. I haven't seen her in years—not since she was a pretty young woman who worked as a dresser for Victoria Frazer. She's only a little older than my wife."

"Really? She looks a great deal older. It was your wife who took me to visit her, as I think I mentioned."

"How did that happen?"

"Your wife seems anxious for me to continue my husband's work on the documentary he was doing about you."

He didn't seem surprised, so perhaps someone had told him.

I continued. "I told her that there's another side of the story that interests me, if I'm to continue Jim's work. Victoria Frazer's side."

He spoke calmly. "How did my wife react to that suggestion?"

"She seemed to think it reasonable, though that surprised me, considering all that happened."

Again he spoke casually and with a seeming openness, as though the subject mattered very little. "Camilla's father was a studio executive, so she understood what could happen in the making of a picture. Of course, love scenes are stronger if the actors like each other."

His manner irritated me. *Like* seemed a pretty weak word, if one remembered what had happened. "Perhaps with Victoria it was a little different."

He ignored that, slowing the car to the pace of traffic through Hickory Nut's steep-sided gorge. In a short distance, he turned the car up a driveway that climbed the hillside on our right. The Esmeralda was set well above the highway and screened by a line of tall pine trees. Roger parked the car and we climbed side steps to a veranda that opened into the lobby of the inn.

We entered a square, open space, rustic in character, contrasting with the Lake Lure Inn's more formal style. This space was rimmed by two floors of galleries, off which guest rooms opened at intervals. At the far end of the lobby, a wide fireplace had been set into the rough fieldstones of a chimney, with a set of handsome antlers placed above the mantelpiece. Wherever possible, whole logs, stripped of their bark, had been used.

Roger Brandt stood looking around, as though lost in his own memories. "The inn opened in 1892," he told me. "But there was a fire that destroyed the original building. It was rebuilt in 1917. It has stood here ever since. Our film company had rooms on the top level, so we had a good view of the gorge and Chimney Rock. I haven't been here in years. After all that happened, my memories of this place aren't very happy, though at the time we couldn't have been more light hearted." He stopped abruptly. "Let's find our table. I asked for one on the veranda."

We were led through an attractive inner dining room and out to where long picture windows formed the front of the inn. A line of tables dressed in turquoise and white invited us, and ceiling fans kept the area comfortable. The wall of pines I'd noticed as we approached the inn protected diners from the intrusion of traffic sounds below. When I was seated, I found I could look out toward the natural phenomenon of Chimney Rock—that granite tower that had separated from the mountain behind to jut out in its own high column.

Menus were presented and I asked Roger to order for us both. At the moment, I had very little interest in food. I wanted to get past his easy self-assurance and stir up whatever he kept hidden underneath.

"Why did you invite me to dinner?" I asked when the waitress had gone.

The shrug of his shoulders beneath his impeccable jacket was still casual. "I liked and admired your husband. And of course I'm still curious about what you thought of the film."

"Tell me about Victoria," I countered. "She seemed so beautiful, so talented—but what was she like as a woman?"

"It's a shame to spoil the illusion, but she could be vindictive—even dangerous."

This startled me. "Betsey Harlan said she was gentle and kind. It's hard to believe—"

He broke in on my words. "You've probably noticed the scar on my wife's cheek? Victoria did that. I really don't care to talk about her, if you don't mind. Let me tell you about the Esmeralda."

He had shocked me into silence, and I tried to listen.

"The road down there used to be the old pony express and stagecoach road—the one route through the gorge. There are all sorts of legends about the gorge—tales of little people, of visions and magic. I've always relished those stories. Earlier film companies than ours came here. Mary Pickford, Gloria Swanson, and Douglas Fairbanks all stayed here. Lew Wallace wrote the novel *Ben-Hur* in a room upstairs."

His voice still held a hint of its youthful timbre as he warmed to his subject, and I was caught in spite of myself. Victoria could wait a little while—I would get back to her.

"Where did the name Esmeralda come from?" I asked.

"Frances Hodgson Burnett wrote a play called *Esmeralda* when she stayed in this area. It's long forgotten now, but Colonel Turner, who built the inn, named it after it. Of course the area appealed to moviemakers because of its marvelous scenery. And now Hollywood is discovering it all over again. You know about *Dirty Dancing* and *The Last of the Mohicans*?"

"I saw where some of *Dirty Dancing* was filmed today, and of course I've visited the Indian village. Gordon Heath told me that's where Jim died."

He spoke gently, with a sympathy I hadn't sensed in him before. "Your husband became my friend. I could trust him. He was a good man."

"Thank you," I said softly. Our wine arrived and when the waitress had gone, I went on. *Tell me about Victoria. I really want to know.*

He sighed as though this was a question he had tired of over the years. "What do you want to know about her?"

"Anything you can tell me. You were in love with her. That much came through on the screen."

"She wasn't always lovable, as I believe I've made clear."

I ventured into more risky territory. "She bore you a baby. That's an accepted fact. So are you telling me you didn't love her?"

For a moment, I had shocked him by speaking so directly. I suspected that people had been pussyfooting around this subject for years. He recovered quickly, however.

"Are you going to make me sorry that I've asked you to dinner, young woman?"

I wasn't going to be put off by this comment and I gave him a look that must have lacked the admiration he expected. I could almost hear the tinkle of silver bells in my purse, as though some misty hand had reached in to touch the bracelet. Soon now—soon.

The waitress brought our soup. I tried to relax and pay attention to food that hardly appealed to me at the moment.

"If you're so interested in Victoria," he said, "there's an old book you might like to read—if you can find a copy. It was published after Victoria's suicide, and it's been long out of print. It was widely read when it first came out. The title was *The Firefly*. That was also the title of Victoria Frazer's last picture before the one she made with me—probably her most famous picture, although sadly it's been uncirculated for decades, like her other films. The author of the book knew her when she stayed here at the Esmeralda. He followed her around, studying her—not always sympathetically."

"Was the book he wrote accurate?" I asked, dipping my spoon into the soup. "How did you come off in it?"

Irritation with me returned. "I warned Victoria against being open with the fellow. I didn't like him. But she was always an off-and-on creature—like a firefly. You could never be sure what she might do next. In a way, I suppose, that was part of her fascination."

"I'd like to find a copy of the book."

Suddenly, he looked doubtful, as though he had just recalled something. "Perhaps it's not a good idea to follow this up, Lauren. All these happenings were over so long ago, and it can only roil calm waters to stir them up again. I don't think your husband meant to do that."

"It's not so long ago, if Jim's death was somehow tied to Victoria's."

Again he looked shocked, but the waitress came with our entrées. When she'd gone, he didn't pick up on my remark about Jim.

Darkness had fallen outside and between the pines I could glimpse the lights of cars following the old road that was now a highway. As the evening wore on, I felt no closer to carrying out my main purpose. I didn't know how to jump into this and perhaps I was hesitant, because I had no idea how he might react to what I had intended to tell him.

Our fresh trout, broiled in country butter, was as delicious as Roger had promised, even though he regaled me with amusing stories of his filmmaking days, part of me still listened to the whisper of tiny bells. I wanted the reality of those bells to be heard. I wanted to see his painful reaction—yet I waited. Not until the waitress took our dessert orders did I force myself to act. My hand shook as I dropped the bracelet abruptly on the table between us.

His look was more than one of pain and shock. "Where did you get that?" he demanded, all the color draining from his face.

"What does it matter? It's the same bracelet that you gave Victoria in the scene in the film, isn't it? She showed her delight and her love for you when you clasped it on her wrist. I don't think either of you was acting."

"She was wearing that bracelet when she died," he said. "I must know how it came into your hands."

"How do you know that? If her body was never found, how can you know that?"

"She always wore it. She told me she would never take it off."

Now I recognized the emotion that shook him—it was fear. Roger Brandt was a frightened man. I wasn't going to give away Ty, but I had more startling news for Roger.

"What matters," I said quietly, "isn't really the bracelet. It's that I am Victoria Frazer's granddaughter. I am your granddaughter."

He recovered himself and smiled at me almost tenderly. "I know. I began to suspect from the first moment I saw you. Why do you think I showed you the film? Why would I have invited you to dinner? It's not so much a matter of features—though your eyes are like hers. There's an overall impression that comes through. Her look is there in your face."

I felt thoroughly disconcerted and perhaps a little frightened because of the door that had opened so suddenly, leaving me with a role I didn't know how to play.

I put a hand out in pleading across the table, feeling guilt along with everything else. "I'm sorry. I've been playing games. I wanted to jar you. You seemed so complacent, so sure of yourself. It never occurred to me that I resemble her so much that you would guess."

His eyes must once have been a bright and penetrating blue. Now their color was pale, faded, and they were haunted by some dread that had taken a toll on him.

He didn't touch my extended hand. "Am I the only one who knows who you are?"

"No. Gordon Heath and I met many years ago. I told him then because he came from this area. But I asked him not to tell anyone, and he hasn't. Now his mother knows, and so do Gretchen and Ty. Though Betsey Harlan is the only one who sensed immediately who I was."

"Ah yes—Betsey. She always had a sixth sense." He was silent for a moment, as though trying to collect himself. My identity hadn't shocked him, but my possession of the bracelet had. "Does Natalie know?" he asked.

"My newly found cousin? I don't think so. And of course your wife doesn't know."

He seemed relieved at that. "Why did you come here after all this time?"

"Natalie summoned me. She believes that Jim was murdered, though she only decided this recently. There's no real proof, but she thought I should come."

Again there was a long silence. His face had changed. It was as if he had gone into some inner space where I could not follow.

The waitress had taken our dinner plates moments before and now she returned with two slices of carrot cake. I waited until she had gone before I continued.

"I came because I wanted to know more about Jim's death. But I also want to know much more about Victoria. My mother never believed that her death was a suicide. She told me that once."

As Roger reached absently for a dessert fork, a woman stopped beside our table. I looked up, startled, to see Natalie Brandt.

She spoke hurriedly to her grandfather. "Gordon said I might find you here. Camilla needs you. She knows who Lauren is, and so do I. Betsey Harlan phoned her—for spite, I think. She wanted to hurt her and she did. You know Gran's heart isn't strong. You'd better go to her right away, Grandfather. I'll take Lauren back to the lodge."

He pushed his chair out and stood up. For an instant, his look turned—not to me but to the silver bracelet that lay in a puddle of light on the turquoise cloth. Then he was gone.

Natalie sat down at his place. "No use wasting good food," she said, picking up a fork. As she ate his untouched portion of cake, she watched me, bright-eyed, with a malice I'd not seen in her before.

"I must say you're rather a nasty surprise, Lauren! *If* you really are Victoria's granddaughter. What does that make *us*, exactly?"

I had nothing to say to that.

I really didn't care to discuss any of this with Natalie right now. "What happened—I mean when Betsey phoned?"

"Grandmother, who is a very strong lady, simply fell apart. It was a good thing my dad was home. He's closer to her than anyone else. She forgives him a lot."

"What is there to forgive?"

"The crime of being dull and unimaginative in *this* family. But it's what Gran said that upset me. She was crying—actually crying!—and she said, 'It's happening all over again, and I can't bear it!' "

"*What* is happening all over again? Even if I am Victoria and Roger's granddaughter, why should she be expecting something bad out of this?"

Natalie's fork pursued a crumb of carrot cake around her plate. "Who knows? I love my grandparents, but I can't deny their eccentricities. So now *you* are part of the legend, Lauren," she added. "How does that feel?"

I hated her cynical tone. "Don't you care about what's happening?"

She regarded me coolly, with no more liking for me than I had for her at that moment. "Perhaps a second spaceship has just crashed and there's nothing I can do except try to save my own sanity."

I said nothing to that. In a way, I had more sympathy and admiration for Camilla Brandt than for anyone else who carried the Brandt name. The more I saw of the Brandts individually, the less I liked any of them. Where was Victoria in all this?

"You're really stirring things up, aren't you, Lauren? Better watch your step."

She sounded more entertained than alarmed, as though she was a spectator observing from a distance.

"Don't you care?" I asked her again. "Don't you care about your grandfather and your grandmother?"

"Of course I do. I love them both, and I'm proud of them. I'm sorry that my grandfather had to suffer the loss of his career because of *your* grandmother."

"So now *we* are supposed to feud? Is that it?"

She laughed, as though my words entertained her further. "Don't be foolish. I like you, Lauren. But that doesn't keep me from feeling that when the curtain comes down on this play, the ending won't matter to me. I'm not really involved, except at second hand."

I wished only that I was not involved. I wasn't able to reject the sense that I was in the middle of some terrible turmoil, whether I wanted to be or not. The knowledge that the scar on Camilla's cheek had been caused by Victoria still shocked and disturbed me.

"I'd like to go back to the lodge, if you'll take me," I said. "And I'm sure you'd like to get back to your grandparents."

"Of course, Lauren," she said, but then wandered off down what seemed to be a side road. "I do hope all that's happened won't interfere with the big party Camilla has been planning."

"Party?" I'd heard something mentioned, but it hadn't really registered. This seemed frivolous to me now.

"She's been working on this for months. It's to be a big fund-raiser for the Lake Lure area. Lake Lure Inn is going to provide the place, since they have a big barn out back that can be used. It's overgrown with kudzu, but Camilla has persuaded the management to clean it up inside and do some renovations. Nobody refuses her when she goes after something. There's already a good dance floor."

I still felt lost, since partying hardly seemed important in the face of her grandmother's collapse. "Is this to be a square dance?"

Natalie smiled. "Can you see Camilla Brandt doing a do-si-do? It will be a ball—a costume ball. Very posh and socially important. The money raised will go to the fire department, the emergency ambulance service, and all the other things that Lake

Lure needs to take care of. Gran has been giving herself to this for months, and it's no little thing if she's suddenly not up to it. The Asheville elite will come, all dressed in expensive costumes. Camilla is paying to bring in a band that will play old dance tunes. This won't be popular with the young crowd, but that's not where the money is. Of course Grandfather will do whatever Gran wants, as usual. If she's up to this now."

"Why does he give in to her? I should think he'd hate being in the center of things in this way."

"Because he loves her," Natalie said simply. "Nothing's ever changed that, and she knows it. Even if her Spanish blood does get riled up over Victoria and the past."

"I wonder where that leaves *my* grandmother?" I said.

She regarded me speculatively. "A suicide, of course. Because she couldn't live without Roger."

I didn't believe that, and I didn't think Natalie did, either.

"When is this affair to be held?" I asked.

"On Saturday night. Camilla has a gorgeous Spanish dress that she used to wear in California—mantilla, comb and all. It belonged to her mother, through whom she gets her Spanish blood. She still has the figure for it, but I haven't convinced her to put a rose in her teeth. And guess who Roger will be?"

I didn't need to guess. Who else would he be but the cowboy actor Roger Brandt? Though I hoped without his horse this time.

"Even if he loves her," she chattered on, "I wonder sometimes why he is still so anxious to please her." Natalie seemed honestly puzzled.

"His infidelity with Victoria, perhaps?"

"It's hard to believe that could still matter after all these years. Though of course because Victoria's body was never found,

171

questions surrounding her death were never really answered."

Natalie spoke lightly, but I shivered, and she gave me a quick look.

"You'll come, won't you, Lauren? Gordon can bring you."

I had no interest in partying and I shook my head, surprised that she was so intent on having me come. "I don't think so. Let's get out of here, Natalie."

But something had caught her eye. She reached to the center of the table and picked up the silver bracelet. "What is this?"

I gave her a bare account. "In the film your grandfather made with Victoria Frazer, there's a scene where he gives her that bracelet. While we were watching the movie, he whispered that he'd actually given it to her then."

"I remember the scene," Natalie said. "It was all very sentimental and pretty."

"You've seen the movie?"

"Oh, yes, but he doesn't know that. *Blue Ridge Cowboy* has always been forbidden territory. Gran doesn't even know that he has a print. Which is funny, because there isn't much she doesn't know. But since it was off-limits, of course I had to see it. When I was about fourteen, I got hold of the right key and ran it when they were away."

I took the bracelet from her and returned it to my purse. It belonged to me now—no matter what reverberations these little bells were ringing down the years.

"Where did you get it?" Natalie asked.

"From Gretchen's brother, Ty. He sent it to me by a small boy who turned up on the balcony outside my room at the lodge. Though I still don't know why."

"That's interesting. Of course the real question is where *he* got it."

"I asked him this afternoon, but he wouldn't tell me."

"If anybody can keep his mouth shut, it's Ty. It's funny to think that he and my grandfather used to be good friends when Roger first came here—before everything went wrong. Ty never forgave Grandfather for what happened to Victoria. But enough of all that."

She signaled the waitress and asked for the check, but we were told Mr. Brandt had signed for it. As we left the Esmeralda, I experienced a strange sense of nostalgia for a time I'd never known. Of course, Victoria Frazer had stayed here, and it was as though she descended the steps with me, still happy, still innocent of what lay in the future. A pretty picture, if it hadn't all ended so tragically.

We walked out to Natalie's station wagon and I got in beside her. As we drove away, I looked back at the Esmeralda set high among the pines.

But no nostalgia filled Natalie. "I have a wonderful idea," she told me as we went down into light evening traffic. "You can come to Camilla's ball dressed as Victoria Frazer! Think what a stir that would cause. Betsey Harlan can probably help. Of course, Victoria was a famous blonde, so you'd have to wear a wig. I'm sure we can get one in Asheville."

She was warming to her foolish idea, and I put a stop to it.

"Of course I won't do any such thing. I wonder if all the Brandts are crazy?"

Her laughter carried an exultant ring. "Of course we are! Just as the Frazers are, Lauren. Only my father is sane, so he's the dull one nobody ever worries about."

As we drove past the lake, the water was only dark glass, with a few ripples of light cast from some boathouse or dwelling.

When Natalie dropped me off and I stopped at the desk for

my key, a note waited for me. Gordon's handwriting was as strong as I remembered. I carried it up to my room to read.

There were only a few words:

> Remember, Lauren. I'll come for you before sunrise. Wear jeans and a warm jacket. Good shoes too for climbing. I promise an interesting experience.
> Sleep well,
> Gordon

This sounded more like the man I remembered, and I couldn't help the sense of anticipation that rose in me. But I must count on nothing, expect nothing. There'd been only that brief time when Gordon and I had existed for each other. I was the one who had gambled away our happiness by betting on Jim. I'd thought that *he* could make me feel "safe"—as my mother's fears and attitude toward life never had. In his way, Jim had been good to me and I had let him down, as well. So I still carried a burden of guilt that I resented and didn't know how to be rid of. Gordon had never forgiven me for that choice, and I couldn't blame him.

Now his note sounded a little softer than his manner had been, and I fell asleep climbing the hills of San Francisco. We'd gone at dawn that time, too, and we'd watched as first daylight touched the ruler-straight line of Market Street far below.

Somehow I must learn how to forgive myself.

T ⋆ E ⋆ N

THE NEXT morning when I went out the door of the lodge, Gordon's car was already parked across the drive. When I saw him, I again felt an emotional jolt, an almost uncontrollable desire to run to him. But I was no longer a young woman of nineteen, even though my heart played tricks at the sight of this particular man and left me in a state of self-conscious confusion.

He got out to open the door for me. I pulled up the hood of my jacket against the cool early-morning air and as an excuse to hide anything he might see in my face.

"The hood's a good idea," he said, his manner friendly but impersonal. "It will be windy and cold where we're going."

"Where are we going?" I asked as we drove along the main road beside the lake.

"Let's just say the top of the world."

By now I knew the road we followed and I guessed where

we were heading. "Chimney Rock? Will it be open this early?"

"That's why I picked this time—no visitors. We'll have the sunrise to ourselves. I have keys since I work for the park."

As I listened, I tried to gauge his mood. Did he remember San Francisco and another sunrise? I wondered.

The little shops and restaurants along the road through the gorge were dark at this hour and there were few cars. The Rocky Broad tumbled over great black rocks below the highway, rushing toward the lake, white foam catching our lights as we went past.

The entrance to the park consisted of two great wings built of fieldstone, with gates in the center. Gordon got out, opened the gates, drove through, and closed them again. Ahead lay a bridge over the river; we crossed to drive up a well-engineered road that wound toward the base of Chimney Rock.

"There are several hiking trails for those who want to make the climb on foot," he told me. "But we'll take the easier way."

The light was still gray when we passed a small visitors' building and continued in hairpin turns until our headlights picked out a wide, cleared area for parking, rimmed around the edge by a low stone wall. Here, in the protection of the cliff above, we were sheltered from the wind. I knew that a tremendous view must lie out there, but in this predawn hour I could see only scattered lights.

We left the car near the wall and Gordon took my arm, guiding me through darkness.

"Chimney Rock goes straight up from here," he told me. "When it's light, you can look up and see the whole column standing above us."

A door had been cut into the base of the cliff and Gordon unlocked it. Dead, cold air from inside the mountain rushed out to us, and I could see nothing but blackness until Gordon reached for switches and turned on lights and the ventilating system.

Dynamite had blasted out this nearly two-hundred-foot tunnel into the mountain. It stretched straight ahead through granite, a low ceiling arching in rough stone overhead. On my right, rock had been cut away to form a low ledge, a foot or two high, into which lights had been set at intervals all down the tunnel. Each sunken lamp threw its reflection upward on the irregular wall, forming an eerie pattern of light and shadow that was rather spooky.

We walked between solid granite walls—the entire creation a remarkable engineering job.

"There's an elevator at the end," Gordon said, his voice rousing echoes down the empty passageway.

When we reached the far door and stepped into the waiting car, he activated the machinery and we moved slowly upward. For a few moments, I had a feeling of the mountain closing around me.

"How high is the shaft?" I asked.

"It's twenty-four floors up. We're still inside the mountain, of course, not in Chimney Rock itself."

When the door opened at the top, Gordon turned on more lights and we stepped into a gift-shop area, bright with counter displays, racks of clothes, and souvenirs.

"Come along," Gordon said, as though I might dawdle. "There's still a climb to the top of the chimney, and we don't want to miss the rising curtain."

We went through doors to an open terrace where a few tables had been placed—for those who might bring lunches or purchase food at the shop's lunch counter. The air felt wonderful after being shut in by all that granite. The sky was just beginning to brighten, so it looked as though we would make it in time.

The steps to the top were wide, with sturdy railings, so I had no sense of vertigo, though they spanned a chasm below. Halfway up, a landing offered a breather, and then we climbed the last flight to the top. Some forty-seven steps. I counted them.

The top of the chimney was formed by a level cap of granite that overhung the column below and was spotted with low outcroppings of rock. Cement paths offered smooth footing among the protrusions. Ahead, at the highest point, stood a flagpole, and I watched as Gordon went over to raise the flag. In this high, windy space, its folds flew out, cracking and whipping in the wind, the colors challenging the slowly spreading dawn.

The outer rim of this wide space was well protected by a decorative iron fence. Inside, two small pine trees seemed to grow out of solid rock—rather scraggly trees that had withstood the storms that would savage this high, exposed place.

Slowly, the sky brightened in the east as a pink blush turned into widespread golden flames that burnished the world. We watched together and I found myself even more aware of the man beside me than I'd been in those long-ago days in San Francisco.

"Thank you for bringing me here," I said softly, savoring the ever-changing colors and the sweet, cool air.

Gordon seemed to have lost the hostility I'd felt in him since our meeting in the Indian village. "Look out there, Lauren." He pointed toward the long, narrow stretch of Lake Lure, where it opened from the gorge. Now I could see the arms of the cross formed by two coves. Rumbling Bald was clearly visible, reflected in water that shimmered with pink and gold, the colors fading as the sun rose. Overhead, the sky changed even as I watched, turning into a shining blue.

Something made me speak as I'd not have dared to under other circumstances. "Do you remember the sunrise we watched together in San Francisco, Gordon? Up near Tamalpais?"

"Why else would I want to show you another sunrise?"

Tears burned behind my eyes, but before I could say anything more, he stood up. "Come over to the other side, Lauren. I want you to see something."

The mountain across from us rose higher than our column of rock, dwarfing it. Its granite face made a sheer cliff, against which I caught fluttering movement. Scores of butterflies fluttered against the rock, and I stared in wonder.

"They migrate at this time of year," Gordon said, watching me.

They looked almost like tiny birds hovering against the cliff. "What a beautiful sight!"

"Let's go down and find a place to have breakfast and warm up," Gordon suggested, breaking the spell.

He had changed the subject quickly from the personal, but I didn't want to leave yet.

"Could we sit down for a few moments? I'd like to tell you what happened after I saw you yesterday."

"Natalie phoned me last night. She seemed upset about your dinner with Roger Brandt."

I told Gordon about it—from watching *Blue Ridge Cowboy* in Roger's company and seeing Victoria on-screen for the first time to the dinner at the Esmeralda, where I'd dropped the silver bracelet on the table between us and Roger had told me he knew I was his granddaughter. I mentioned the book that had been written about Victoria Frazer—*The Firefly*—and said I wished I might find a copy to read.

"I'm sorry Natalie arrived when she did," I finished. "He and I were on the brink of a really important conversation. But after she came with her news, he could think only of Camilla. He left quickly, and then Natalie drove me back to the lodge."

I must have shivered, and Gordon noticed. "Let's go down, Lauren. Hot coffee will help."

How could I ever forgive the young girl I used to be for not being wiser? I stayed where I was, looking up into Gordon's eyes, letting him see what was in my own.

He shook his head at me sadly, but when he spoke, his words were kind, though he made it clear that long ago was long ago.

"You were only nineteen. You were so young. Even though we were almost the same age, I was older and ready for what I wanted. But I wasn't all that smart, either. I wanted you to fall in love with me as I had with you."

"Do you think I hadn't?"

"I don't think either of us knew much about love at that point in our lives. First love doesn't always survive the clear light of logic. I shouldn't have blamed you for being so unsure. You chose what you thought was right for you. Coming with me might have spelled disaster. I expect it's just as well that you chose a sensible course, even though I was angry with you at the time."

I answered him, reckless now, wanting only to speak the truth and make him understand—if ever I could understand myself.

"What I did was cowardly. I married Jim—which I should never have done. But by the time I came to my senses, you were gone and I knew that what we had shared was over. So I tried to make the best of things. That was all I could do, but I never got over you and I never forgave myself."

I couldn't look at him now. I turned my head away and fought back a dreary impulse to cry.

He drew me up from the rock and touched my cheek gently with the palm of his hand so that I had to look up at him. "Let it go, Lauren—cut it all loose. That's what I've been trying to do since you came. I know now how useless anger is. We can't go back and change anything, but we can give up resentment and self-blame."

There was nothing I wanted more. With all hesitation gone, I put my arms around his neck and kissed the deep crease near his mouth that I knew so well. When he held me tightly, it was as though I'd come home to where I'd always wanted to be.

In that intense moment, I was acutely aware of everything around me: the butterflies, a soaring cloud in the sky, the high rock that put us at the top of the world—all these made up a moment I would never forget. When he kissed me, we were not only together, as we were meant to be, but we were a part of everything around us. Now I could respond to the fierce tenderness of his embrace, and I didn't ever want him to release me.

"We'd better go down," he said against my ear. "You're shivering and it will take time for the sun to warm us up here."

"I'm ready to go back now," I said. I would never lose him again, no matter what.

But as we moved toward the steps that led down from the chimney, he stopped me, his hand on my arm. "Listen! Someone's coming. Someone who's climbed up one of the trails on foot."

We waited as a man appeared on the steps, and I saw that it was Ty Frazer. If he had suffered a dislocated shoulder yesterday, he showed no sign of discomfort now. He wasn't even out of breath. I felt only dismay at the sight of him. Ty belonged to that whole world of problems that had brought me to Lake Lure, and I didn't want to face them now.

"Caught you!" he cried in obvious triumph. "I brought Finella some kudzu before her shop opened this morning and she said this was where you'd be. I wanted to talk to the both of you. But especially *her*." He glowered at me from under shaggy brows, and his very excitement alarmed me. He seemed a different, wilder creature than the man Gretchen and I had visited yesterday.

I made an effort to distract him from whatever he intended. "How is your shoulder, Ty? I thought your sister said you shouldn't move around until it healed."

He shrugged off my words. "Gretchen has the *gift*. She can heal better than she knows. She thinks it's kudzu and all that stuff she uses, but it's her hands that do the trick. I didn't keep that gunk on for long. Gretchen's spirit is what counts—that and what's inside my own head. Victoria told me that I must come and talk to you."

His look grew a little glassy, and I waited in alarm. Gordon's arm tightened around me.

"She came to me in a dream last night. She won't let me be. Minute I get to sleep, there she is. She won't let me alone till I do what she wants. She wants you, Lauren."

I kept my voice low. "What do you mean, she wants me?"

"You're her granddaughter. Give her a chance and she'll get inside you. She scares me when she sneaks into my dreams. I think she wants to make me pay."

"Pay for what, Ty?"

He shook his head so vigorously that his hair and beard lifted and then settled. "I don't owe her—she owes me. For everything she did and didn't do—pretending to be a loving sister and then leaving me high and dry."

I looked at Gordon as Ty began to hop about excitedly, but he shook his head, indicating that we'd better listen. Now I knew what it was that so alarmed me about this strange man. It was fear that drove him. Just as fear had touched Roger last night. Ty was deeply afraid of something about which he didn't want us to know. Perhaps he was trying to warn me or scare me off with this wild tale about Victoria.

He stopped in front of Gordon. "None of those Brandts are good people. *She*"—he nodded toward me—"needs to watch out for them. Put her on a plane for California—get her away from here!" He stared off toward lake and sky. "You hear me, Victoria. She's going away! It ain't good for her to stay around here. Look what happened to you—and to me."

"I'm not going anywhere yet," I told him quietly. "But if you know something that will help me to find answers, then *you* can free me to go."

"Roger won't let you have any answers. He's the Keeper. But if you go away now, you can stay alive—the way Jim Castle didn't manage to do."

He was beginning to frighten me. "And Victoria? What happened to Victoria?" I asked.

Ty went off on a tangent. "You think Victoria was everything wonderful and beautiful—that she didn't deserve what happened to her. Isn't that so, Lauren? Your grandmother! My beautiful, talented, wonderful sister!"

"Isn't that the way you saw her?" I asked.

He threw up his hands. "Ask anybody who knew her back then! She was a magnet for trouble."

"Betsey Harlan is still devoted to her. That counts for something, doesn't it?"

"Never mind Betsey. Just ask Camilla Brandt. She can tell you about Victoria."

I thought of Camilla's scarred cheek. "It's possible that Roger's wife is prejudiced. I'm asking you, Ty."

He came so close to me that I could smell the earth and forest odors that were part of his very being. He belonged as much to the mountains as some small wild animal. Yet he had been the one to send me Victoria's bracelet—the bracelet that had caused Roger Brandt to go white when he saw it.

"Hear me real good," Ty said, his face almost in mine, so that I drew back. "Natalie Brandt came to Finella's shop early this morning while I was there. She told us what happened last night at the Esmeralda. You sure stuck your neck out, didn't you, Lauren? I never meant for you to show that bracelet to Roger. Victoria wanted *you* to have it."

"Where did you get it, Ty?"

He wasn't going to tell me—I could see that—and he ignored my question. "Now Camilla knows who you are!"

"Why are you so scared?" I challenged. His eyes seemed as bright as a chipmunk's as he peered at me intently. "Victoria's the one who kept Betsey from marrying me. Did me a favor, maybe. Back then she was the one who was going to pay for me to go to college. Then I could have married Betsey. Her folks wouldn't look at me the way I was—young and pretty much good for nothing. Victoria cut off the money and that finished me."

The truth about my grandmother must lie somewhere in between the stories I'd heard about her. Right now, I knew only that I had to learn more.

"Ty," I said, "last night my grandfather told me about a book that was written about Victoria Frazer—*The Firefly*. Would anyone in your family have a copy?"

"That was a book full of lies. Gretchen wouldn't have a copy in her house, and I don't have any place to keep books."

"Did you read it, Ty?"

"Books don't matter now. Victoria wants you to visit her. But you better not go—" He broke off dramatically, as though promising dire consequences.

"Tell me where to find her, Ty."

"She's in a lot of places. She can get inside people—the way she does in my dreams. She made me come here today. She wants you to help her."

Gordon had heard enough and he tried to change the subject. "Natalie called me last night, Ty. She told me that Camilla was sick. Have you heard if she's better?"

Ty answered shortly. "I wouldn't be hearing stuff about the Brandts."

"If you know what happened to Victoria, Ty, please tell me," I urged.

His eyes took on an angry gleam. "Why don't you ask your grandpappy? He knows better than anyone else." He broke off and ran toward the steps that led down from the top of Chimney Rock. We had to let him go.

"Maybe he's got something when it comes to putting you on a plane for home," Gordon said.

I shook my head, wishing that Ty had never climbed up to this rock. The magical moments between Gordon and me had been interrupted and we couldn't recapture them now.

"You know I won't leave," I told him. "I need to know what happened to Jim. And to my grandmother. I feel as though I'm getting close to something, and I owe them both that much. And perhaps I owe it to Victoria to find out what she was really like." I smiled uncertainly. "Perhaps that's what she wants—for me to

185

know, for me to help set the record straight. Roger Brandt is remembered even today, but she's been forgotten. I wonder if it's up to me to change that? I don't believe all the things Ty says about her. In the long run, maybe he didn't like Victoria. And right now he seems wild and disturbed, so how can he be a good judge of anyone?"

Gordon shook his head. "Don't dismiss Ty too easily. There's more to him than you might think—even in the times when he seems a bit off."

My thoughts, however, were already wandering from Ty as an idea began to take hold in my mind.

"I have a notion, Gordon. Natalie says there's to be a costume party held at the Lake Lure Inn. I told her I wouldn't go, but I've been wondering if I might be able to stir up some of the secrets about Victoria Frazer—and even about Jim—if I picked up her suggestion. Will you be there, Gordon?"

"Of course. This is a civic event, and Finella would never let me off. If you want to go, I'd like to take you. But first, tell me what you have in mind."

"Natalie wanted me to dress like Victoria Frazer, and at first I rejected that. But if I followed it through, I might be able to startle a few people and force something into the open."

"I don't like that," he said quickly. "You could make yourself a target."

"If you were with me, I'd be all right. And Betsey has just the dress I might borrow." I was beginning to feel excited—as though something urged me into this. "It's a gown Victoria wore in *Blue Ridge Cowboy*. That ought to cause a stir!"

"No! It's a foolish idea. You don't look like any of the pictures I've seen of Victoria. She was blond and you're dark. No one could possibly confuse you."

I knew he was setting himself against this because he wanted to protect me, keep me out of possible trouble. But a vision had begun to possess me and I wouldn't listen.

"I'd wear a wig, of course. Don't you see? That first moment of shock when I appeared, looking—if only for an instant—like my grandmother, might tell us something."

He gave up for the moment, though he was clearly not convinced. "Let's go down and have breakfast."

I was hungry and also eager to do anything that would keep me in Gordon's company. He seemed to have drawn back from me just a little—perhaps we'd gone too fast—but I wasn't really worried. I could still feel his arms around me.

At the little lunch counter on the shop level, Gordon picked up rolls and butter and bought mugs so that we needn't drink coffee out of Styrofoam cups. We sat near long windows that looked out toward Lake Lure, shining in the morning sun—its entire length revealed from this high place. I could see the massive shape of Rumbling Bald, as well—that mountain of secrets that was always a magnet for my eyes.

It was good to be with Gordon quietly. In spite of Ty's interruption, I was sharply aware that something new had come to life between us. We had both changed.

His next words surprised me pleasantly. "Finella asked me to invite you to our house for dinner tonight. Will you come?"

I liked Finella and I would go anywhere to be with Gordon. "I'd love that." But there was still that one track in my mind. "How will *you* dress for the party?" I asked.

There had been times long ago when he could look playful—nothing like the serious man he had become. It was this glint I saw in his eyes now.

"Let's just wait," he told me. "Maybe I'll surprise you."

I had to let it go at that, and I turned in another direction.

"I wonder if there's any way I could get hold of a copy of *The Firefly*?"

Gordon considered. "There's an antiquarian bookshop in Asheville that might have a copy. I could phone and find out."

Phoning was too easy. I wanted to stay with Gordon as long as I could manage it. "Let's just go," I said. "I'd like to see the shop, anyway." I knew my own eyes were dancing in the old way—as they'd done when Gordon and I embarked on some little adventure. Once he had found that look irresistible, and it didn't fail me now.

He leaned across the small table and kissed me. "Finish up and we're on our way."

We went down in the elevator, walked back through the tunnel and out to Gordon's car. He chose the high road over the mountains to Asheville and we followed the Blue Ridge Parkway for a while. It was a road of hairpin turns, and when the trees opened up, there were far-flung vistas of distant valleys and mountains. The many turns slowed us down, so the trip to the city took nearly an hour.

Gordon drove to the old downtown section, where he parked near a pedestrian mall that wound its course among elderly buildings of interesting geometrical design. A short walk took us to where a sign hung over a door, indicating the Captain's Bookshelf.

High, steep stairs led to the second level. Originally, Gordon told me, the bookshop had been started by a retired naval captain, and now it was run by his son and daughter-in-law.

This was the sort of old bookstore I'd always loved. The walls were solid with ancient volumes and there were counters and stacks, as well as a couch and comfortable chairs to encourage browsing. On the far end wall, a fanciful dragon made of patches of Japanese obi silk formed a dramatic decoration. In the center of the shop, an enormous rubber plant that was practically a tree dominated the space.

Gordon knew the proprietor and called her Megan. I quickly recognized her interest in a myriad of subjects and her knowledge of the books that crowded around her. When Gordon asked whether she had a copy of *The Firefly*, she looked surprised.

"What an odd coincidence. That's the second request I've had today. A man called earlier and said he would come in to pick up our one copy. He didn't give me his name or say where he lived, but he should be in any minute now. If you like, I can let you see the copy before he comes."

She gave me the book by Dennis Ramsay, and while Gordon explored the shop, I sat down to look through it. The jacket had been torn and mended with tape, but the pages were intact. There were a few photographs and I looked through them at once.

The author had devoted the early chapters to Victoria's childhood, and for the first time I saw pictures of my great-grandparents, whose names I'd never even known. Because of the strange circumstances of her birth, my mother had known little about her family. There were pictures of Victoria with her brother and sister, and she had been a beautiful child. Gretchen looked a little stodgy; it couldn't have been easy for her, growing up with so stunning an older sister. Ty looked small for his age but bright-eyed, as if he could be naughty.

I was most interested, however, in later pictures, when Victoria had become a successful screen actress. Her parents had apparently died while the children were still young, so they had never known about her fame.

The writer pointed out that Victoria Frazer, a slightly younger contemporary of Garbo, had possessed a special quality of her own. What she might have achieved if she had lived would never be known. *The Firefly* had been her most impressive starring vehicle, and the author claimed that her magic could flash on and off—like the light of a firefly—though it had never burned more brightly than in the picture she had made with Roger Brandt—her last.

Dennis Ramsay warmed a bit maliciously to his subject at this point as he went into detail about the love affair between Victoria Frazer and Roger Brandt. Dipping into these paragraphs, I wondered how he could possibly know such things and how much had been created out of his own imagination. He seemed more disapproving of Victoria than of Roger, who he indicated was devoted to his wife.

I was startled to read that Betsey had taken care of Victoria for the last three months of her pregnancy. It seems Victoria needed a secluded place where the press wouldn't find her. If she could keep her condition a secret, which she managed to do during the filming of *Blue Ridge Cowboy*, then her career might continue unaffected. The baby had been born at Betsey's house and from there it was taken by a trusted friend to the couple in California who were eagerly awaiting my mother's arrival.

My sympathy turned wholly to Victoria and I had little patience with Roger. I had just come to Victoria's supposed suicide and the resulting scandal that had ruined Roger's career. But before I could read further, I heard steps on the stairs. A moment later, Roger Brandt walked into the shop. I was screened from his view where I sat, and he didn't see me. I gave up the copy of the book to Megan reluctantly.

While it was being wrapped, I went to stand beside Roger. "Good morning," I said. "I see you needed a copy of the book you were telling me about last evening."

He hid any surprise he might feel at my presence. "So it seems," he said shortly.

"Why do you want a copy after all these years?"

He looked off toward the silken dragon winding its colorful way across the end wall. "To keep it out of your hands, of course. Ramsay wrote a number of lies into his account, and I'd hoped they were long forgotten. I should never have mentioned the book to you. Now *you* are stirring up unhappy occurrences all over again."

"Lies about you, or about Victoria?"

I had seen that same expression of angry distaste on the screen—usually followed by some violent action. But he could hardly draw a gun and shoot me. He wasn't even on a horse.

"Lies about my wife," he said.

I hadn't expected that, and I was silent. He smiled wryly, pleased that he had startled me. Now I was all the more curious about whatever part Camilla had played in the famous tragedy.

"How *is* your wife?" I asked.

He surprised me with his own question. "Where did you get that bracelet?"

Ty's earlier visit made me hesitant to tell him, but I could find no real reason not to answer his question. "Victoria's brother, Ty, gave it to me. But that's all I know."

What that might mean to him, I couldn't tell. He thanked Megan, picked up his package, and walked out of the shop. Far from being accepted as his granddaughter, I was clearly less than nothing in his eyes.

Gordon had stayed out of this exchange, but he had been listening. "I'd certainly like to know what's in that book," he said. "Do you know where we could get another copy, Megan?"

"I don't think I can get you one. It's been out of print for quite some time, but you might look up the author," she suggested. "I believe Dennis Ramsay is still alive and living out at Fairfield Mountains at Lake Lure. Perhaps he would loan you a copy."

Gordon and I looked at each other, and I knew we were again on our way.

"We'll have lunch first," he said, "and then we'll look him up. That's a good tip—thanks, Megan."

I felt a new stirring of excitement. Dennis Ramsay, whether I approved of what he had written or not, had lived at the time of all those happenings and he had known the principal players.

As we walked back to the car, Gordon told me about Fairfield Mountains.

"It's a residential resort on Lake Lure and Bald Mountain Lake. There are homes for family living, a golf course, and a beach. It's exclusive and well protected. You don't just walk in. I'll phone when we get to the restaurant and find out if Ramsay will see us."

Gordon seemed more relaxed than he'd been earlier, and I began to relax a little myself. We were sharing something in a search we could make together.

E ★ L ★ E ★ V ★ E ★ N

WE DROVE up Sunset Mountain high above the city. Grove Park Inn, Gordon told me, was one of the grand old hotels of the South. It had opened in 1913 and had received distinguished guests from all over the world. William Jennings Bryan had given the opening address, and presidents had stayed there. It had been modernized considerably over the decades, but the basic rocks with which it was built could never be changed.

A winding road took us to the top, where I had my first view of the astonishing building. Thousands of tons of rocks of all sizes, from huge boulders to smaller stones, had been carried up the mountain and painstakingly fitted into the walls—by Italian masons, Gordon said. The visual effect of the massive structure of gray rock was overpowering. One had almost the same sense of awe that would be felt at viewing some natural phenomenon.

Windows had been set into the walls at intervals, overhung

by a brown roof of surprising curves and scallops. Two more high rows of windows had been set into the roof itself.

Inside the great hall, more stonework was evident, framing doorways, mounting stairs, and set into gigantic fireplaces. We walked down a long corridor to one of several dining rooms, where we were seated at a table from which we could look out over Asheville.

When we'd ordered, Gordon went off to telephone Dennis Ramsay. "Wish me luck," he said. "I didn't know the man was still alive, so he must keep a pretty low profile."

I waited eagerly for Gordon to return. More than ever, I wanted to know why Roger Brandt had tried to keep Mr. Ramsay's book out of my hands.

Gordon came back quickly enough. "We don't exactly have an appointment, but we'll take a chance that we can see him. He was asleep when I called and I talked to his granddaughter, Carol Ramsay. Apparently, he has made it a rule for some time not to discuss anything about *The Firefly* or the events that made him write it. She said his memory isn't as sharp as it once was and that he has become rather frail. But when I was insistent and told her who you are, Lauren, she gave in."

As we ate our lunch, Gordon made an effort to distract me from my growing concern.

"I've heard," he said, "that a scene from *Blue Ridge Cowboy* was filmed in a ballroom here in the Grove Park Inn."

I remembered the scene where Roger Brandt had ridden his palomino into that room, scattering the dancers, waltzing with Victoria and then taking her up onto his saddle. She had risen so gracefully that I'd wondered how many takes it had required to achieve that smooth ascent.

At any other time, I would have wanted to see the real ballroom, but now something more important drew us, and we ate quickly. When we were on our way back to Lake Lure, Gordon said there was one more stop we might make to see whether we could find a copy of *The Firefly*—in case the author failed us.

Mountains Library was not far from Fairfield grounds and staffed by volunteers. There was just a chance that it might have the book we were looking for. Though of course it would be a plus if Ramsay would agree to see us.

Again we followed the high, winding road from Asheville until we descended into Hickory Nut Gorge and drove on past Lake Lure. Along the road, kudzu had made beautiful sculptures, hiding everything that lay beneath. Trees, old shacks, abandoned cars—all disappeared under the mantling of lush, destructive green. Ty Frazer would never run out of vines to harvest, and it was certainly time for the South to wake up to the way kudzu might be put to use.

The little library was set close to the road and interesting in itself. Three small six-sided huts had been joined to make a whole. Inside, the carpeting was bright and there were comfortable chairs. Shelves with colorful book jackets added to a cheerful atmosphere. Paintings by local artists had been hung wherever there was wall space. While a volunteer searched the shelves for a copy of *The Firefly*, I looked at the paintings. One in particular caught my eye and I recognized Natalie's style.

Again she had painted the Indian village from an angle that included the ominous stake, with longhouses stretching back beyond it. At first glance, the scene seemed empty of any human figure. Yet I had the curious feeling that someone was watching me from around the corner of one longhouse. I moved my eyes quickly from one spot to another in the painting, as though I might surprise something I hadn't seen at first glance. Of course there was nothing there, but the effect of Natalie's curious spell reached out to the viewer.

I studied the picture carefully once more, and when I glanced sidewise from the corner of my eye, I caught the impression of a misty figure that hovered there—not quite in view. Gordon came to stand beside me, and I pointed out the illusion.

"I'm never sure how she does it," he said. "In fact, I wonder if Natalie herself knows what can be present in her painting."

"She's good—but unsettling. I can see why your mother has a hard time selling her work."

The librarian came to tell us that they owned one copy of *The Firefly*, which had been donated by Dennis Ramsay. It had sat on the shelf for years, only to be checked out just an hour or so ago.

Gordon and I looked at each other. Roger, of course.

We drove to the main gateway into Fairfield Mountains. The guard had been told to expect us, and he gave Gordon directions for finding the house where Dennis Ramsay lived with his family.

We found it easily, set on a rise of ground and apparently built from local timber, with a cantilevered deck that looked out across a lake on the highest level.

Carol Ramsay had told Gordon on the phone that her parents were away and she was looking after her grandfather. She waited for us at the rustic front door as we climbed the incline to reach her. She was a round-faced, pretty young woman who greeted us anxiously.

"I'm not sure I should have let you come," she told us immediately. "He's awake now, but not feeling too well. . . ."

I felt that she was about to turn us away, but Gordon spoke smoothly. "Perhaps we'll be good for him, since we're interested in his writing. As a journalist, he should want to meet Victoria Frazer's granddaughter."

She was still uncertain. "I've had second thoughts about this. If I'd known where to reach you, I'd have told you not to come."

"Was Roger Brandt here?" Gordon asked, and everything fell into place.

"Well, yes. He hoped I would keep you away from my grandfather if you came."

Gordon persisted. "Why don't you let your grandfather decide whether he wants to talk to us or not?"

"All right—we'll find out. But please don't stay if he gets the least bit upset."

We followed her out to the cantilevered high deck, where Dennis Ramsay lay stretched in a deck chair in the sun. In his youth, he must have been a big man, but now corpulence had taken over, so that his face was heavy with jowls and his flesh had grown ruddy.

"Grandfather, you have visitors," Carol told him. "They'd like to talk to you about your writing."

That seemed to bring him wide awake, and he looked us over curiously. "Are you connected with a paper?" he asked. "Is that why you want to talk with me? Nobody's bothered for a long time."

I decided to tell him straight out. "I'm Victoria Frazer's granddaughter. I know that you wrote about her in your book *The Firefly*. Not many people are left who actually knew her, and I've wanted to find out more about my grandmother."

He reached to a table beside him and put on thick-lensed

glasses, the better to see me. I couldn't tell whether he was accepting or rejecting me. His question sounded cautious. "What do you want to know about her?"

"Anything you can tell me." I pulled over a chair and sat beside him while Gordon drew Carol down the deck, leaving me alone with the author.

"I'd love to hear whatever you remember about her, Mr. Ramsay," I went on. "I know so little, since my mother was sent away days after her birth."

He closed his eyes. "Yes, I remember. I didn't much like Victoria, but she fascinated me and I thought it was time someone wrote about her. I suppose I fell all over myself when I first met her and she consented to let me interview her. Later she turned against me. Nobody really got near her except Roger Brandt. Maybe I was envious of him at first—until I got to know Camilla and saw how badly he was treating his wife. What Victoria saw in that cowboy, or what Camilla saw, for that matter, I'll never know."

"Roger Brandt is my grandfather," I reminded him.

He closed his eyes behind the glasses, shutting me out. "At least that's how the story goes."

I quickly called him on that, startled. "Don't you believe what was said?"

"I didn't say I didn't. As their granddaughter, I suppose you want to glamorize Victoria and Roger, but that's not what I did in writing the book. *The Firefly* is also about the beautiful woman they both betrayed."

"Camilla Brandt?"

His sigh suggested a wistful memory, and I watched him closely as he continued.

"Camilla was strong as well as beautiful and she could hold her own well enough. She knew when to give Roger his head, and I don't think she ever really worried about Victoria. He'd had a wandering eye before."

"This time there was a baby," I reminded him.

"That must have been hard for Camilla to take, but she stood by him when all that scandal broke into the open and his career went down the drain. A lot of good Victoria did him then. It would have been convenient for everyone if she had simply disappeared, but since she upped and died, everything became known."

"Drowned in Lake Lure?" I said. "A suicide?"

"I never believed that, either. All that propaganda the studio tried to put out to make the story sound romantic! A lot of good it did."

"But you wrote about Victoria—not Camilla?"

"Of course. She was the one who would sell my book, and Camilla never wanted to be written about. Strong, noble women aren't as interesting to write about as those with a great deal of self-love who are flamboyantly wicked."

I spoke quickly, indignantly. "I can't believe that Victoria was wicked. What do you think she did?"

"Ask Ty Frazer and Betsey Harlan. Ask her sister, Gretchen. And of course Camilla could tell you, if she was ever willing to talk. It was all too neat—the suicide. What I asked in my book was who most wanted her out of the picture. Are you sure you want to dig into all this? How can it matter anymore?"

I was silent for a little while, wondering how much to tell him.

"There was another death," I said. "My husband, Jim Castle, died a little more than two years ago under mysterious circumstances. He was making a documentary on Roger Brandt's career."

Ramsay stopped hiding behind closed lids and stared at me with a bright, curious look—still the journalist. "Of course! That's who you are—Jim's wife. He came to see me a few times and he seemed to want to talk more about Camilla than about Victoria. I suppose because Roger was the subject of his film."

I spoke softly. "You'd fallen in love with Camilla, hadn't you?"

He answered me indirectly. "I couldn't see why Roger would stray from a woman like Camilla and take up with Victoria Frazer. Roger came to see me one time while I was working on my book. I was staying at the Esmeralda at the time, and maybe I had had a few drinks one night and said a few things about Victoria. He got pretty nasty and I had to throw him out."

Interesting, I thought. "You knew them all, didn't you—Ty, for instance?"

"Of course. I always liked Ty, even after Betsey turned him down and he took to the hills. He has a good heart, no matter what happened in the past, and he loved Victoria—even after he found out how much his love was misplaced. *She* never loved anybody but herself. Ty still comes to see me now and then and Carol always lets him in, though my son doesn't think much of him."

"And Gretchen?"

"It was pretty hard on her when Victoria disappeared. I guess she'd lived her life through her older sister for a long time. Gretchen still comes to see me, too. I have arthritis, high blood pressure—the works—and she helps me, though she scolds a lot, too. She tells me I have these problems because I haven't respected the *temple,* as she calls the body. But she brings out her pots of goo and touches my swollen joints with her hands—and I'm better for months after she's been here."

200

I wanted to draw him back to the subject of Victoria, but I could see that he was tiring. Before I asked any more questions, I wanted to make sure I had a copy of his book.

"Mr. Ramsay, would you loan me a copy of *The Firefly?*"

He studied me doubtfully before he looked away again, as though he couldn't meet my eyes. "You won't like what I wrote about your grandmother."

"That doesn't matter. Whatever she was like—and some people think she was an angel—I want to know her a little better."

He made up his mind. "I'll do more than loan you a copy. I'll give you one and sign it for you. It's not often that I get to play author these days." He spoke to his granddaughter, who was still talking with Gordon down the deck. "Carol, can you find a copy of *The Firefly* for Mrs. Castle?"

When she went off on her errand, he had nothing more to say. I asked a question, but he seemed not to hear me, and when Carol returned with the book, it was as though he had forgotten who I was. She had to remind him of my name and how to spell it.

It was time to leave, so I thanked him, though I'm not sure he heard me. Carol came with us to the door.

"I'm sorry," she said. "He can fade out like that when he tires—sometimes in the middle of a sentence. He did very well to talk to you this long. You caught his attention."

"I think he wanted to talk about Camilla Brandt," I suggested.

"Of course." She smiled affectionately. "His great love! In his imagination, I'm sure she was that. I'm very fond of him. In his day, he was a top journalist. He even won an award or two, and I have an album of clippings—pieces he wrote for various papers. Though he never did another book after this one."

We thanked her and went out to the car, and Gordon explained what Carol had told him.

"Roger was in a fierce mood when he came here. Carol was even afraid of him. But she felt indignant at the same time. He was going to such extremes to keep the book out of your hands that she decided to let us in. Now that you have the book—what?"

"I'd like to go back to the lodge and read it carefully."

He looked uneasy. "Okay. Let me see anything that strikes you. And, Lauren—don't go wandering off anywhere alone. I feel uncomfortable about Roger's behavior."

I agreed, but wished I could recapture that wonderful feeling I'd had on Chimney Rock. Roger and Dennis Ramsay had taken over.

Gordon left me at the lodge and said he'd come back at six to take me to Finella's. The moment I reached my room, I sat down to examine my treasure more carefully than I'd had time to during the drive. The jacket was old-fashioned and suggested the lake, with Rumbling Bald in the background. I wasted no time on jacket copy, however, but turned first to the surprising dedication. The words were brief:

> *For Camilla Brandt*
> *with the respect*
> *and admiration of*
> *the author*

What was surprising was that Dennis Ramsay had declared his admiration for Camilla in so open a manner. The dedication itself would make anything he wrote about Victoria suspect and perhaps prejudiced.

Now, with Roger's warning to Carol in mind, I read carefully from the beginning.

Ramsay was anything but admiring when it came to the woman about whom he'd chosen to write the book. Only as a screen actress did he give Victoria any credit. There he recognized her fascination and admitted to feeling something of her spell himself. Nonetheless, through most of the book, Victoria and Roger came through as shallow and untrustworthy. No wonder Roger had dismissed it. Victoria, especially, was the firefly of the movie. Still, Roger's behavior seemed extreme.

I came upon an interview Ramsay had done with Victoria, where he'd quoted Victoria in detail. He had asked about the coming marriage between her brother, Tyronne, and young Betsey, Victoria's dresser. Victoria had said carelessly that such a marriage would never take place.

Ramsay set down her very words: "I would never allow my darling Betsey to marry someone like Ty. He is undependable and filled with ridiculous notions. I will see to it that Betsey realizes exactly what she might be getting into."

However, though I read carefully until it was time to meet Gordon, nothing surfaced that gave any indication of why Roger had been so anxious to keep the book out of my hands. Whatever it was must still lie ahead; I would get back to it later.

I dressed somewhat absently for my visit to Finella's house because Ramsay's words still haunted me, left me troubled. What had Victoria Frazer really been like? What might she have done to bring on her own death? Assuming, of course, that Jim and Ramsay were both right and that her death had not been a suicide. Was this what Roger didn't want me to think about?

There were other matters to consider, but I put off my main

concern for now—my day with Gordon and what it had, or had not, meant. There had been those moments up on Chimney Rock when the old feelings we'd had for each other had seemed renewed in a fresh way.

I could hope only that tonight would be a pleasant experience—as Finella would probably make it.

T ✶ W ✶ E ✶ L ✶ V ✶ E

GORDON AND FINELLA lived on a tiny island on the lake. We drove across a bridge to a road that circled the small wooded area. Bright leaves were falling, whipped by a wind that had risen after a calm day. Since land was at a premium here, houses were built at various levels. Finella's was on the water, so Gordon left his car near the road and we went down wooden steps to the inevitable boathouse with a deck area above.

Finella's preparations were attractive. There was still light in the sky, but hurricane lamps had been placed about on the big square deck. A round table, covered with a yellow cloth and set with colorful dishes, stood in a corner where the view down the lake was best. Thanks to the island, the wind that whipped the water to froth farther out bypassed this sheltered spot. It would be pleasant to dine outdoors.

Gordon and I were not the only guests. Natalie and Camilla

were already there, sitting in outdoor chairs.

At the sight of Camilla. I felt immediately uneasy. If she had collapsed last night in order to get her husband away from Victoria's granddaughter—and his—how would she greet me this evening? I needn't have been concerned. Both she and Natalie behaved as though nothing had happened last night to upset anyone. I still had no idea how Roger had reacted after he got home.

In any case, this supper appeared to be a means of bringing the three women together for further discussion about the coming costume ball. I'd been invited simply because I was here. Gordon went to help his mother with the chef's salad she'd prepared, and then set the bowl in the middle of the table. As we sat down, I saw that a fifth "guest" was present. Already at his place sat a life-size dummy figure, limbs sprawled, vacant of face.

Natalie looked delighted at the sight of him. "So Ezekiel is back." Then she explained to me. "We've nicknamed him that. He was one of the stand-ins that was thrown off the cliff at the end of *The Last of the Mohicans.* His arms and legs are articulated and can be worked by remote control so as to give a lifelike appearance as he goes through the air. These dummies are pretty valuable, and locals were beating the woods to find them after they'd been tossed over from the top of the falls. Who discovered this one, Finella?"

"Ty came across him in a remote area and brought him to me. I think I'll display him in my shop for a few days before I send him off to California to his rightful owners."

"He spooks me a little," Natalie said. "I think he knows more than he's telling us."

"I remember the filming," Camilla said. "For once, I was

invited to view some of the scenes in the Indian village—though so little of what I saw appeared in the final picture."

As Finella brought out a chilled bottle of white wine and a loaf of warm bread, I watched Camilla in both doubt and admiration. She looked as beautifully composed as ever, and it was hard to imagine her collapsing as she'd supposedly done last night.

"The burning at the stake was so cleverly managed," she went on. "The illusion on the screen was perfect."

"I painted that same scene," Natalie said, "though I had to do it from my imagination."

I told Natalie that I'd seen her watercolor of the empty Huron village that hung on the wall at the little Mountains Library, and then asked the question that puzzled me.

"When you were working on that painting, did you have a sense that someone was watching you?"

She sipped the wine Gordon had poured and smiled ruefully. "I never meant to paint anything shadowy into that picture, but when I was finished, there it was! Though it was only something I caught out of the corner of my eye. I don't much like it that something can take over when I'm painting. I want to be fully in control."

"Natalie has a special vision," Camilla said, "though she doesn't always appreciate it." She took the bowl of salad from Finella, helped herself, and passed it along. "Natalie's gift is one I'd love to cultivate."

"You have your own gifts, Gran," Natalie said, and I was aware of the look of affection that passed between them.

Gordon listened as we talked and ate, though he had little to say. There wasn't a moment when I was not sharply aware of him beside me at the table.

The three women began to talk about preparations for the coming ball and I found myself watching the twilight view out over the lake, paying little attention until Natalie spoke to me directly.

"Of course you're coming, aren't you, Lauren?"

I wanted to give away nothing that I was planning for that night, so I merely shrugged. "I'm not sure. There would be so few people there I'd know." I held my breath, hoping she wouldn't give away the suggestion she'd made that I come as Victoria. There would be no point to my plan if the shock value of to such an appearance was spoiled.

Natalie interested herself in a plate of succulent shrimp and tomato wedges set in a nest of bright green kudzu leaves and then went on.

"It's going to be an exciting night. You mustn't miss it, Lauren. You might even learn more about us than you want to know." She laughed wryly at her own comment, but her grandmother caught her up.

"What do you mean by that?" Camilla asked.

"Nothing, really. You and Grandfather will be the center of attention—and that's excitement enough. I've started a watercolor of you both dancing together, with the crowd standing around watching. I've even begun to spot in a few faces among the watchers."

"Am I there?" I asked curiously.

"Maybe. I haven't gotten very far. Though I've discovered a monk standing just beyond the dancers. There's a hood over his head, so I can't make out his face. That's when I stopped painting—because I began to have a bad feeling about the monk."

"Who do you think might come dressed as a monk?" Gordon asked.

208

Before Natalie could answer, Camilla broke in. "It's only a painting, for heaven's sake! Let's talk about something else. Lauren, I understand that you and Gordon visited Dennis Ramsay this afternoon. What do you think of him?"

I must have shown my surprise, for she smiled.

"The Lake Lure grapevine works quickly. Carol Ramsay called to ask my advice about you."

"Advice?"

"She felt that you might upset her grandfather. I told her you were just trying to follow up on your husband's research and that if Dennis didn't mind, it was fine. Of course you won't be here very long, as I told Carol. So one visit isn't going to matter."

Too many people seemed to want me gone, and I dug in my heels. "I'll be here for as long as I need to be," I said, and heard my words echo hollowly in the odd silence that followed. They were all looking at me, and suddenly I wanted to ruffle Camilla's calm assurance.

"Mr. Ramsay was kind and quite willing to talk with me. He didn't seem to think much of Victoria Frazer. Perhaps because he was in love with you in those days, Mrs. Brandt?"

All around us, the light was fading, so the hurricane lamps on the rooftop deck softened our outlines. I hadn't disturbed Camilla in the least. Her smile was fond.

"A dear man, and a good writer. He was there when I was in need of a friend."

There when Roger was not? I wondered. Gordon gave me a warning look, but I paid no attention. "What kind of friend was he, Mrs. Brandt?"

Natalie laughed softly, entertained by what was happening.

"You're still young, Lauren," Camilla said. "Perhaps you haven't discovered that there may be a time in a woman's life when she needs a man who will be a helpful friend and who asks nothing more. Have you started to read the book he loaned you?"

"Yes—it's fascinating. It reads like fiction."

"Much of it is fiction."

This time, it was Natalie who spoke. "Which parts, Grandmother? I read some of the book years ago—before you took it away from me."

"You were too young for it, dear. Dennis liked to exaggerate, to embroider. Sometimes he distorted the truth."

This time, Gordon pressed her. "In what way, Mrs. Brandt?"

Her answer was casual—perhaps a little amused. "I'm afraid Dennis had a crush on me for a time, when we were all young. So perhaps he wasn't always fair to my husband in the book."

Was that the answer? I wondered. That Roger's determined actions were only an effort to protect his fragile ego? "Has the grapevine reported that my grandfather has been snapping up copies of *The Firefly* from here to Asheville? And that he went out to Dennis Ramsay's to persuade him not to see me?"

She still seemed unperturbed. "Roger can play dramatic roles at times. He gets carried away, so perhaps that's what happened. The book upset him when it was published—much more than it did me."

Because it had been so critical of Victoria, whom Roger still loved? "What is in that book that he doesn't want me to know?" I asked.

She looked away from our small group, off toward Rumbling Bald. "Why don't you consult *him*, my dear?"

Roger wasn't likely to tell me anything, and she knew that perfectly well. I stared at the mountain, too, wondering how many secrets were held by that sleeping giant.

Finella had had enough of this curious dueling; she rose to clear away the dishes. Natalie got up to assist. Gordon was talking to Camilla about the coming ball, so I joined the others in helping clear the table.

All through the meal, the dummy from the movie had seemed to watch us. Long weathering outdoors while he was lost in the woods had left its traces. He looked a bit battered and his clothes were beginning to shred. None of this mattered so long as his inner machinery continued to work. Perhaps his next dive would be off the top of some high building on the West Coast.

"You must live an adventurous life," I remarked whimsically as I folded the yellow tablecloth. When I joined the others in the kitchen, Finella shooed me back outside, explaining that I was the "real" guest and that I must sit and relax.

"This won't take long, Lauren. We'll just pop everything into the dishwasher. So go talk to Gordon and Camilla."

But when I returned to the deck, Camilla was leaving. Gordon followed her into the house as she stopped to tell Finella good night.

I stood at a side railing of the deck, looking up at the rising moon—a plump moon that cast a shimmering face on the water. Voices drifted across from the opposite shore. Above Finella's house, the windows of two higher dwellings were dark, their summer people gone.

Wisps of mist had begun to gather near the water and I watched as they thickened around the lower part of the boathouse. Not far from where I stood, steep steps led down to a strip of dock, almost invisible now in the veil of white. I decided to walk down toward the water and enjoy the sights and sounds of this beautiful night.

I was halfway down when a voice spoke out of nothingness and I froze. "Come down, Lauren. I have something to show you."

The voice seemed to come out of misty darkness at the foot of the steps. It was only a whisper and I couldn't tell whether it came from a man or a woman. I peered down into opaque depths through which a watery moon wavered.

"Who are you?" I called. "What do you want?"

"Hush!" the voice warned. "I will speak only to you. You want to know how Victoria died, don't you?"

I caught my breath, but I would not put myself at risk. I ventured down three more steps, trying vainly to see whomever was down there. The speaker was silent now, hidden by the silvery floating veil. The unseen movement of lapping water had a hypnotic effect and I began to feel disoriented. Distant sounds from the house reached me and I heard Gordon's voice. I shook my head to clear it, and, without warning, a strong voice sounded in my head—as clearly as though the word had been spoken aloud: JUMP!

I obeyed the command instinctively, even though it meant leaping out into space from these high steps. Because I was moving away from the blow when it fell, it only grazed my shoulders. Heavy and hurtful, it would have been much worse if it had struck across the back of my head. As I dropped into space, a flash of awareness went through me. Now I knew how Victoria had died.

Cold water closed over my head, enveloping me, and I seemed to drop endlessly before I could change my plummeting descent and fight my way, sputtering, to the surface. I paddled in the water and searched the lighted area of dock and boathouse for any indication of who had struck me. Through the mist, which was translucent now with the lights behind it, I could see that stairs and railing stood empty. Pilings below the dock were only a few feet away, but I didn't want to swim into those shadows, lest my attacker be hiding there. Nor would I dare swim toward the nearest shoreline, where the bridge to the island ended. But the water's chill was growing painful, and, despite the mist, I knew my whereabouts were all too visible.

Far above, I could see the lighted window of Finella's kitchen, and I began to shout, calling Gordon's name. With kitchen clatter going on, how could they possibly hear me? In a moment, I would have to swim to the dock and take a chance that my attacker was gone.

Then I heard someone running down the steps, calling my name, and I put more volume into my voice. Gordon ran along the dock to where I paddled fiercely against the cold.

"I'm here! Here in the water! Help me, please!"

He kicked off his shoes and dove in to swim over to me.

"Oh, Gordon!" I cried between chattering teeth, and clung to him.

He put a hand under my chin and towed me to a ladder that ran from the dock to the water. As I hung on to its rungs and looked up, I realized that this ladder bypassed the steps and continued to the top deck over the boathouse. My mind was clear now, no matter how frozen my body felt. Whoever had called to me from the foot of the steps could have climbed this ladder to come around behind me up there.

Then Gordon was pulling me to safety, and the moment my feet touched the dock, my legs turned to rubber. He picked me up and carried me through a doorway at the land end of the boat-house. I smelled fresh sawdust and varnish as he laid me down on a cot covered over by an Indian blanket and turned on lights. This was where he worked on his drums, and I felt safe for the first time as he wrapped the blanket around me and shouted for Finella.

She came down at once and took over, asking no questions. "Can you carry her up to the bedroom, Gordon? I'll get her out of those wet things."

I tried to tell them I could walk, but Gordon picked me up again, and I relaxed with my head against his shoulder, perfectly willing to be helpless. When he set me down, blanket and all, on Finella's bed, he bent over me and rubbed his cheek against mine. I looked into his eyes, surprised, but he left quickly. His mother helped me out of my wet clothes and gave me an enveloping terry-cloth robe to put on.

"Now then," she said, "something hot to drink. Then you can talk. I want to hear what happened."

Apparently, both Camilla and Natalie had left right after dinner, and I needed to talk to only the two of them. Gordon, too, had changed from his wet clothes and had put on a soft old sweatshirt and a faded pair of jeans.

Hot herbal tea restored me a little. I sat at the kitchen table, warmth seeping through me, calming me as I told them both what had happened.

"Something told me to jump," I finished, feeling weaker now that I had gone over what had happened, realizing how close to death I might have been. "Perhaps *Victoria* warned me. Perhaps she wouldn't let it happen again—not to me."

Finella accepted my notion quietly, but Gordon shrugged this idea aside. "You sensed someone's presence, and now we have to find out who was there. Someone wants you gone because you're coming too close—just as Jim may have done. You've got to go home, Lauren. Get away from here and let it all go."

I shook my head weakly, warming my hands around the hot cup. "If I'm that close, then I'm close enough to find out the rest."

He gave me a worried look and went back to the dock to see whether he could find any traces of an intruder.

"You haven't any idea who called to you?" Finella asked when we were alone.

"Not the faintest. But there are only four people left from Victoria's generation—Gretchen, Ty, Roger, and Camilla. Not counting Betsey, who is helpless and who loved Victoria most of all."

"We shouldn't limit the search to that group," Finella said. "It could have been someone younger who wants to protect an older member of the family."

"You mean Justyn or Natalie?" This was possible, but it didn't lead me anywhere. Natalie would never have harmed Jim—and his death was an important part of this whole dreadful puzzle. Of course, I had no clear idea of where Justyn's loyalties lay or how he felt about anything—except that he disliked Ty Frazer and didn't approve of me. Just as he hadn't approved of Jim.

Gordon came back to report that he'd found nothing. Whoever it was hadn't come by boat, since a boat with a motor would have been heard and a rowboat, while fairly silent, would not have been a fast, efficient means of getting away. It would be easy enough to leave a car up near the road and come across the bridge to watch the goings-on at Finella's house. Or perhaps the person had some other reason and I had simply offered an opportunity that was too good to pass up when I appeared on the steps.

Finella went to get my clothes from the dryer, and Gordon sat next to me, drinking a mug of coffee, looking a bit disoriented himself. I remembered how tenderly he'd carried me, how worried

215

he had been, and I touched his hand lightly. "I won't do anything foolish or risky, I promise."

"You might not even know it was foolish or risky." He did his best to glower, but I knew now how he felt about me.

When I'd dressed, I thanked Finella and was grateful for her warm hug and kiss on the cheek. Gordon drove me to the lodge and insisted on coming up to my room to check it out. I promised I would lock myself in, and when he stood outside my door, looking more uncertain than I'd ever seen him look before, I kissed him quickly and closed the door before he could react. If he was still fighting against the past, that was going to end.

When I was ready for bed, I settled myself against the pillows with Dennis Ramsay's book, still curious about what it was that Roger had not wanted me to read.

Ramsay's infatuation with Camilla was more evident as the book progressed and it prejudiced me against what he had to say. He saw Victoria only through Camilla's eyes.

In my haste to find answers, I stopped reading carefully and began to search, scanning the pages for the answer I sought. One passage must have upset several people when it appeared in print. Camilla, Ramsay wrote, had possessed a spectacular Spanish temper. When the love affair between Roger and Victoria became too obvious and was more than she could take, she'd proceeded to indulge in a petty revenge. *Petty* was my word, not Ramsay's, and perhaps it was no small thing to Roger Brandt that Camilla had taken a pair of shears and cut up her husband's favorite Stetson hat. He had come upon her in the act, and the fight between them had nearly blown off the roof. Ramsay wrote:

> I was outside on a balcony at the higher level of the house at the time, and I heard the whole thing. The violence

in their voices alarmed me, and I tried to go to Camilla's aid—I thought he might injure her.

But both she and Roger turned on me, and I backed out quickly. At least the heat between them subsided at my interruption.

Roger took the shears away from Camilla before she could stab him with them, and he swept the remains of the Stetson into a wastebasket. For the rest of the film, he had to wear a newer hat, without the well-worn marks of the one that had appeared in the earlier scenes of the picture.

I put aside the book and thought about what I'd read. In spite of the ugly violence that had flared between them, Roger had never left his wife. Had he, in the end, wanted only to protect her? Or was she in some way protecting him? Certainly, they seemed locked together in some love-hate relationship that perhaps still existed. I wondered if this was the scene he didn't want me to read.

All that night my dreaming was uneasy, and I woke up early, ready for the next step I meant to make. When I telephoned Betsey to ask if I might come out to see her, she sounded pleased and not at all surprised. I could come any time I liked, she told me.

I had no difficulty following the route to the valley where apple signs abounded and was able to locate Betsey's farmhouse easily. She was out on the porch in her wheelchair, waiting for me when I drove into the yard, and her eyes were bright with an anticipation that made me suddenly uneasy. I thought about turning my car around and just driving away. But, of course, that would have been too sensible.

T * H * I * R * T * E * E * N

BETSEY WAS in a lively mood when she greeted me. She had dressed in a multicolored gown that completely enveloped her small person—a gypsy sort of dress that belonged to the past—plus a pair of cowboy boots that were clearly hand-tooled. She had wound a turban of white silk crepe around her head. I recognized at once that it was the same turban Victoria had worn in *Blue Ridge Cowboy*.

As I came up the steps, she held out both hands to greet me warmly. "I was waiting for your call. I knew you'd be coming today."

By this time, I could accept that Betsey had talents of her own that one didn't question.

Her thin, sweet-faced granddaughter came out of the house to hover anxiously, but Betsey waved her away. "Lauren will look after me, dear. I'll call if I need you."

I held the screen door as Betsey wheeled herself inside. Her legs might not carry her anymore, but her arms were strong and helped her to move vigorously.

In her own bright room, she added a further colorful touch that reminded me of paintings I'd seen by Matisse.

"Sit down, Lauren." She gestured toward the chair where I'd sat before. "I hope you like my costume. It really is a costume from a movie. Victoria arranged a bit part for me in Roger Brandt's movie that he made at Lake Lure after *Blue Ridge Cowboy*. I played a gypsy who could tell the future. When my bit part was done, she bought this dress for me to keep."

"I recognize the turban," I said.

She nodded dreamily. "It hasn't been worn since I wound it around Victoria's head in preparation for that ballroom scene. The one where Roger Brandt rode in on his horse. They filmed that at the Grove Park Inn in Asheville, you know. Ever since Victoria died, I've kept the turban with the dress I showed you. You've come for that gown, haven't you?"

"How did you know?"

"I have my ways."

"No wonder they cast you to predict the future in that movie. What else do you see?"

The brightness went out of her face for a moment, but she quickly regained her composure. "Let's just talk about the costume party they are holding. Of course you must wear Victoria's dress—it will keep her from being forgotten. Bring it out of the closet now and try it on. You're about her size, though perhaps a little taller. That won't matter, since it doesn't need to drag on the floor. I've mended the place where Roger tore it."

I went to the closet and drew out the garment bag that protected the treasured gown.

"You can dress in my bathroom. There's a full-length mirror

out here, when you're ready. Hurry, so I can see how you look."

I hooked the bag over the shower rail and took off my slacks and blouse. A full white satin slip hung in the bag with the dress and I put that on. Its thin straps sat perfectly on my shoulders and I pulled the gown over my head carefully. There'd been no zippers in common use in those days, and tiny pearl buttons ran down the back. I went to work fastening those I could reach. Clearly, no one had ever put this dress on without help, and I returned to Betsey and knelt before her chair.

Though her knuckles were bumpy with arthritis, she managed to fasten each tiny pearl to its loop. There was no décolletage to this gown; Victoria's perfect face had been enough to show it off. Even before I looked in the mirror, I knew my own shortcomings.

When I stood up, I saw tears on Betsey's cheeks as she looked at me. "The last time I fastened those buttons, Victoria was wearing that dress. She looked so beautiful."

"I know," I said humbly. "I saw her in the film when Roger Brandt showed it to me. Imagine—he has kept a print for all these years. He seemed deeply moved when we watched it together."

Betsey shook her head impatiently. "He wasn't moved because of my beautiful lady, but only because *he* played that silly cowboy role. Narcissistic—that's what he always was." She broke off, flicking her fingers as though brushing him away. "You look well in that dress."

"I know I don't resemble my grandmother, Betsey. But perhaps I'll startle a few people when I wear it."

She looked at me critically. "Your hair is too dark. She had hair like a canary's wing—soft and golden and beautiful. She never did anything to touch it up, the way some of those other actresses did. So now you must wear her turban to cover your hair. The turban was *my* idea for the picture—to show off the lovely sculpture of her head. I made it myself, and I showed her how to wear the folds tight to her head, crossing gracefully, with no knot at the top. I tucked in the ends at the back so it showed only the shape of her head. Garbo wore a turban just like this a few years later, and I suspect her costume designer got the idea from me."

Betsey began to unwind the long white bands from around her own small head and motioned for me to kneel again—this time facing her.

When I was on her level, I could count every wrinkle in her face. The creases, I suspected, were not marks of sadness, but had been earned by wisdom, by life, and perhaps most of all by laughter. In spite of losing Ty and Victoria and a husband of many years, she had clearly not been a sorrowful woman. Even her present handicap was something she handled with simple courage. Her breath touched my face with a faint odor of mint leaves, and on impulse I leaned forward and kissed her cheek.

"I know why Victoria loved you, Betsey."

"We did fine together. You know she stayed with me, hiding away here at the farm until the baby was born? Her studio approved of that. Of course they wanted to hush everything up; an unmarried woman just didn't have a baby in those days. She did as they instructed, but she couldn't let Roger off so easily. After the baby arrived, she went back to the lake for a little while to stay with her sister, Gretchen. I suspect she was giving Roger one last chance to leave Camilla and do right by her. I never knew exactly what happened, only that she asked me to take the baby away, because by that time she wanted to be sure that Roger would never get his hands on her. I'm the one who carried your momma out to those good friends in California. She told me to do it right away because she was afraid she wouldn't be able to let her go if she looked into that little baby's eyes again. She died while I was gone."

I held very still, listening to these revelations. She paused in her winding and sat with an end of white crepe in her fingers, her gaze on something far away.

"You must understand the truth, Lauren, or you can't wear this dress honestly. Victoria wasn't always an angel, even though she looked like one."

"I can accept that," I assured her. "I've been reading a book by Dennis Ramsay, and even though Ramsay was in love with Camilla and prejudiced against Victoria, some of the things he wrote about her must have been true."

"Dennis was a fool! He turned to Camilla only because Victoria wouldn't give him the time of day. But no matter what nasty things she could do, she was always good to me."

"Of course *you* must have worshiped her, supported her, and perhaps she needed that."

"I *loved* her," Betsey said, "and there weren't many people who did. Only Ty and Gretchen. Though Ty came to resent her because she cut off the money that would have sent him to college."

"How could she have done anything so cruel to her own brother?"

"In the long run, it was the right thing to do. Maybe she knew him better than anybody else did. She knew he'd never stick it out through four years of college."

"She kept him from marrying you."

"Thank God she did! Imagine what my life would have been

like if I'd been Mrs. Ty Frazer! First love can be pretty idiotic. Maybe you've found that out by this time."

It wasn't always idiotic, I thought. Sometimes it was right—though one might not have the wisdom to recognize that fact when it happened. What I wanted now was a second chance.

"What about Gretchen?" I asked. "Did she really love Victoria?"

"Yes, in her way. Trouble was, she wanted her older sister to be more perfect than Victoria could ever be. Even though she was the youngest, Gretchen was the little mother in that family, and maybe she had better sense than the other two. She hated it when Victoria got pregnant, and she hated Roger for what he did to her sister. After Victoria died, disappeared—whatever—she wanted to keep the baby. But Victoria had other ideas and Gretchen couldn't get it back."

"Do you think Victoria drowned herself because she couldn't live without Roger?"

Abruptly, Betsey returned to winding the folds of white crepe around my head, and I knew she wouldn't talk about this anymore. The smooth overlapping folds had to be exactly right and they took all her attention.

"I'll teach you how to do this," she said. "Now go look at yourself in the mirror."

The pier glass across the room gave back the reflection of someone I didn't know. Here was an illusion I hadn't expected. The full white gown with its high, molded bodice made me look almost glamorous. The turban was the last touch to make Lauren Castle disappear. I wasn't sure I liked this. If I wasn't Victoria and I wasn't Lauren Castle, who was I?

Betsey uttered a soft humming sound of satisfaction. "You

don't *look* like her—but there's something. . . . Your head is the same shape, and the way you hold it reminds me of her. And your back is as straight as hers was. But that's about all. Yet there's something—an *essence*—that *is* your grandmother."

She paused, suddenly troubled, and then went on, "I hope this won't worry anyone too much."

I intended to answer her, but for an instant an unexpected delight rushed through me, then was as quickly gone. My reflection in the glass frightened me more than it pleased me—I suddenly felt as though Victoria herself might step into my body when I wasn't looking.

"I wonder if she's around—watching," I said, only half-joking.

"Of course she is. She can't let go when there's so much unfinished business."

"You don't think she drowned herself, do you?"

"It's better to leave all that alone, my girl. Let Victoria take care of it in her own way, if that's what she wants."

"Perhaps I shouldn't wear these things to the party?"

"That's up to you. I don't think anyone will take you for her, but they'll recognize what you're wearing, and you may make quite an impression on more than a few of her contemporaries."

"What do *you* think I should do?"

Quite suddenly, she covered her face with both hands. "I wish I could see what lies ahead. Sometimes I can, but now it's all misty—the way the lake can get at times."

"I know," I said. "I fell into Lake Lure last evening." I told her what had happened—all of it.

She kept her hands over her face as she listened. When she took them away, she'd clearly made up her mind. "Don't go to the party. Take those things off and leave them here. Let me unbutton you now."

While she worked on the buttons, I unwound the length of crepe from my head and folded it neatly. Then I went into the bathroom and put on my own clothes. I didn't return Victoria's clothes to the garment bag because I knew what I meant to do and no one was going to dissuade me.

"Do you have something I can put these things into, Betsey?" I asked briskly. "If you'll let me, I'll take them back to the lodge now."

She knew I had made up my mind, and she didn't oppose me, although she looked unhappy. "There's a canvas tote bag at the bottom of the closet. Use that."

When everything had been folded into the bag, I bent to kiss her cheek again. "Thank you, dear Betsey."

She blinked at me, owl-like, and closed her eyes. I doubted that her trick of suddenly falling asleep was real, but it was better to accept it and go away.

"I'll let you know what happens," I told her as I left, though she gave no sign that she heard me.

I drove back to the lodge on automatic because my mind was busy going over all that had happened. I wanted to tell Gordon about the dress, but since he had been uneasy about my going to the ball, I knew I'd better not. I still didn't know what he planned to wear that evening.

I parked my car, picked up the bulging tote bag, and went inside. Mrs. Adrian saw me and beckoned urgently. I stopped at the desk and she handed me a phone message.

I didn't look at the slip until I reached my room. It appeared that Finella had been trying to get in touch and wanted me to call her as soon as possible.

First, I took Victoria's dress and turban out and hung them in my closet. I'd folded the gown carefully so it wouldn't wrinkle, and it hung smoothly enough—a slim ghost from the past. Waiting to possess me—to take me over?

From the moment I had tried it on, I had believed that I would delight in wearing this gown to the costume ball. Anticipation of the stir I might cause had brought a tingle of almost mischievous excitement. I especially wanted to see Roger's and Camilla's faces when I walked in. Yet now I felt suddenly reluctant. There had been moments lately when I'd almost sensed some restless spirit hovering close—as though waiting. If I wore this dress, would I open a door to some unknown place, so that *she* could come in?

But that was nonsense. I was allowing the atmosphere, the very "legend," of Lake Lure to affect me. Someone who was far from being a spirit had struck out at me last evening. Only the flash of warning in my mind had saved me. My enemy was real enough, and I began to feel more angry than frightened. I must be very close to something or such an attack would never have been risked. If only Jim had shared whatever knowledge he'd unearthed. Or—perhaps he had? What if he had shared it trustingly with the wrong person and sealed his own fate?

I closed the closet door, and when I phoned Finella, she asked me to come to the shop at once. "Ty is here and I've never seen him so upset. He thinks Victoria is after him and that only you can persuade her to leave him alone. I can't talk sense into him and he won't leave until he sees you. So please come over right away, Lauren. This is more than I can take."

Finella had always seemed perfectly able to deal with whatever happened, so her plea alarmed me. "Of course. I'll be there in a few minutes."

I left Victoria's ghost behind and went out to my car. A few minutes later, Finella met me at the door of her shop. While her manner was still disturbed, she tried to maintain a semblance of calm.

"How are you, Lauren? I've been concerned about you."

"I'm fine. One shoulder carries quite a bruise, but that's all. I went to see Betsey this morning and I'd just gotten back when I spoke with you."

Ty heard us and came scurrying across the shop. "Better you stay away from that one!" he told me. "She'll give you all the wrong ideas. She let Victoria fool *her* most of all."

"I can make my own decisions," I told him, sounding sharper than I intended. "Why do you want to see me?"

"You know why. She tried to knock you off those stairs yesterday, didn't she?"

This was likely to be rough going. "Let's sit down where we can talk," I said, and led the way back to the couch where I'd sat so recently with Camilla Brandt.

He trotted after me, but when I sat down at one end, he dropped to the floor and sat with his legs crossed, looking up at me.

"All right," I said. "What *is* this about Victoria? *She* certainly didn't try to knock me off those stairs at Finella's boathouse yesterday."

Finella had come with us, clearly interested, though she didn't sit down.

"They can be all over anywhere—all at the same time."

"They?"

"Spirits."

"I don't believe in spirits."

"You mean you haven't felt her around?"

I didn't want to admit that to Ty. "I'm like you—I have an imagination that runs away with me."

"Why did you go to see Betsey?"

"That's between Betsey and me, Ty. I'm still not sure why you wanted to talk with me."

"Victoria will listen to you. So tell her to let me alone. She didn't treat me right when she was alive, and I don't want her tormenting me now."

"Just how am I supposed to tell Victoria anything?"

"Stop holding her off. Just let her come in."

"What if I don't want to do that?"

"You better try. She can tell you things you need to know. *If* she feels like telling you the truth. She used to lie a lot in the old days—my loving sister!"

"Betsey seems more generous toward her, Ty. She admits that Victoria wasn't always kind, but Betsey loved her and admired her good qualities."

"What good qualities?"

Old bitterness was so deeply a part of his nature that I didn't try to argue with him. "I'm not sure I want to let her in, as you say. If you're right and there are spirits around us, it may not be a good idea to encourage them to become real."

The telephone rang and Finella, who had been listening with interest, went to answer it.

Ty leaned toward me, his arms on crossed knees. "You can reach her right now, Lauren. Close your eyes and let your thoughts drift. Here—this will help you."

He fumbled in the knapsack he carried and drew out a dried twig. "It's rosemary. You know what that's for, don't you? Remembrance."

"But *I* don't have any memories of Victoria or that time. What do you expect me to remember?"

"Don't worry, you'll know. Go ahead—sniff the rosemary and close your eyes. *She* will remember."

"Not here," I said, and dropped the sprig into my purse. "I'll take it with me and perhaps I'll try it later."

Finella returned and shook her head at Ty. "That was Gretchen. I told her you were here, and she says you're not supposed to be running around with that bad shoulder. She's out shopping and she's coming over to get you right away."

Ty looked alarmed. "I don't want to see her. She'll put me back inside a house—where I don't want to be. Just tell her I'm fine and she needn't go chasing me around."

"She isn't coming just to see you," Finella told him. "Lauren's the one she most wants to see."

"Then I'm off!" Ty gave me an intent look. "Just think about what I told you. She won't talk to me anymore now that I've given her to you. So tell me what she says if you get through."

He started toward the door, but he wasn't quick enough. Gretchen must have been phoning from close by, because she came hurrying into the shop.

"I'm okay," he assured her. "It's Victoria you need to worry about now. She's loose again, and she's going to make everybody who ever crossed her pay."

Gretchen snorted. "Sometimes, Ty, you've got about as much sense as Siggy. Less, in fact."

He gave her a look that was far from brotherly and flung himself out of the shop.

At once, Gretchen turned to me. "Come along, Lauren. It's time I showed you something."

I'd had enough of both Frazers, and when she reached for my

arm, I pulled away. "I'm not going anywhere unless you tell me why."

Startling me, she put a hand on either side of my head. "Just be quiet for a minute, Lauren. There's too much turmoil now for you to think clearly."

In spite of myself, I stopped resisting. When she took her hands away, I felt somehow calmer and more relaxed. Whatever resentment was left in me had dissolved at her touch.

Apparently, Finella had seen Gretchen do this before, for she nodded her reassurance. "You'll be fine, Lauren. Whatever Gretchen wants to show you must be important, so come and see me later."

The bell on the shop door sounded musically and she went to greet a large group of customers who had just come off the tour bus parked outside. I followed Gretchen out the door.

"We'll go back to the lodge first," she told me. "I'll meet you in the parking lot."

My actions had begun to feel strangely normal. "Are you part witch, Gretchen?" I asked.

"Only about one percent," she told me, and her smile reminded me of Siggy's grin. Perhaps it was true that we come to resemble the animals we love.

Her car was parked not far from mine and I followed as she drove uphill over the familiar road to Rumbling Mountain Lodge. There she put her car into her own garage, while I left mine in the space reserved for guests. As she emerged from her garage, she waved me over.

"We'll go down to my house and use the boat." She walked ahead of me so quickly that I could ask no questions.

When we reached the house at the foot of the walk, a curious sight met us. Siggy was trying to come out through his doggie door, but he'd foiled his own efforts by carrying a handbag of Gretchen's in his mouth. It was too wide for the opening and he was stuck, with only his snout protruding.

Gretchen laughed. "He's trying to leave home again. If we give him time, he'll figure it out and turn the bag sideways. He's plenty smart. Here, let me give you a hand, Sigmund."

She reached in and relieved him of the bag. He trotted through, looking up at her hopefully. "You can leave if you like, my boy, but you can't take my good bag. You've got an old one of your own. Go and get it."

Siggy sat back on his haunches, the tip of his tongue out and his little piggy eyes entreating.

Gretchen threw up her hands. "Oh, all right—come with us. I don't know how you always know when I'm taking out the boat, but you can come if you'll behave."

He trotted happily down to the boathouse and went around to the side of the dock where the small pontoon boat was moored. "In you go," she told the pig, and he launched himself heavily onto the boat, setting it rocking. When it had quieted, Gretchen got in and gave me a hand. We sat side by side, as we'd done when we went to visit Ty. As before, Siggy sat at the back of the boat where he could watch the wake, which apparently fascinated him.

"I hope you're not going to leave me somewhere this time," I said, but my tone was calm and I wasn't really worried.

She had the grace to look ashamed. "That wasn't a positive thing to do. Usually, I'm pretty good at rejecting negative actions, but that time I got upset."

She started the outboard and there was no more talking as we headed across toward Rumbling Bald. Justyn's sight-seeing boat was coming down the lake, but Gretchen steered calmly in front of it, waving at him insolently. He slowed to let her cross, though I thought he gave us a troubled, questioning look as we headed toward shore.

I'd wondered whether we could be going to Roger's house, but the stretch of shore Gretchen approached seemed empty. As we drew near a rickety dock, I saw that the same rough sort of path that had run past Ty's shack followed the lake here, as well. Gretchen tied up to a rotting post that didn't look too secure.

"You stay here and mind the boat," she told Siggy.

He whimpered a little, but, with his bulk and short legs, he couldn't get out on his own. He watched unhappily as Gretchen and I started along the overgrown path. The dam was ahead at some distance, and, through an opening in the trees, I could see the roof of Roger's house.

Gretchen seemed sad, or perhaps *grim* would be a better word, her manner far from reassuring. I knew this was no time for questions, though I had many. Her "witch's spell" had stopped being effective and I found myself apprehensive, though unable to do anything but go along.

The shoreline turned in to accommodate a little cove where no houses had been built. Gretchen stopped on the path ahead of me.

"The tour boats have it wrong," she told me. "This is where Victoria died."

I froze on the path behind her and she turned to face me, her expression blank—as though she held whatever she might be feeling under stern control.

"It was time for you to know, Lauren—now that I know who you are. There are too many lies being told. You need to know the truth—or at least part of it. There's only one person who could know it all. *This* is where we found her."

The shock of this new reality held me still, frozen.

Gretchen knelt on the path and moved her hands through the weeds as though she could touch what had once lain there. A snake wriggled away and slid into the water, but she didn't move. I suspected that no snake would choose to tangle with Gretchen Frazer. I asked no questions but waited tensely for her to continue.

After a moment, she looked up at me. "She was dead when we found her. Roger and I. I think she died immediately from a blow to her head." Gretchen sat back on her heels and covered her face with her hands. I saw the glint of tears and knew that remembered grief could be as painful as grief in the present.

A blow to the head? That was the message that had come to me yesterday when I'd plunged into the water and had *known* how Victoria died.

Gretchen continued, her voice muffled. "It was toward evening when we found her. Roger and I were walking along this very path you and I just took. We were angry with each other and we walked over here so no one would hear us argue.

"I was wild because of the way he was treating Victoria, but he couldn't take criticism from anyone. He had the gall to tell me she had enjoyed their little escapade as much as he had. *Escapade!* Then we came around that curve in the path and she was lying there. She loved to wear white, and her dress shone in the dusk, with a bit of her skirt drifting in the water. Even in the fading light, I could see the red stain in her hair and the blood on her dress. I can still see it!"

Gretchen seemed to be forcing herself to remember, and I could only wait in horrified silence for her to continue.

"Roger practically fell apart. I don't think it was because he really loved her, but because her death frightened him into seeing what lay ahead. Everything the studio had hushed up—their affair, the birth of the baby—would come out now and the fingers of accusation would point to him. Victoria's murder would never be hidden. Unless—"

She broke off and rose from her knees, brushing off her jeans. "It was time for you to know," she repeated. "Your grandmother didn't drown. Someone utterly evil murdered her. Part of me knew that at the time, even while part of me wondered if *she* had caused this to happen. Sometimes I still wonder. Who was good and who was evil? When Victoria died, a beautiful light went out of the universe. Until now, I've returned to this place only in my worst dreams. When there's been an act of violence, the very ground can stay haunted for a very long time."

She turned to go back to the boat, as if that was all she had to say. I ran after her and caught her by the arm. "Wait! You have to tell me the rest of the story. You can't stop now. What happened after you found her?"

"I made a terrible mistake." She turned to face me. "I listened to Roger. He told me that she mustn't be discovered like that— murdered. He said her career, everything she had accomplished, would be forgotten in the lurid scandal of her murder. It would be better if she was thought to have simply disappeared. Her body would never be found and people could only speculate about what had happened to her. He took the white sash from around her waist and caught it around the pilings of the dock down there so that part of it floated in the water. Then he told me that he knew a place where we could hide her body, a place where it would never be found. But he couldn't carry her up Rumbling Bald alone—the way was too rough. So I would have to help him. I began to see how terrible it would be for all of us if she was found like that, and I was afraid."

"For Ty?" I whispered.

She ignored my question and continued her story. "While we were struggling up the mountain, I thought of a letter Victoria had shown me but hadn't mailed yet. It would sound like a suicide note and we could use it."

I could see how the plan must have evolved—it was all a way to keep the damage to a minimum—or so they hoped. The lake was deep in some places, and even divers might never find what was down there. But who had most needed protection? Victoria or the last person she had seen that long-ago afternoon?

Perhaps at that point, Roger might still have thought his career and reputation could be saved. He hadn't seen that a baby plus a missing young star thought to be a suicide would be enough for the press to run with and blow everything into the open. I felt sure the uproar must have been far worse than either he or anyone else expected.

"Where did you take her?" I asked softly.

Gretchen stared up at the great dark mountain crouching above us. "It was a terrible climb, but I wouldn't let her be dragged—even though she was impossibly heavy. By the time we reached Roger's cave, it was dark. He had a flashlight and we managed to take her inside, deep inside. In a sense, we buried her in the heart of the mountain and left her there. The cave is still her tomb."

"Did you ever go back?"

"Once I tried to find the cave, but the opening is only a slit in the rocks and it isn't visible unless you know what landmarks to look for. Roger knows, but I would never ask him. We both went through all that ordeal that lay ahead as though we'd never been on the mountain that night. Once we'd conspired to hide her murder, there was no going back."

Her story left me shaken. "Why have you told me now?"

"So you will stop stirring things up and go home. Just let it be, Lauren. What difference can it make to anyone today? Let her sleep in peace. The mountain makes a noble tomb."

I rejected this at once. "I don't think she's at peace. I don't believe that anyone connected with Victoria is at peace. Jim died. Perhaps he died because he'd found the cave and Victoria's bones and knew that she'd been murdered. Now there's been another attack. On me."

She caught up my words. "What do you mean—an attack on you?"

I told her then—the whole story of how I'd barely escaped the same sort of blow that must have killed Victoria. Gretchen listened in stony silence, but if she had any thoughts about this, she gave nothing away. When I finished, she stepped into the boat and helped me aboard without saying a word. Siggy was beside himself with joy—as though he thought she might never return. He wiggled, rocking the little boat on its pontoons. Gretchen scratched him absently between the ears and he calmed down. When she started the outboard, talking was impossible, so we crossed the lake in forced silence.

On the other side, she turned off the motor and boosted Siggy onto the dock. Before she could escape, I stopped her.

"I'm glad you told me this, but now we *must* talk. You've been thinking about all this for years, and you must have come to some conclusions."

She took my hand in hers. "You're my blood kin, Lauren. I held your mother in my arms when she was a baby. I feel connected to you, and I worry. I've been worried ever since you came. But there's nothing more to talk about. Now you know what I know."

I had to leave it at that. But just as I was about to start up the walk to the lodge, I remembered something and turned back.

"There was an odd piece of green material with Jim's letter that Natalie gave me. Do you have any idea where it came from? Do you think Jim found it with her body?"

She answered me with what little patience she could summon. "I wish I knew, Lauren, but I don't." She threw up her hands wearily. "Can't you just let it go? I've already told you all I know."

There was no point in pushing her further. She went inside abruptly and I returned to the lodge. Once more in the quiet space of my room, I sat down to consider all that I'd learned. From the beginning, I'd believed Jim's letter, believed that Victoria was murdered, and now I knew this was so. But the puzzle was larger than ever.

I went over to my window and stood staring out at the lake. I thought of Natalie and her paintings and particularly the one of the spaceship that Finella had in her shop. I repeated the title Natalie had given it, sounded the syllables out loud—*Star Flight*— and a new thought occurred to me. What if her title carried a double meaning? What if it was a play on words, since another *star* had taken flight?

Ty's sprig of rosemary was still in my bag. Feeling only a little silly, I took it out, lay down, and closed my eyes, holding it to my nose. The scent of the herb was still strong and I allowed it to envelop my senses. When darting lights behind my lids subsided, a strange vision framed in cavernous darkness began to form on the screen of my mind. Shimmering with movement as I watched, a sparkling white ribbon of water fell vertically down the center of my dream picture.

Ty had reminded me that rosemary was for remembrance, but what was I remembering? The only waterfall I'd seen was the one that fell over the cliffs opposite the Indian village where I'd heard a drum playing. Was this memory or prophecy?

A sharp mechanical ringing broke into my reverie. I reached for the phone.

"Lauren?" Gordon sounded excited. "I've found out something pretty interesting. There's someone you ought to meet. Can I pick you up in about fifteen minutes?"

He sounded like the young man I remembered, and I knew everything was right between us. I told him I'd be ready. The waterfall could wait.

F ★ O ★ U ★ R ★ T ★ E ★ E ★ N

GORDON WAS still excited when he picked me up and his mood reminded me of San Francisco. There was satisfaction for me in thinking that we might really be able to have a second chance. Now I knew what I wanted.

He explained our outing when we were on our way toward Chimney Rock. "We're going to see a man I've known for a long time, though I never recognized his connection with Victoria and Roger until Justyn tipped me off. I have a feeling that Justyn is trying to get back at his father in some way."

Just before we reached Chimney Rock village, Gordon pulled in before a long, low building that had once been a lumber warehouse. A sign outside read DOLL HEAVEN. We went in through a wide door and I looked about in delight.

Dolls were on display *everywhere*—dolls of every size and shape and age. Tables and counters and shelves were crowded with a fascinating doll population—rag dolls, bisque dolls, old kid dolls with china heads, Kewpies with fat stomachs that dated back to early in this century. But I knew we were not here because of the dolls.

A middle-aged woman who obviously recognized Gordon came toward us. "Hello, Amy," he said. "This is Mrs. Castle. Lauren, Mrs. Osborn."

She held out a friendly hand. "I remember your husband, Mrs. Castle. What can I do for you, Gordon?"

"Is your father-in-law in? Do you suppose we could see him?"

"He's always in these days, and he enjoys company. He'll be glad to see you. Go right ahead. You know the way." Nevertheless, she gave us a curious look as Gordon led the way back through the shop.

"He'll like it if you recognize him," Gordon said to me. "See how long it takes you."

I was puzzling over what he could mean when I passed a glass case that caught my eye and stopped to look. The display was of two dolls and a china horse—clearly a palomino. The female doll had long golden hair and wore a white dress; the man was clearly a cowboy. The actors in the legend had been carefully reproduced.

Gordon drew me on. "You can come back and look later. If you want to."

We stopped before the open door of what appeared to be a small office.

"Hello, Gerald," Gordon said. "I've brought someone to see you."

An elderly man turned from his desk, and when he saw me, he got to his feet in a courtly manner. Gordon introduced me, and while Gerald Osborn was shaking my hand, Gordon surprised both of us.

"Lauren is not only Jim Castle's wife—she is the granddaughter of Victoria Frazer and Roger Brandt."

As startled as I was, Osborn peered at me through his glasses and then took both my hands in his. "Yes—I can see it. Your eyes are like hers." He sounded wistful, as though the discovery made him sad.

"You knew my grandmother?" I asked.

He waved a hand toward the wall, and I saw several framed photographs of Victoria Frazer, though none of Roger. I recognized some shots from *Blue Ridge Cowboy*, though mostly in scenes where Victoria was alone. One of them was signed "To My Darling Jerry."

Gordon was still waiting for some recognition on my part, but nothing clicked. I went closer to the wall and moved from picture to picture. One was of a young officer in the uniform of the First World War. In another, the same officer held a beautiful young woman in his arms—Victoria. And of course I knew.

"You're the actor who danced with her in *Blue Ridge Cowboy!* In the ballroom scene. I remember how beautifully you danced together before Roger rode onto the scene."

Pleased, Osborn came to stand beside me. "Yes—that scene was shot at the Grove Park Inn. You must have seen the movie?"

"My"—I hesitated and then went on—"my grandfather showed it to me. You and Victoria danced so perfectly together that I was almost sorry when Roger came riding in so dramatically to take her away from you."

Osborn's eyes were bright as he remembered, but there was sadness in his look.

"I was so sorry for Victoria that day. It was dreadful that she
had to be so humiliated. Roger could be short-tempered, and they
had such trouble shooting that scene. It wasn't Victoria's fault.
She'd never even been on a horse before, and she couldn't get up
into that saddle gracefully. Much later, of course, we all realized
she must have been five or six months pregnant at that time, which
is shocking to think about. Anyway, it looked as though he were
pulling her apart, and she was making terrible faces. She was
terrified of the horse, and of course Roger was impatient because
he wanted the scene to be right. The palomino got skittish and we
all knew it was hopeless. Roger decided that they'd have to get
Victoria into the saddle offscreen. By that time, she was in tears.
I knew how much she wanted to please Roger, and he wasn't even
thinking about *her*—just the movie. I tried to comfort her, but I
wasn't the one she needed just then."

He stopped as though lost in time. Of course he, too, must
have been in love with Victoria, as so many men had been, and this
could only be a painful memory for him.

"What happened?" Gordon asked gently.

Osborn sat down at his desk, not looking at me now. "I'm not
sure I remember the details clearly anymore. Everything got out
of hand, though I never blamed Victoria for what she did. It was
Camilla Brandt's fault, really." He paused and the silence in the
room grew. Finally, he pushed himself up and said, "I'm sorry—I
can't talk about it."

Amy Osborn had come to the door, her disapproval clear.
"He hasn't been well," she whispered to Gordon.

Osborn pulled himself together. "You'd better see Dennis
Ramsay, Mrs. Castle. He left a lot out of his book because he was
in love with Camilla. If he wants to, he can tell you."

We thanked him and let Amy Osborn draw us out of the room. "I didn't know you would upset him," she said reproachfully. "All that ancient history—but he still feels it."

Back in Gordon's car, we looked at each other. "Let's go see him," I said.

"Right. We won't phone Ramsay this time—we'll just go and take our chances. I have a feeling that a few more pieces may fall into place."

It was past lunchtime, but we didn't bother about food. We were both intent upon learning more about what had happened. I'd begun to feel a real sympathy for Victoria and new anger against Roger for his insensitivity. I had watched that scene in the picture and I'd seen Victoria rise gracefully, competently, onto his saddle. So how had it been managed if everything was going so wrong on the set?

When we reached his house, Ramsay came to the door. His granddaughter was out and he seemed glad to see us.

"Have you read my book?" he asked me at once.

"Most of it, and it was fascinating," I told him. "Though I think you were too hard on Victoria."

"Not as hard as she deserved," he said curtly. He stepped out of the doorway to invite us in.

Gordon wasted no time. "We've just talked to Gerald Osborn and he thinks you can fill us in on a part of the ballroom scene that you didn't write about."

"Come on back to my workroom," he said readily. "I'm writing about that very thing now."

He led us into a small room that held a desk, typewriter, bookcases, and a slant table with a chair before it. A handful of typewritten pages lay stacked beside the machine.

"I'm slow these days, but I've been working on a new book about the whole Lake Lure legend for over five years. I want to set down the *whole* story this time. Too much had to be left out of the first book."

Because of threats from Roger? I wondered.

"I'm not sure why any of this matters anymore, or if anyone will be interested in reading it. Please sit down and tell me why you're so interested in what happened so long ago."

"I want to know more about my grandmother," I said. "Is that so strange? Mr. Osborn described the scene where he waltzed with Victoria Frazer and Roger Brandt came riding in on his palomino. He told us that Victoria had trouble getting up on the horse, but that's all he would tell us."

Ramsay sat down before his slant board, picked up a pencil, and began to scribble idly. He seemed to be doodling something that looked like a military saber.

"I didn't see everything that happened. Some of the time, they were in Victoria's dressing room with that woman who used to look after her clothes and makeup. What's her name—Betsey Harlan? I had to coax *her* to tell me what happened. All I can repeat is what Betsey told me."

He closed his eyes and leaned back in his chair.

"Victoria came off the set in tears and Camilla Brandt, who was there that day, followed her into her dressing room. They exchanged words and things got emotional. Victoria didn't want to take off that beautiful dress, but Camilla *made* her. By this time, Victoria was tired and her makeup was ruined by her tears, so she didn't have much choice. Camilla put on the dress and came back to the set. When she appeared, it might have been Victoria her-self—just for a moment. The dress fitted her perfectly—they were about the same size. And she'd wound that white thingamajig around her head to hide her black hair. The camera started and Roger mounted his horse and pulled Camilla up onto his saddle without a hitch. With no close-ups, no one could tell that it wasn't Victoria. Camilla was right for that scene—she knew horses and she knew riding."

He broke off, just as Osborn had done—an old man remembering his youth and an old love.

I pressed him for more. "What happened when the scene was done and Camilla went back to the dressing room?"

He added a few scrolls to the saber that had taken shape on his paper. "All right—but mind, this isn't something I saw for myself. It's what Betsey told me, though later she denied the whole thing. Camilla got out of that white dress and *threw* it at Victoria. Then she put on her own clothes and started to leave the room. That's when Victoria went crazy. There was always a vicious streak in her. She picked up a letter opener from her dressing table—a miniature army saber—and she stabbed Camilla in the face with it. It all happened so fast that Camilla didn't have time to defend herself."

Ramsay paused wearily.

"Victoria had managed to slash Camilla across one cheek. We all heard her cry out, but we just assumed those two were going after each other in a fit of jealousy. The wound bled all over the place, Betsey said. When Roger came running in and saw his wife's face and the bloody letter opener in Victoria's hands, he struck her so hard across the face that he knocked her down. Then he took the towel out of Betsey's hands and tried to stanch the flow himself. When it stopped a bit, he drove his wife to Asheville to a hospital. In those days, they didn't have great plastic surgery—

that skill had to be developed through a few more wars. So Camilla carries the scar to this day. She covers it up with makeup, so only a bit of puckering shows, and she's still so beautiful it doesn't matter. Of course, what Victoria did turned Roger right back to his wife."

"You've seen Camilla recently?" I asked.

"She comes to visit me now and then. We've remained friends over the years. She liked what I wrote in my book—she thought I was very fair."

"I'm sure you were," I said. "To *her*. But were you fair to Victoria?"

Being fair to Victoria wasn't important to him. "Whatever happened to *that* one, she had it coming, Mrs. Castle. You need to recognize what Victoria Frazer was really like—totally self-enamored. Of course, after what she did to Camilla, Roger never felt the same way toward her again. But she was already carrying his child. Frankly, I think he still cared for her, but the passion was gone. I'd have liked him better if he'd blamed himself a little more. It was all because of him that it happened. The classic situation—two beautiful women and one man."

Ramsay was warming to his subject now, as though he was enjoying writing this second book." I emphasized all this in my last chapter—and Roger must have hated it. I placed the blame where it belonged—with him."

Which, of course, was why Roger hadn't wanted me to see the book. Vanity still prevailed.

It was time for me to ask the pertinent question. "Mr. Ramsay, who do you think murdered Victoria Frazer?"

His smile had a cold, hard twist to it. "You'd run out of fingers trying to count the people who hated Victoria."

"Betsey and Gerald Osborn and Gretchen didn't hate her."

"Perhaps not, but how many others did?"

I couldn't answer that—I had only my own instincts to go on.

Once more the old man had tired, so we thanked him and left before his granddaughter returned.

Back in the car, Gordon sat with his hands on the wheel. I still felt shaken by the story Dennis Ramsay had told.

"How do you feel about Victoria now, Lauren?" Gordon asked gently.

"Sorry for her. It was her nature, I suppose, to behave in uncurbed ways, but I don't believe she was ever a vicious person. She was pregnant with Roger's child and she loved him. She was under a lot of stress. I'm sorry for Camilla, too. She never asked for the situation she found herself in. It was a very human triumph for her that she could ride, when Victoria couldn't."

"So where do you go from here?"

"Will you come with me to see Betsey Harlan again?"

"Of course. If that's what you want, but Ramsay says that Betsey later denied her own story."

"That's why I want to see her."

"Then let's go." He put an arm around me and held me close for a moment, so that I knew I wasn't alone. We wound down to the valley floor and the apple farm. Betsey's young great-grandson came to meet us before we got out.

"Great-grammaw's sick," he informed us. "I don't think my mother wants anybody to visit her today."

My first impulse was to leave and not trouble her. She was so old and frail. Yet I sensed in Betsey a certain tough core, and I wondered whether she was really too ill to see us for a few minutes.

"Where is your mother?" I asked.

He nodded toward the rear of the house. "She's working in her vegetable patch."

The boy followed us as we walked around the house to where a woman in jeans was weeding. She looked up, knowing at once who I was.

"You can't see her," she told me flatly.

"There's only one question I need to ask," I pleaded. "If we could see her for just a moment—we'd go away quickly after that."

Her "No!" was vehement. However, before we could turn away, a querulous voice was raised loudly enough to be heard through the open window above our heads.

"You let her in right now!" Betsey ordered.

Her granddaughter threw up her hands. "It'll be worse if I try to keep you away now she knows you're here. Go on in, but don't stay long."

"You'd better see her alone," Gordon said as we walked away from the granddaughter. "I'll pick up some apples for my mother."

I thanked him for understanding. He kissed me lightly before turning away and my spirits lifted. He was on my side now. He was with me, giving me courage, whether or not he approved of what I intended.

This time, I went in through the back door, knowing my way to Betsey's room. She lay beneath quilts, as though she was cold, but her eyes looked hot and feverish. I tapped on her open door and went in.

"It's good to see you, Lauren. I guess you know by now what I told Dennis, don't you?"

"I know what he told me, but I think there's more."

One small claw of a hand gestured to a rocker beside her bed.

"Sit down. I'm not as sick as they think. I just don't want to listen to them scold."

I felt a little better about my insistence. She, at least, had loved Victoria, and there must have been more behind the stabbing than I knew.

"What do *you* think happened?" She folded down the edge of a quilt, the better to peer at me.

I repeated what Dennis had told us—that Victoria had snatched up a letter opener and slashed Camilla across the cheek.

Betsey became suddenly agitated. "That's what I told him, but it wasn't true. She didn't do that. She never would have—she was a gentle lady."

"But then, how—"

"You should have seen me in those days. I had spunk— plenty of spunk. I couldn't stand it that Camilla took that last scene away from my lovely lady and then came back to the dressing room to gloat over what she'd done. I'm the one who went crazy and slashed her face. And I've always been glad I did. Maybe I'd have killed her if I'd been strong enough."

I rocked in the chair, agitated myself, not sure I believed her. "But Roger came in and saw Victoria with that little saber in her hands."

"Sure! She'd taken it away from me before I could hurt Camilla even more. And she took the blame, as well. When she saw what Roger believed, she didn't even try to defend herself. She did that to save me. The Brandts would have had me arrested and sent to jail. But they wouldn't touch Victoria."

"Why not?"

"She was going to have his baby, she was his lover, and this would be an even bigger scandal if it came out. Think what a field day the press and fan magazines would have had if it was known that Victoria had slashed Roger's wife across the face. So they had to keep it quiet. And, of course, Camilla never told *him* the truth."

"But if Camilla knew what really happened, why does she treat you like a friend? You disfigured her for life."

Dark eyes twinkled maliciously. "I did a good job, didn't I? But don't you see—she's had to keep an eye on me over the years, to make sure I wouldn't spill the beans somewhere along the line. She wanted Roger to go on believing in what he thought Victoria had done. So she tried to keep me quiet with kindness and forgiveness and gifts. Forgiveness!"

There was no question as to where Betsey Harlan's loyalties lay. She went on with gleeful spite.

"I gave Dennis Ramsay the wrong story. But he didn't publish it, anyway. He was crazy about Camilla, and she didn't come out so squeaky clean, either. Getting up on that horse gave her a way to tell off Victoria. Which might have been all right—but she really rubbed it in."

"I can hardly blame her for that."

Betsey went right on. "In a way, she got Roger back because of what he believed. Or a piece of him, anyway. You can't tell me that any man who ever loved Victoria Frazer could really get over her."

I remembered how moved Roger Brandt had seemed when we had watched *Blue Ridge Cowboy* together. The love scenes had shaken him. Though, in the end, Camilla had been the one to hold him. Perhaps he even felt he owed her because Victoria had scarred her face.

"Why didn't you tell him the truth after Victoria was gone?"

"Camilla would have denied it and he'd have believed her. What good would it have done?"

"What if I was to tell him the truth now?"

"Let it alone, Lauren. The truth would probably destroy Roger. I don't have much use for him, but telling won't help Victoria now. And finding that he'd given up—maybe the great love of his life—because he wrongly suspected her would be enough to send anybody over the edge."

"Thank you for telling me all this. And for being so wise. You've given my grandmother back to me. Whatever else she did, this was generous and brave, and I admire her for it."

"Nobody really understood that she was a good, rather simple person who followed her emotions. She never realized what it would be like when all that fame hit her. She came from these mountains, so how could she know? She ran from it, even while she enjoyed it. We're all pretty mixed up, aren't we?"

This was true enough, and I smiled. Betsey's hands came out from under the quilt and reached for mine.

"You've brought Victoria back to me, too. Brought her into this room where she had her baby. Gretchen was too critical and straitlaced, and though she'd have taken her in, Victoria didn't want to stay with her. And, of course, the studio wanted her hidden away until the 'problem' could be put up for adoption. They had a lot of money tied up in those two careers. Anyway, Victoria was better off with me, who really loved her. Your mother was born in this room, so it was right for you to come here. Everything we've talked about and done has been right, except for one thing."

For a moment, I was lost in my own feelings. My mother had uttered her first cries in this very room—and because of her I was here now and alive.

"Except for what?" I asked.

"I should never have let you take Victoria's dress and the

turban I made for her. I don't think you should wear her clothes to that ball and remind everybody about the past. There's somebody out there, Lauren—the person who killed Victoria."

"Do you know who it is, Betsey?"

"If I did, do you think I'd have kept still all this time? I didn't talk to your husband much when he came to see me, but from things he said, I think he was getting too close and that was dangerous. I don't want that for you."

"I don't see what harm can come to me if I startle a few people. That's all that can happen. I'll be with over a hundred people. Perhaps I'll even get Roger Brandt to dance with me!"

"He wasn't the only one who danced with Victoria in the movie, you know."

"I know. I met Gerald Osborn this morning. He's another one who was once in love with my grandmother."

Betsey was staring at me in a strange way, and I broke off. "What is it? What's the matter?"

"Sometimes I can see ahead a little, and that happened just now. I could see a storm—lightning flashing around you. And I could see fire. But I don't know what it means, and nothing else comes to me. Lauren, I'm afraid for you."

I bent to kiss her cheek, murmuring reassurances even though her words chilled me. "I'll be fine. When I bring Victoria's things back, I'll tell you all about what happened at the ball."

She seemed to sink into herself again, not falling asleep but closing herself away.

I returned to Gordon and told him everything that I'd learned from Betsey Harlan. And I held on to his hand while he listened gravely.

F ⋆ I ⋆ F ⋆ T ⋆ E ⋆ E ⋆ N

THE LONG mirror on my bathroom door gave back a reflection I hardly recognized. The dress was perfection—only yellowed a little from age, a creamy white. The smoothly wound turban hid my dark hair, its folds crossing gracefully in a peak on my forehead. I knew I would never do justice to my grandmother, or to Camilla Brandt, who had also worn this dress. I felt awkward and much too uncertain about what I meant to do.

Had I expected that magic would take place and transform me when I dressed like Victoria Frazer? How could I ever carry this off?

Nonetheless, words seemed to whisper through my mind. *Relax. Be yourself. You'll do fine.* The inner advice was sound, and I raised my shoulders with a certain defiance. The reflection in the mirror changed very little, but my confidence returned. This was only a game, really—a masquerade—and I needn't feel concerned.

I'd made no attempt to imitate the makeup of Victoria's day. Though she hadn't painted on a Cupid's bow mouth, she had worn the face that was fashionable in the thirties. No matter how I dressed tonight, my face belonged to my own generation, and I used touches of blush and lipstick accordingly.

When I stepped back from the glass, the tips of my low-heeled white shoes caught my eye, making me smile. Entirely inappropriate, but they were all I had to wear. Most of the time, the long skirt would hide them, so it didn't matter.

As a last touch, I clasped the silver bracelet around my wrist and enjoyed the sound of tiny bells as I moved.

It wasn't time yet for Gordon and Finella to come for me, so I went outside to stand at the railing and look over the lake. The sky had darkened early, turning the water to black marble, veined here and there with lines of yellow light from houses along the bank.

Down the walk at Gretchen's, windows were alight. I was just as glad that she wasn't expected to go to the ball. I was sure she would have resented seeing me in her sister's dress. Ty, of course, shunned most human company, and he would never appear at such a gathering.

Off beyond Rumbling Bald, lightning brightened the sky and I heard faint thunder. It was far away, but I thought of Betsey's vision and felt a little uneasy. It would be too bad if a storm spoiled the festivities, but at least we'd be inside and dry before it broke.

Once more I had the curious sense that the mountain waited, watching me. Now I knew the exact place on the far shore of the lake where Victoria had been found. And I knew that her body had been carried laboriously up to a cave on the mountain. I suspected that somehow Jim had found that cave and discovered more than it was safe for him to know.

I shivered in a cool breeze that rose suddenly and I went inside. I was in time to hear the phone. Gordon was waiting for me downstairs.

Aware of the theatricality of this moment, even smiling a little to myself, I started the grand descent down to the lobby. A man waited for me at the foot of the steps, and the theatricality was not wholly mine. For just an instant, I thought that Roger Brandt had come for me in his full cowboy regalia. Certainly the outfit was his: pointed boots, leather chaps, a blue shirt with a scarf knotted jauntily at the throat, and, of course, a wide-brimmed Stetson hat that hid the face of the man who wore it—until he looked up at me.

Gordon's grin was wide; he looked pleased over surprising me. "How do I look, ma'am?"

I continued down the stairs. "You look like the right escort for Victoria Frazer."

He watched me all the way down and held out his hands when I reached the bottom step. "You're beautiful," he said. "But you're not Victoria. And I want you to know I like Lauren a lot better than what I've been learning about Victoria."

The clasp of his hands was warm, and although he didn't touch me in any other way, I felt as though he had drawn me into his arms. I was happier than I could remember being in a long while. My emotions were too close to the surface and I must be careful. Not with Gordon—not anymore. But because of whoever might be watching me.

Over one arm, Gordon held a long white rain cape, borrowed from Finella, and he put this around my shoulders. We went out to where Finella waited for us in the car. When I looked into the backseat, I saw with delight that her costume consisted of kudzu leaves—cut from cloth that was almost the exact green of the plant. She even wore a wreath of skillfully sewn leaves tucked into her red hair.

Gordon smiled at his mother. "She's a true mountain spirit, isn't she? I just hope nobody gets hungry and tries to pick her leaves."

We laughed and chatted as we drove down from the lodge. The storm was still far away. Perhaps it would bypass Lake Lure altogether.

When we reached the inn, the space in front was already filled. Costumed guests were going up wide steps and through the building to the far door opposite the barn. Gordon drove behind the long white stucco building and found a place in the unpaved alleyway between the inn and the barn.

Lights had been placed all around the area, and I could see that the sides of the barn were covered with walls of lush kudzu vines, so that the barn seemed to wear its own costume. A red carpet ran toward steps that led to a side entrance; we climbed them and went inside.

A band was playing tunes that belonged to the years of the lodge's famous past. In the twenties, songs from World War I would still have been played in this room. Years later, during the second war, I'd been told, the lodge had been turned into a convalescent home for soldiers.

Tonight, the interior of the old building had been transformed from whatever its past life had been. High cross beams had been covered with bright-colored strips of plastic that hung in streamers, catching the light from shaded bulbs. The long room, with its polished dance floor, stretched to the band platform at the far end. No one was dancing yet, but the great space was already filled with costumed guests, and the sound of voices echoed in high, dark spaces above the lights.

On the platform, a young woman in a nurse's uniform from World War I was singing "It's a Long Way to Tipperary." When she finished, there was a smattering of applause, but I had the feeling that the room waited for something else to happen. The stars of the evening had not yet appeared.

I'd checked my cape near the door, and Gordon and I stood for a few moments unnoticed while Finella went off to find her friends. When we finally started down the room, our costumes were recognized and there was a burst of applause.

The legend was well remembered. Perhaps there were even those who recognized my dress and turban as being authentic, though few would know who I really was.

There were too many people for me to note whether anyone was especially startled. Not that it mattered. Gordon and I knew exactly whom we needed to watch.

I recognized quickly that this was an older, well-to-do crowd with long memories. Probably a number of these people came from Asheville and recalled the great days of Lake Lure. Their costumes were elaborate but not always original. There was Little Bo-Peep and Red Riding Hood and a few gentleman pirates. One Marie Antoinette appeared to be having trouble with her wig and the red devil escorting her had tangled himself in his tail.

Near the edge of the floor, a monk stood huddled in robe and hood. Who was it who had mentioned a monk to me?

Young people had come dressed in a variety of imaginative costumes, but in many ways they seemed only sightseers at this antique spectacle. Gordon and I, like a number of others, were somewhere in the middle, willing to take part but not really belonging. We found chairs near the edge of the floor, where we could watch, and I began to sense the feeling of something electric in the air. That sense of waiting had grown. I knew why the dancing had not begun.

Justyn and Natalie came in first—Justyn in his captain's cap and the seafaring garb of a sailor; Natalie dressed simply enough in an artist's smock and beret. Justyn held the door for the two who followed, and I could hear the indrawn breath of the waiting crowd.

Camilla came through on Roger's arm and they stood together, waiting for the applause that began very quickly. The band struck up the "Habanera" from *Carmen* and the elder Brandts moved regally down the room, the crowd parting to make way.

Camilla wore a full-skirted black gown with a cascading overlay of creamy lace. Her dark hair (the gray long banished) was piled beneath a black lace mantilla, held in place with a high amber comb and pinned with a yellow rose. A circle of diamonds at her throat caught the light and diamond earrings dripped from her ears, almost to her shoulders. Soft lighting flattered her and careful makeup almost hid her scar.

Roger whirled her proudly down the long room, and the silver buckles on her high-heeled black satin slippers shone beneath the hem of her gown, twinkling in and out as she moved. I became even more conscious of my inappropriate white shoes only partially hidden beneath Victoria's long gown.

In no way would I ever look as beautiful, as stunning, as Camilla Brandt. Perhaps that was how Victoria Frazer had felt when comparing herself with a younger Camilla—a woman who was already Roger's wife. I knew why I was having these thoughts. *Go away!* I told the whisper in my mind. I wanted none of Victoria's thoughts prompting me tonight.

In his own way, Roger matched the elegance of the woman

in his arms. Wearing well-cut black trousers and a short Spanish jacket, he suggested a caballero. His frilled white shirt and the scarlet cummerbund that bound his still-trim waist made him seem far younger than his years. He was a match for Camilla, and never a cowboy!

"They're so beautiful together," I marveled to Gordon.

He was less impressed. "In their own way, I suppose. But they make me nervous—they look like puppets dancing. Come on, let's start things going. Look who we are—Roger and Victoria!"

I didn't want those two to see me yet, and I felt a last-minute panic. I wanted to hold back—even to run away before I was discovered. In spite of the purpose behind my own masquerade, I knew that everything would be spoiled for those two the moment we came into their view. So I waited, not moving, until others began to dance. Only then did we slip in among the many couples, to be lost in the throng. The band changed its tune; the ball had begun.

For only a moment I had put aside my reason for wearing Victoria's dress. Now I began to turn my head as we moved among the dancers, so that I would never lose sight of Roger and Camilla. They still hadn't seen me. The moment of confrontation was coming, and now I didn't hesitate.

We needed only to let the crush of other dancers move us forward. Everyone wanted to approach Roger and Camilla Brandt, and even if he had wanted to, Gordon couldn't keep us apart. They moved in a charmed circle with a space left around them, so they were not crowded. I pressed my hand on Gordon's shoulder; he understood my signal and swept me closer. We entered the cleared space and became suddenly conspicuous.

Roger saw me first, and his expression froze into shock—

perhaps even alarm. Then the actor took over and he smiled at me over Camilla's shoulder—a glittering smile that didn't conceal how badly he'd been shaken. I guessed his intent as he turned Camilla away in a wide circle, so that creamy lace swirled about her.

I couldn't allow that space between us to grow, and it wasn't the back of her head I wanted to see. My pressure on Gordon's shoulder increased, and though he was not altogether willing, we quickened our matching steps, moving faster than the music. When we had swung about them and Camilla could not fail to see me, I raised my hand and allowed the chime of little bells to sound clearly beneath the music of the band.

Camilla heard and turned her head. I saw the horror of recognition in her face. For that instant, I was Victoria for her, and she faltered in her husband's arms. He tried to turn her away, but there was steel in Camilla's spine, in her soul, and her recovery was swift.

Because she'd stopped dancing, Roger was forced to stop and let her go. In that moment of arrested time, I was once more sharply aware of every detail around us: the high, dusty rafters of the barn, with the bright ribbons streaming out of darkness overhead; the whisper of dancing feet; the beat of the music; and the rising heat—for me—of the great room, so that I grew breathless. And always I heard the silvery chiming of bells that came out of the past to possess both Camilla and me. No one else had stopped, yet somehow the dancers moved away from us and we were left in our own exclusive moments of time.

Camilla stepped away from Roger and spoke directly to me without raising her voice. "You are a fool, Lauren. And perhaps as stupid as your grandmother, since you have no idea of the power you are setting loose. Invoking ghosts from the past is a dangerous game—not one I'd recommend to children."

The look she gave me was disdainful and chilling with its promise of disaster. Then she spoke calmly and coolly to Roger, slipping her hand through the crook of his arm. "I would like to go home, please."

For a moment, I think he didn't fully realize what had happened. He covered his wife's hand with his own and looked at me—a sad, resigned, almost fearful look. *He* had never really thought I was Victoria, except for a moment, but he was beginning to see what I had done.

They walked the length of the dance floor together and couples stepped out of their way. The bandleader, realizing that the guests of honor were leaving unexpectedly, signaled for a small fanfare. The incongruous sounds accompanied Roger and Camilla as they went out the door. I saw wind catch at the skirt of her gown, whipping it out in billows as they disappeared from view.

Gordon's arm held me suddenly close. "Are you all right, Lauren?"

I'd felt feverishly hot, but now I was cold, shivering. I was far from all right. My challenge had been given and taken. I had seen Camilla's horrified look at the first sight of me, but she had recovered quickly—so where did that leave me? She had simply dismissed me as though I'd been a child playing games.

Gordon's arm guided me toward a chair on the far side of the room. I felt sick and more than a little confused, so it was a relief to sit down. When I spoke, it was with new conviction, though my voice cracked a little.

"It *wasn't* Camilla," I said. "And it *wasn't* Roger. So who?"

Gordon shook his head gravely and I knew he didn't care about the past—but only about me. "I don't want *you* to be hurt. That's all that matters now."

I was grateful for his concern, but I knew this wasn't the time to give up—no matter how weak and shaken I felt. We hadn't watched for the reaction of anyone but Roger and Camilla at the sight of us. All my sensitivities had been tuned in toward them— yet no sense of guilt had come to me. I knew only one thing about them: They were both frightened people—Camilla no less than Roger. Beneath masks they'd put on so quickly to conceal whatever they felt had been a fright that was very real—fright but not guilt.

Gordon was watching me, increasingly concerned. "I'll get you some coffee. Stay here, Laurie hon, and I'll be right back."

Laurie hon—he'd used to call me that, and the same tenderness was there in his voice. Tears came into my eyes, and I was wiping them away when two people stopped in front of me. I looked up at Justyn and Natalie. Both wore angry faces as they looked down at me.

"I hope you're pleased with yourself!" Natalie cried. "Hurting two old people like that!"

This was hardly fair, and I stiffened to answer her. "*You* are the one who suggested that I come as Victoria!"

"That was a joke. I never dreamed that you'd wear that dress. I never thought you'd manage to look like *her*. That was a cruel thing to do."

I didn't think either Roger or Camilla had been innocent of cruelty to my grandmother.

Justyn had no patience with this talk about dresses. "Your husband got what was coming to him, Mrs. Castle. And now

you've stuck out your own neck. I hope you'll get out of here
before anything else happens."

Justyn's hatred of Jim was clear. His daughter had fallen for
the charms of a married man, and he could never forgive that. Yet
I couldn't see Justyn as a murderer.

Natalie put a hand on his arm. "None of this matters anymore. *She* doesn't matter." She looked at me scornfully and then
away. "Dad, we need to get home to Gran. She'll need us now."

I watched them go off and tried to get myself in hand.
Gordon was probably standing in line somewhere trying to get me
a cup of coffee, but I couldn't wait here for him. I felt unable to
breathe. Fresh air was all I wanted—just to fill my lungs. But
before I could move, a man stopped before me.

"Victoria?" he said, and I looked up in alarm, to see that he
was smiling at me. I recognized Gerald Osborn in the uniform of
an old war.

"Will you dance with me?" he said. "We seem the perfect
couple tonight."

I knew he would be dancing again with Victoria—an old man
reliving moments from the past. At least I could give him this, and
perhaps help my own discomfort. I rose gladly.

The band was playing an old fox-trot, and he was still a
beautiful dancer. I followed him easily, but once more I began to
feel disoriented and queasy. When we neared the door, I stopped.

"I'm sorry, Gerald, but I don't feel very well. I'd like to step
outside for a breath of air. I'll be all right—really. Gordon's bringing me coffee. Will you tell him where I am, please?"

He reluctantly let me go and I went out into the whipping
wind and held on to the railing of the landing. The storm was
closer now—down near the far end of Lake Lure—and I raised my

face to cold, reviving wind. The bands of Victoria's turban seemed to have tightened about my head, so that I could hardly bear the pressure. I wanted to unwind those folds and cast away from me everything that had ever belonged to Victoria Frazer. When Gordon came, I would ask him if we could leave immediately.

Lightning stabbed above Rumbling Bald and thunder boomed soon afterward. At least the rain held off. I should never have worn these clothes; I should never have opened so direct a door to the past. I had hurt people who didn't deserve to be hurt by me. I wished that Gordon would come quickly. I didn't want to be alone, but neither did I want to go back into that hot swirl of color and sound inside.

Someone started up the steps from the ground, and I was glad to have my uneasy mood interrupted. It was the man in the monk's costume whom I'd seen inside. His brown robe whipped in the wind and he clutched the hood tightly over his head. I waited for him to pass me and go into the ballroom. Instead, a strong hand reached from one brown sleeve and grasped me rudely by the arm.

Even as I pulled back in surprise, something was pressed over my face—something with an odor that brought back the terrors of a hospital stay from my childhood.

That time, too, I had dreamed wildly and vividly, with visions that took me into a fantasy world. Memory was gone. Time had no meaning. Yet out of the void around me, a voice spoke my name insistently, calling me back.

S * I * X * T * E * E * N

I FELT sick and dizzy, and only half-aware of what was happening around me.

"You *must* walk," a voice said. "I can't carry you."

It was more like stumbling than walking, but I managed to move my feet. In a moment, I was pushed roughly into the backseat of a car and forced to lie down. The cloth came over my face again and stayed there, but after a while, with the bumping of the car, it slipped off. There was fresh air blowing in from a window in front and I lapsed into a half-conscious state. It was then that I discovered that my wrists and ankles had been tied.

The monk appeared to be driving, but time fell away and it was hard to keep my eyes open. The storm had worsened, and when we stopped, I could hear the thrashing of wind high in the trees.

"You'll have to walk again!" the voice said. "I'll untie your feet."

When the monk bent over me, I could smell a strong, familiar odor, but I was too muddled to place it. I was hauled from the car, and immediately I fell to my knees. Headlights illuminated the clearing ahead and outlined the ghostly shapes of longhouses where light touched them. Suddenly, my eyes fell on the pale shape of the stake that Natalie had celebrated in her painting and I bent forward on my knees and became deathly sick.

Strangely, the hand that had pushed me around now held my head and a voice murmured encouragingly.

"That's right—get it all out of your system. Then you'll be fine again. I want you to have a clear head, Victoria, so you'll understand exactly what is happening. That's only fair, you know, considering all you did to hurt Ty and me."

Gretchen! I caught again the scent of those poultices and ointments she dealt with.

Recognition brought shock and a powerful new wave of fear. Gretchen thought she was talking to Victoria! Those I had meant to startle hadn't believed for a moment—but Gretchen, whom I had never suspected, thought I was her sister! When the dizziness lessened, she pulled me to my feet, supporting me as she urged me into the clearing. The headlights cut a path, so that darkness was pushed back on either side into the high, thrashing trees. As I stumbled along, trying to clear my mind, a strong gust of wind almost blew me down. Lightning slashed the sky above Hickory Nut Gorge and thunder crashed around us. Without Gretchen's arm thrusting me along, I might have fallen, far too weak and sick to move alone.

As we reached the dusty path that branched among the longhouses, I heard a sound so clear and strong that it struck its own signal beneath the clamor of the storm.

For a moment, hope leapt in me. It was Ty's drum! I tried to shout, to call out to him, but my voice was weak.

"Don't do that," Gretchen warned. "It's no use. He can't hear you. Anyway, he knows you're here. I asked him to come to witness what's going to happen. This is *our* revenge, Victoria— Ty's and mine. We thought you were dead, but you fooled us. You always did like to fool us, make us feel like oafs and simpletons. You should have been a better girl, Victoria!"

My grandmother's name, spoken with such venom, wiped away my grogginess and I realized my danger. I had no idea what Gretchen intended, but I had to convince her that I was not Victoria. Even though she was obviously demented, I must try to pull her back to *my* reality.

"*Listen to me!*" I cried, only to have my words blown away as the night exploded around us. Somewhere a tree went down. Nevertheless, she had heard me and I could hear her laughing close by. The wind died suddenly and she spoke into my ear.

"No, Victoria—now it's *your* time to listen! This is your trial, you know—just as witches were tried long ago. It's your turn now—because you always were a witch." Gretchen's voice had a singsong quality to it that I found terrifying.

She was leading me toward a circle of stones where upright wooden poles had been placed. Not a real stake, of course, but one that had been used for a make-believe burning.

"I'll show you how it was done in the picture," she told me cheerfully. The very change in her was alarming. It meant that she was altogether confident, sure of Victoria's punishment. My own weakness held me captive.

"I was here, you know, when they filmed that scene." She suddenly grew angry when I stumbled. "Pick up your feet, Victoria! Step over the stones."

Somehow I managed to stop my forward motion and stand

against her. "NO! I'm not going any farther! I'm *not* Victoria. Look at me! Please, I'm Lauren!"

"I wish you could see your face. That's almost reward enough—the way you look. You're frightened, aren't you? Do you think I'm really going to burn you at the stake? It might be fun, I admit, but you needn't worry. I just want you to stand over there and listen to me and be afraid. In case I should change my mind. . . ."

The sound of Ty's drum grew louder because of a lull in the storm. Gretchen forced me on, prodding me from behind, and I stepped over the circling stones. My own movements took on a dream quality—totally unreal. In a moment, I would wake up from this nightmare. She pushed me against the upright poles of the stake and untied my wrists. I tried to use my hands to fight her off, but the ropes had cut my circulation and they were numb. She pulled one arm high over my head to secure it to a crossbar. And as she did so, I heard the bells on the bracelet I was wearing. Gretchen heard them, too. She reached up to pull it from my wrist and then flung it away into the rain.

"I never want to hear that again!" she cried, and I understood why she'd been upset that time when she'd left me with Ty.

If only I could throw off the nausea and weakness that came in waves, but my knees sagged and I could feel the pull of my own weight on that one arm. I tried to calm down by telling myself that when she'd played her wild scenario through, some semblance of sanity would return and she'd once again become the Gretchen whom I knew.

If only Ty would stop beating the drum so that he could hear me. I even thought helplessly of Gordon, who would have no idea what had happened to me, even if Gerald Osborn had managed to deliver my message.

Something had apparently distracted Gretchen, for she hadn't secured my other arm to the overhead pole. One hand was free and the feeling had returned to my fingers. I reached up and frantically tore the bands of the turban from my head.

"Gretchen—look! I'm Lauren Castle. I'm not Victoria Frazer! I'm *Lauren!*"

She saw my dark hair whipped by the wind, but only laughed again. "Don't try to fool me. Of course you're inside Lauren's body. I know that. I've seen you look out of her eyes, Victoria. I've known you were there all along. So *now* are you ready to listen?"

Under the fury of the newly rising wind, she came very close to my ear, and I could hear her clearly as she told me all that Victoria had done to her and to Ty. Or what *she* thought Victoria had done—the older, beautiful, successful sister who had ignored the small, plain Gretchen when she was young. Victoria had been intent only on the fulfillment of her own ambition. She had destroyed lives, turned brother against sister; *everything* that had caused Gretchen pain throughout her life was Victoria's fault.

"You destroyed our lives!" Gretchen cried. "You cared only about yourself. Camilla Brandt hated you, too—because of the way you bewitched Roger. If Camilla'd had the guts, she'd have killed you long ago."

I listened and I shivered in cold and fear.

"I only wanted you to love me. Our parents were gone, and there was no one else. Only you and me and Ty. And you were so beautiful. . . ."

I heard the pain of a long-ago child in her voice. Perhaps she would talk herself out soon and this nightmare would end.

However, deep down I knew Gretchen had brought me to this place for a purpose I dared not think about. If she'd only wanted me to listen, then anywhere at all would have served.

Again the wind died down and took on a waiting quality. The rain still hadn't come. I heard her clearly, though her voice was low.

"Afterward—after you were gone—I had to atone for what I'd done. To take a life is a wicked act. No matter how evil you were, I had no right. That was when the power came into my hands and I found I could heal those who were suffering. I could *save* lives. That is why I've been allowed to live. In payment for one life, I have helped hundreds. God forgave me and granted me a gift that I have used faithfully and gratefully. That gift must be preserved. It's all I have. Then you came back, and you were about to show Lauren everything—just as you showed Jim Castle. They would have destroyed me and ruined my gift. I couldn't let that happen. They had to be stopped and you had to be stopped all over again. And for good, this time."

She stared up into the darkness of rolling black clouds laced with lightning and did not flinch when a tremendous clap of thunder sounded close by.

"Jim should have known that what I can do is more important than anything you'll ever do. I didn't want to kill him, but by stopping him I've saved the lives of those who will need me. Now I must stop you. I see that more clearly than ever."

She stepped back from the circle of stones surrounding the stake. I watched as she ran to a smaller circle where wood had been piled for burning. She picked up a branch with dead leaves on the end and set it afire with the lighter she'd brought. Then she touched the burning end to the pile of dry wood and kindling, so that it burst into flames, whipped to life by the wind. But *that* circle of stones was not where I stood.

My left hand was still free and I began to struggle frantically with the rope that tied the other hand high over my head. The oily-feeling rope was stiff and tightly knotted.

I hadn't made much progress when she came running back to me, her face alive with a terrible excitement. Ty's drum sounded louder now and more ominous. He was helping his sister, after all.

"This is how they did it in the picture," she cried. "They built a fire like that in the smaller circle and then shot the scene through those flames to where the actor was tied to the stake. If I had a camera and shot this scene from over there, it would look as though you were burning. But *I'm* not making a movie."

Gretchen ran to pull a second torch from the blaze she'd started, then came back to me.

"We can make this much more realistic. I have only to touch this to the sticks at your feet. Then it will *feel* real."

I must not faint. Somehow I must hold on to my own reason—when hers had gone completely. I tore at the rope that held me and at last it began to give.

"Wait, Gretchen! This isn't the way—you're not finished. Show me the cave! Show me where you left Victoria." If I could distract her, I might have time. . . .

But she only laughed and lowered the torch to the wood piled at my feet. The flames caught, smoldered, and smoke curled upward, making me cough as I lurched away, straining against the loosened rope and holding my long white skirt as far from the smoldering branches as I could.

Ty's voice came suddenly out of the darkness beyond headlights and fire. "You don't want to do that, Gretchen."

She paid no attention, her interest fixed on the small spreading flames. I could already feel a pulsing of heat near my legs.

"Help me, Ty!" I shouted.

I could see him clearly now—a strange figure in the dancing light that surrounded him. He held out his hands, palms upward, raising his eyes toward the black sky.

"I've been playing my drum, Lauren!" he called to me. "I've been asking for help. It's coming right now!"

Big drops splashed on my face, hissing in the fire at my feet. Suddenly, sheets of rain poured from the sky, long overdue.

Gretchen shook her head angrily and began to scream at him over the sound of the rain. "Look what you've done, Ty! Now this isn't going to work. You might as well cut her loose!"

Ty cut the rope with a pocketknife and caught me as I sagged. He carried me out of the stone circle and over to where Gretchen stood. "Take her to the car and put her in the front seat—now!" she yelled.

When I tried to struggle, he tightened his grip on me, probably too afraid of Gretchen's anger to disobey. I tried to speak to him calmly, but Gretchen heard me. "Be quiet. You'll come with me to the cave, and you'll be still—or I'll put you under again."

I couldn't allow that; I had to buy some time. "I'll come. I want to see where Victoria is buried."

"Go away, Ty," she told him. "You've messed things up enough."

We'd reached the car. He opened the door and then faded into the darkness, again obeying her, as he'd so often obeyed his strong, younger sister. She pushed me onto the floor of the front seat and ordered me to crouch there as she got behind the wheel. "I've got to be able to keep my eye on you. Don't give me a reason to put you under!" When she'd turned the car around in the clearing, we went bumping down the hill at a greater speed than was safe.

All my focus was on escaping. I would wait for the right moment and hope I was successful. Perhaps when the car slowed, I could get the door open and hurl myself out. Gretchen was clever; it was hard for me to move, cramped as I was under the dashboard, and my hope began to fade.

I heard the windshield wipers working at top speed as sheets of rain slammed into the car. I was already soaked before I got in, and Victoria's long dress clung, hampering my movements.

Perhaps Ty would go for help. But how far could he get on foot? How could he reach anyone in time? Time for what? Would the cave be *my* tomb, as well?

Once we reached the highway, the car picked up speed as we headed toward Lake Lure.

"Be careful. I know what you're thinking," Gretchen warned. "You'll kill yourself if you jump out. That's not the answer. Not yet. I want you to meet your grandmother. It's time—just as it was time to show you where she died."

At least she seemed to know who I was for the moment.

"It's just as well"—she sounded pleased with herself—"that there wasn't another accident up there in the Indian village. The first death was an accident, you know—Victoria's death. I never meant for that to happen. I followed her along the lake as she was walking toward Roger's house."

Abruptly, Gretchen switched pronouns again, chilling me.

"Do you remember how we quarreled? How scornful you were! You *asked* for punishment. I had my walking stick with me, and I was so angry that I used it. But I never meant to kill you. Afterward, I let Roger find your body, and I said what I could to point toward his wife's guilt. She had every motive, and he believed what I said—so of course he had to protect her. We hid your body in the cave to save Camilla! That was the wonderful joke—that he stayed here at Lake Lure because that house guards the way to the cave. All these years he has never let her know that he believes she's a murderer. What a laugh! Now you can bring it all full circle."

So when she'd showed me where my grandmother had died, the story she told me had been only partially true. Roger wasn't trying to protect his reputation or Victoria's; he thought he was protecting Camilla! Once more I tried to reach Gretchen: "You can't undo old history, Gretchen. There's no way to change what happened so long ago. I'm Victoria's granddaughter, and I had no part in any of this."

She braked so suddenly that I dared to peek over the dash as we skidded on wet pavement and came to a sliding stop only a few feet from a dancing, gesticulating figure in the middle of the road. Ty! Of course, he'd known the shortcuts down the mountain that allowed him to get here ahead of us on the road.

Gretchen reached for my arm with a steel grip and rolled down the window on her side. "So you won't go away, will you?" she called to Ty. "If you feel you must come with us, get in the car."

He moved agilely to open the rear door and got in. Gretchen spoke over her shoulder. "Take her with you in back, Ty. She makes me nervous up here. Climb over the seat, Lauren."

At least I would be able to see where we were going if I was in back with Ty, and perhaps he would help me get away if there was an opportunity. We were already moving fast again, and I fell clumsily into the seat beside him. Rain clattered on windows and road, and under its cover, Ty whispered to me.

"I knew of a ranger's phone near here and called Gordon. I told him where she'd probably take us."

I slumped back in the seat and closed my eyes, too grateful and relieved to be able to do more than squeeze Ty's hand.

The dark rain made Lake Lure nearly invisible when we reached it, though light showed brightly around the inn, where the party was still in full swing. Gretchen followed the winding road that led around the lake and across the dam. We saw no other cars, and Ty was quiet and watchful.

Once he whispered to me, "I don't know how she'll manage this."

Below Roger's house, she drove through a blind cut into the woods and on to where an empty house stood. When she'd pulled into the driveway, she spoke over her shoulder.

"Get her out, Ty. And keep ahold of her. She mustn't get away now. Just relax, Lauren. Don't worry—I know you're not Victoria, though it's been fun to scare you a bit."

I didn't believe her. I suspected that she went in and out of a state of delusion. She would still mix me up with Victoria—and that was dangerous. How would Gordon ever know where to find us? He probably didn't know where the cave was.

"Now we climb on foot," Gretchen said. "You go first, Ty. You know the way. We'll put her in the middle so she can't get past either of us. That'll keep her from playing any tricks. If she's smart, she'll behave."

I saw that she'd brought her walking stick from the car, and I shivered.

We seemed to be climbing a thread of path through thick underbrush. Ty found his way like some woods creature that could see in the dark. Rain pelted us, but the thunder sounded farther away now. Gretchen had brought a flashlight, and that helped a little.

My long dress clung to my legs and hampered me. I was still

very weak. At times, I took hold of bushes to pull myself up. Even if it had been possible, I would no longer try to get away. I *wanted* to know what lay in the cave toward which we were climbing. That was my destiny. I had come here to find Victoria.

Some distance up the mountain, Ty stopped, so that I bumped into him. Gretchen played the thin beam of her flashlight over the rocky face of a cliff.

"Good for you, Ty," she said. "I'd never have found it in the dark. Go in first. I know you stored some lanterns here years ago."

Ty seemed to disappear into a sheer face of rock, and Gretchen prodded me with her stick. "Go on! Follow him. There's a slit up there you can get through real easy."

By reaching out with both hands, I felt the ragged fissure of the opening and found my way in. I was soaked through and cold, and it was a relief to be out of the rain and wind.

Ahead of us, Ty had lighted two lanterns that threw very little radiance into a high-roofed cave, spacious and hollow. I was fearful of what I might see, but only a featureless brown void opened around me. From deep inside the mountain came the muted roar of rushing water.

Gretchen listened, pleased. "That's the waterfall. This rain's been enough to stream through all the crevices and flood the inner river. Too bad it's so late, Lauren. I'd like to show it to you, but we haven't time."

Ty said, "This is where Roger and Justyn came for shelter the night they saw the spacecraft hit the mountain. That storm was real bad—worse than now. They ducked in here to get away from hail the size of golf balls. I was out in it—I know."

Gretchen laughed—an unsettling sound that echoed in the cavern. "Roger knew to seek shelter in this place because he'd come here before. This is where we carried Victoria. I never wanted to come back, but you come here often, don't you, Ty?"

"Somebody had to look after her," Ty said. "This is where I brought Jim. I showed him what's up there."

"That was a mistake, wasn't it?" Gretchen said. "Because he would never have kept still about what he found. Now we'll show Victoria's granddaughter—and *she* isn't going to tell anyone, is she? Lead the way, Ty."

I still felt weak and shaken, and when Gretchen shoved me again, I stumbled after Ty. Most of all, I feared her walking stick. I could easily become its next victim.

Compelled by his sister's voice, Ty began to climb what at first appeared to be a sheer rock wall. "We won't need lanterns up here," he said mysteriously. "Come along, Lauren. It's easier than it looks."

In lantern light, my own shadow grew to monstrous size as I followed him along grooves in the rock. Partway up, he disappeared into another, higher chamber and again I followed him. This was a larger cave than the one below, and as I emerged into it, the sound of rushing water grew very loud, its voice filling the mountain.

As Ty had said, we needed no lanterns or flashlights here. The entire space seemed alight with an eerie greenish glow—not as bright as daylight but luminous in its own way.

"My God!" Gretchen's voice rising above the sound of rushing water sounded awed, and I knew that this was something as strange to her as it was to me. When I went farther onto the floor of this second cave and saw what waited for us there, a trembling started inside me. On a natural rock platform ahead of us, a bier had been placed.

For a moment, Gretchen had dropped behind, and Ty held out his hand to me. "This is why you came here, isn't it—to find your grandmother?"

Suddenly, I was as fearful of this place as I had been of the stake in the Indian village. But no escape was possible, and I let him draw me up to the level of the rock plane that held the bier. Beyond lay empty black space where the green light didn't reach. Now the sound of water falling precipitously into unseen depths became a rumbling boom that echoed through the cave.

Gretchen came to stand beside me, and I could still feel her shock. "It wasn't like this when Roger and I brought her here!" she cried.

I expected to see Victoria's bones stretched out upon the flat ledge of rock, but nothing of what remained was visible. A blanket of lush green vines covered her—beautiful and healthy, growing in a place where there was no sunlight, earth, or water. Great kudzu leaves shone with their own green light, eerie and unnatural.

As my eyes became used to the luminous green, I found its source. On each side of the bier was a small heap of greenish material, from which the vine seemed to have taken sustenance. Now I knew where the snippet of strange cloth Jim had left for me had come from.

"Tell me what happened, Ty!" Gretchen demanded.

He managed to raise his voice so we could hear. "All those years, I kept bringing vines to cover her, even though they just withered and died. But after that—whatever it was—crashed on the mountain, everything changed. Maybe something from that wreckage came down here before army intelligence arrived. Maybe they found the upper cave to hide in until their kin could come and get them. I sort of think they found *her*, and they left something of themselves here for her when they went away. So for all these years, she's had a proper shroud."

Like Gretchen, I felt awed by a mystery that was beyond earthly understanding. Gretchen and Ty had been shouting, but now that they were silent, the crash of falling water filled my very being. I remembered the vision I'd had of a waterfall—a warning vision!

Ty shouted again: "I climbed out through there once to stand on the edge. There's no bottom. The waterfall feeds the river and cuts its way underground from the top of the mountain straight down. Sometimes when you stand outside on Rumbling Bald, you can hear the sound of rushing water."

"This is Victoria's tomb." Gretchen's voice struck a high, clear note, and I heard her clearly. "Yours will be *out there*, Lauren. You'll just step into space and be gone. It will be quick and easy. No one will ever find your body, just as Victoria's was never found."

I felt a sharp pain as her stick poked into my back, and once more I swung around to face her. "No, Gretchen! You've done enough! This has to stop now."

I think she would have struck me with the heavy knob on the end of her stick, but something strange seemed to happen around the bier. It was as though a green mist rose from beneath the vines—or perhaps it was only a thickening in the air.

Whatever it was, Gretchen saw it, too. Perhaps her own feelings of guilt, which could doubtless shake her at times, made her see it more clearly than I did.

She thrust out her hands to push nothingness away, but the thickening that quivered in the air did not subside. Whatever she saw caused her to shrink away, to step backward, and then backward again, her movements violent and jerky.

Ty's mountain-trained ears must have heard something from the lower cave, for he shouted suddenly: "Gordon? Are you there, Gordon?"

My heart jumped in wild hope as Gordon—and Roger with him—climbed up into green light. I learned later that he had gone to my grandfather to try to find me, and Ty had reached him there. Now, however, it was still Gretchen who held us transfixed.

Perhaps she never knew how close she was to the edge. Or perhaps she knew very well and, in the face of greater terror, made her choice.

The next step took her backward into space, and I could hear her cry, lost in roaring emptiness, as she went down. There could be no echo of her plunge into whatever river flowed beneath the mountain. The waterfall that came rushing out of some high place swallowed up all other sound.

Gordon sprang up to the platform where I stood with Ty. He simply held me as I fell into his arms. I pressed my face against his neck and tried to stop trembling.

Roger climbed up to stand beside us. He wore a spectacular cape that belonged to past glories, but he no longer looked like the dashing actor he had once been. All make-believe was gone; he was an old man possessed by shock and sorrow.

I didn't try to speak aloud above the roar of water, but I spoke to *her* in my mind. *You're free now, Grandmother. Wherever you are, you're free of what held you here.*

No green mist stirred among the leaves, but a deep feeling of some loving presence filled me.

Together, Gordon, Roger, and I went down to the quieter area of the lower cave. There my grandfather held out his hands to me and I put my own into his.

"I can let *her* go now," he said, and I understood. "But I don't want to let you go, now that I've found you."

"I don't think Lauren is going anywhere," Gordon said, his arm still around me. "I hope she will stay here with me."

I had no doubt at all that this was what I would do.

Ty had followed us down, more subdued than I'd ever seen him. When he spoke, it was as if only to himself.

"I reckon it had to be. She couldn't go on playing at being somebody she knew she wasn't. She was blessed in some ways—and she was cursed. She couldn't live with that forever."

He seemed to collect himself and see us now, though he showed no emotion. There was a question I had to ask. "How did you know about Victoria, Ty?"

He no longer hesitated about answering. "I was in the woods when Gretchen and Roger carried her into the cave. When they'd gone, I found her. I saw the wound on the back of her head and I knew it was made by Gretchen's stick. She fooled Roger, but she didn't fool me."

"Why didn't you tell someone?" Roger's voice was faint.

"She was my sister. They were both my sisters, and I didn't *hate* either of them. Victoria was wearing that bracelet with the bells, and I took it off her wrist so as to have something of her to keep. I sent it to you as a signal, Lauren—to pick up or not. When you brought it across the lake to me, Gretchen knew where it had come from and it threw her pretty badly."

There was one more question I must ask. "What about Jim?"

"I showed him the bracelet and I brought him here to the cave. She was only bones under the kudzu, but when he looked at her skull, he knew it had been murder. He cut off a piece of the green stuff to see if he could find out what it was. Gretchen knew he was getting too close and she found a way to stop him in the village that day."

Emotion came through in Ty at last, and after a choking pause, he continued.

"Gretchen was right, you know—even at the same time she was wrong. She helped so many people with her healing. But when she brought you to the village tonight, Lauren, I knew it had to end. Justyn was catching on—getting suspicious—and I didn't want *him* after her. Roger, you were always on the wrong track. Now you know it was never Camilla. You were protecting each other—and you were both wrong."

"I know that now, Ty," Roger said sadly. "Finally, I know. Tonight after we left the ball, Camilla and I talked for a long while. I should have talked to her about Victoria's death years ago. But because of what I thought she had done, I was afraid of what I might learn. And all the while, she believed that I was guilty, and she couldn't speak of that to me."

Ty spread his arms wide, palms up, as he had done in the Indian village when he was asking for rain. Perhaps the gesture was a benediction now. "Go back to your lives—all of you. I'll stay up there for a while with my family."

We left him there, and Gordon helped me out through a slit in the rock. The rain had stopped and the wind had died down. Moonlight edged the clouds, pointing our way, as we took the difficult path down the mountain. Roger came with us partway and then disappeared in the direction of the Brandt house. Perhaps he was the guardian now of a new legend that would spring up around Lake Lure.

"We'll go back to Finella's," Gordon said to me. "You'll stay with us for now. I can get your things tomorrow and report that

Gretchen is missing. Maybe Ty will take her pig."

On the way down through the last stubborn mountain growth, I puzzled aloud over what I had seen in the upper cave.

"Those vines, Gordon—they were growing without light or water!"

"There are cracks in the rock," he said. "Light and water *can* come through. But I'd rather believe in miracles."

I accepted that, and we went out on the shore of the lake and stood together near the water.

"Where shall we build our own house?" he asked me calmly.

I knew my smile was one of joy, of wonder. I, too, believed in miracles.

"On Lake Lure, of course," I said.

Perhaps there was peace now for Victoria Frazer. And peace, at last, for Roger and Camilla Brandt. For Gordon and me, a new life was beginning, but this night would haunt me for a long time.

We didn't look back as we left the moonlit lake. I had learned in my life that it was better not to look back.

Moonlight touched the moving water and struck sequins from its surface. No misty traces gathered now, though the dark reflections of Rumbling Bald held even more secrets than they had in the past.

About the Author

Phyllis A. Whitney was born in Yokohama, Japan, of American parents, and has also lived in the Philippines and China. After the death of her father in China, she and her mother returned to the United States, which she saw for the first time when she was fifteen. This early travel has exerted a strong influence on her work; many of her novels are set in areas she has visited in Europe, Africa, and the Orient, as well as in the places she has lived.

Phyllis A. Whitney is the author's maiden name. (The *A* stands for Ayame, which is the Japanese word for "iris.") She is a widow and lives near her daughter in Virginia. In 1975, she was elected president of the Mystery Writers of America, and in 1988 received the organization's Grand Master Award for lifetime achievement. She is also the recipient of the Agatha Award for lifetime achievement given by Malice Domestic.

Since 1941, when she attained her first hardcover publication, she has become an international success. More than forty million copies of her novels are in print in American paperback editions. Her novels for adults now number thirty-seven, and her devoted following has made best-sellers of most of these titles, including *The Ebony Swan, Woman Without a Past, The Singing Stones, Rainbow in the Mist, Feather on the Moon, Silversword,* and *Dream of Orchids.*